ALTER ROAD

A Wartmann Universe Story

MARK JAMES

NORTH
ARROW
PRESS

ALTER ROAD

Edited by Pete J. Gerardo
www.petejgerardo.com

ISBN 978-1-969608-06-3 (Paperback)
ISBN 978-1-969608-07-0 (Kindle Edition)
ISBN 978-1-969608-08-7 (EPUB Edition)

Cover design by North Arrow Press
Interior layout by North Arrow Press

North Arrow Press
Annapolis, Maryland
www.northarrowpress.com

Printed in the United States of America

PROLOGUE

The firefighter removed his oxygen mask and helmet. His hair was wet with sweat despite the cold.

"It's bad in there, Chief," he said. His face was grave. Too grave for a man his age. Behind him, a ladder crew sprayed water down on the house from above.

Chief Nelson nodded solemnly. He already knew as much. Three separate cars were parked in the driveway and along the street in front of the house. A bicycle and toys lay on the front lawn.

A deafening *swoosh* marked the complete collapse of the house into itself. The young firefighter recoiled and looked back, distraught. Nelson stuck his arm out, blocking him from dashing back to the house.

"They're out," Nelson assured him. "The firefighters— they're all out."

Angry flames leapt high. Swarms of glowing embers danced across the night sky like angry fireflies amid the falling snow.

"Oh, God!" someone had cried out. Nelson looked over his shoulder. A crowd of neighbors had gathered on both ends of the street. The house falling in on itself caused a stir.

"Didn't anybody come out?" an elderly woman asked. "Anyone at all?"

"What about the children?"

<center>~~~</center>

André Murray stood on the curb and surveyed the smoldering remains of what was probably a Starlight Bungalow Sears Catalog home, like so many of Detroit's working-class neighborhoods, nearly all of which were just over 100 years old.

The Fire Chief had called him directly the evening before.

"We have a problem, Mr. Mayor," Chief Nelson had told him. The crowd on the street had grown in size as the firemen battled the blaze, and they had grown increasingly distraught.

Of course, people get upset when they see a home on fire, and especially if it is their neighbor's. But this particular fire—and the crowd's reaction—was *different*.

There was a tension in the air. An *anger*.

It was palpable.

And so here was André Murray, the Mayor of Detroit, his Fire Chief Charlie Nelson, and his Chief of Police, JD Wiggins. Murray's Chief of Staff and a handful of uniformed police officers rounded out the entourage.

Nelson was right. There *was* anger, and André worked hard to placate the neighbors who had gathered again despite the frigid cold of the early morning.

"This has got to *stop*," snapped a woman.

"How many of us gonna die before you *do* something?"

The questions were coming fast.

"How many fires now? Huh?"

"Whatchya gonna do?"

Wiggins discreetly called for more officers. The people were hostile.

Wiggins' phone buzzed in his pocket.

"Wiggins," he barked. His head snapped up and he looked to the end of the street. Sirens blared in the distance.

He grunted and marched up to André.

"Mr. Mayor, we have to *go.*"

A line of police cars and the Mayor's SUV pulled alongside, sirens blaring, and both climbed in.

"What's going on?" André asked.

He soon got his answer.

~~~

The Mayor's convoy sped down Alter Road and swung a hard right onto Jefferson Avenue. Jefferson paralleled the Detroit River from Lake St. Claire to downtown.

It was here that the Mayor got his answer. His convoy came under a barrage of rocks and bottles as they sped through the intersection.

The mayor looked at his watch. It only just after 8 a.m.
~~~

It was going to be a long day.

PART ONE
Slow Burn

Chapter 1

Jason Reid hopped into his work van and flipped through the printout on his clipboard. It was his schedule for the day. He had two energy-efficient thermostat installations to do, two apartment units and a house to be hooked up for power, and four scheduled shutoffs.

It was company policy to work through the shutoffs first and work your way down to the efficient thermostats. It was all about the money, Jason suspected. Shut off those who aren't paying to stop even one more penny of energy outflow, add new clients to get that income inflow—which included the initial connection fee—and, lastly, delay any savings on the part of environmentally-conscious consumers by installing energy-saving thermostats last.

Jason drove east on Jefferson Avenue. Reaching over, he turned up the radio.

It was Johnny Cash. *How high's the water, Mama? Four feet high and rising.*

There was a crowd of people milling about alongside the road after he passed the sprawling—and now closed—Jefferson North Assembly Plant, where the vaunted Jeep Grand Cherokee was once built. Jason glanced at the time display on the dashboard: 8:25 a.m.

It was unusual for a crowd to be out at such an early hour. Or to be standing alongside the roads like they were.

An eerie feeling settled over him as he stopped at a traffic light. He was drawing a lot of stares. Something was up. The light turned green and he drove on.

Jason slowed as he neared another group standing on both sides of the road, and he was careful to give them a wide berth. A boy sprinted forward and hurled a bottle at his van. Jason swerved. He felt two *thunks* against the van, and stole a look into his side mirrors. The teenager had landed a direct hit, as had a second teen. Both of them chased his van for a full block before giving up.

Yet another crowd of a dozen or so people stood in the street ahead of him, and Jason slowed to a crawl. As he came upon them, they parted without looking to let him pass, but their faces and demeanor turned hostile when they did look.

They swarmed around the van, forcing Jason to stop. The van took more *thunks*—they pounded on its front and sides. The windshield spiderwebbed. The driver side window smashed inward, and arms reached in.

"Get the fuck off me!" The driver side door was yanked open, and he was pulled into the street, scraping his hands and knees on the pavement. He covered his head as the crowd pummeled him with kicks and punches.

The van, now driverless, rolled to the right and bounced against the curb. Turning back onto the street, it glided along until it struck a light pole.

"Kill that muthafucka!" Jason scrambled to his feet and ran. He absorbed a couple of more punches before he got away.

The group turned their attention to the van and pummeled it with rocks and whatever debris they could find. Jason slowed and stole a look back. They attacked the van, yanking at the doors and breaking the windows. He turned and walked east at a fast pace, still the focus of too much attention.

"Yo, man, get the fuck out of here!" yelled an older black man. A small boy ran up to Jason and hurled a pebble at him. Jason instinctively threw his arms up in defense, but he was too late, and the pebble skipped off the top of his head. He stumbled and fell.

"Get outta here, boy!" the older man now snarled at the kid. The boy fled down the street to join the others now setting fire to the van.

"Come on, white boy," the man said, offering a hand to help Jason stand. "Let's get your crazy ass outta here before you get yourself killed."

~ ~ ~

Wiggins worked the phone. He issued a "Code Blue" for the Fifth Precinct—the signal for an emergency "swarm."

The Jefferson/Mack neighborhood was not a high-crime area, at least by Detroit's standards, but the early crowds that had assaulted the Mayor's convoy had also attacked a GLEE utility van.

Calls were coming in that crowds were gathering at other intersections as well. Morning commuters were being pelted with rocks and debris.

"Code Blue" was a swarming order. For the next thirty minutes, police units from all across Detroit sped, lights flashing and sirens blaring, to the Jefferson/Mack neighborhood. The intersection of Alter Road and Jefferson Avenue was of most concern; this was where the crowds first formed and where the Mayor's convoy and the GLEE van were attacked.

A police helicopter took flight above.

Wiggins was anxious, but it wasn't long before reports started coming over the radio from the helicopter above and units arriving in Jefferson/Mack.

His angst was justified: it wasn't just the intersection of Alter Road and Jefferson Avenue that crowds were accumulating. They amassed a few blocks over at the intersection of Alter Road and Mack Avenue, and further north at Alter and Warren.

The whole neighborhood was erupting.

~ ~ ~

Back at City Hall, Wiggins huddled with André and his staff. "I issued a 'Code Blue'," Wiggins reported.

"Will it work?"

Wiggins leaned back in his chair. He shrugged. "If this was ten years ago, I'd be a little more confident in saying yes. But we just don't have the personnel we used to. Still, if we can calm things down enough in Jefferson/Mack, that would free up units to swarm other areas if necessary. It might be a game of Whac-a-Mole for awhile.

"I need to cancel all leave," Wiggins continued, "and call in all shifts. We need all hands on deck."

André stood at the window behind his desk and looked out on the city. He watched snow tumble lazily from the gray sky. He grunted.

"Let's not get carried away just yet," he said. "I still have some levers to pull."

André looked back to Wiggins. "Do you know who lived there—in that house on Alter Road?"

Wiggins shook his head.

"Mrs. Bernadette Price. She was a Michigan Teacher of the Year—*twice*—and won the NEA Foundation Award. It was presented to her by the President just a few years ago. *Everyone* knows her. Hell, my own kids had her. She's a goddam institution."

"Nelson said the house was full?"

"Yep," André sighed. "The neighbors said her daughter, five grandchildren, son-in-law—all of them—had moved in after getting evicted from their apartment. They had only been there a few days."

André sat heavily in his chair. "At least nine bodies in that house."

"Jesus." Wiggins shook his head.

~~~

André was armed with numbers in hand: more than 300 fire-related deaths so far this year, and it was only mid-February. Usually, it was forty-five to fifty for the *whole year*—which was tragic enough. The surge was surely a direct result of GLEE's crackdown.

He picked up the phone.

"I'm sorry, Mr. Mayor, but Mr. Desmond is not available." It
~~~

was Desmond's executive administrator.

Charles Desmond was chief executive of Great Lakes Energy Enterprises—or GLEE, the regional electric utility company—the ones shutting people's power off for late payment. It had been an unusually brutal winter—even for Detroit's standards—but they offered no quarter.

"Surely he is available if GLEE is in a crisis. And let me assure you, GLEE is in a crisis. Please do tell him to call me as soon as he can."

"Yes, Mr. Mayor, of course, I will—"

André disconnected. He rubbed his face and head.

On his desk radio, a jazz tune ended and the host chimed in with the early morning headlines. When the announcer mentioned GLEE, André leaned in.

The timing was extraordinary.

The first part of the news segment was dedicated to an interview with Mrs. Louise Jackson, a fifty-five-year-old woman who had lost her granddaughter to a house fire two months earlier.

Damn. Talk about timing.

She held a daily vigil outside GLEE Tower to call attention to their policy of shutting off power for late payments. Her vigil had started solo, but it had grown to more than fifty people on any given day. Some days, usually weekends, as many as 200 people would show up alongside Mrs. Jackson.

André stared into space as he listened. He was well aware of Mrs. Jackson and her vigil. GLEE's globetrotting CEO,

Charles Desmond, had personally called André and asked him to do something about the vigil and the growing crowds.

The gall.

André had pushed back and pressed Desmond to do something about the damn shutoffs.

That was only a few days ago. *Was that Wednesday last week? The week before?*

It was a testy conversation, but Desmond had agreed to implement a relief program for low-income households. He also promised a telephone hotline for customers in shutoff status. Neither hadn't gone live yet.

Chapter 2

Ian Nguyen was up at 5:30 a.m. He did his morning wake-up routine of brushing his teeth, getting dressed, and downing a bottle of Red Bull before meeting up with his long-distance track and cross-country teammates for a 6:00 a.m., fifteen-minute shuttle to Belle Isle in the middle of the Detroit River. Once there, the team ran twice around the roughly five-mile circumference of the island, and were back on campus in time for Ian to take a quick shower, down a muffin, surf social media, and check his emails before his first class at 9:00 a.m.

Social media was abuzz about a fire in the Jefferson/Mack district of Detroit, accompanied by hashtags like *#Endthe-Shutoffs* and *#NoPowerNoPeace*. Ian skimmed a breaking news article about the fire, tweeted by the *Detroit Free Press,* in which an entire extended family had perished. His breath caught in his throat when he saw the name of one of the victims presumed killed in the fire: Mrs. Bernadette Price. That was the name of his 9th grade social science teacher, who had taken an interest in him and made him think about college. As he read the article, it was pretty apparent that his former teacher and the Mrs. Price in the article were one and the same.

In class, Ian's mind wandered as the professor lectured about endoskeletons. He nodded as though he was paying attention, but memories from high school and Mrs. Price wouldn't wait. It was Mrs. Price who got him into cross country running, an offhand suggestion for him to find both a place of inner solitude and something to focus his hyperactivity and simmering anger on.

He had had a tendency to resort to fists at the first sign of anti-Vietnamese or anti-Asian sentiment, real or perceived, among his mostly black and Latino classmates. Running calmed him. His teams, both in high school and now in college, were a diverse group, and he learned he had a lot in common with his fellow runners and students.

His cell phone vibrated repeatedly in his hoodie pocket, and he glanced at it whenever he could while the professor lectured.

Text messages and emails rolled in, most of them about Mrs. Price, but he couldn't read any of them without getting noticed. He fidgeted; the class seemed to drag on longer than the scheduled fifty minutes. Glimpses at the clock confirmed that time *was*, in fact, moving, but at an excruciatingly slow pace.

When class finally let out, Ian headed for the Student Center. He navigated through unusually busy pedestrian traffic to get into the Center and tried to find a place to sit. At last, he found a spot, and sat with his second Red Bull of the day to read his emails and texts, trying to learn more about what had happened to Mrs. Price. When he finished, he texted Sarah. In addition to being a runner on the women's cross country and track teams, Sarah was active in the campus Amnesty International group, serving as its vice president. It was another reason he liked her. She was passionate about social justice and human rights. And she was a fellow runner.

Ian: Did you hear the news about Mrs. Price?
Sarah: Yeah, I've been texting you. We're protesting outside SC right now.
Ian: I'm inside. Price was my 9th grade teacher!

Sarah: No way!

Ian: I'm on my way out. See you in a few.

~ ~ ~

Out in front of the Student Center, roughly three hundred students were gathered at Fountain Court. Many were between classes, but the majority seemed to be just hanging around.

"Yo, Ian!" someone called to him.

It was Walter Clay. A decade older than Ian, Walter was dreadlocked, well-dressed, and bespectacled. He looked like a hipster intellectual—but he was genuine. He was a first-year Ph.D. student in Physics, and was president of the campus Black Lives Matter chapter.

With Walter were several other BLM members and two athlete friends of Ian's, both football players. Each offered Ian with a brief embrace and a "What's up, brother?"

Trevor, a cross-country teammate, stepped out of the crowd and bumped shoulders with Ian. Right behind him were more cross-country runners, but on the women's team: Sarah, Tina, Dakota, and Michelle.

"Hey there, big guy." Sarah punched Ian in the shoulder. *Big guy.* Ian weighed no more than 140 pounds soaking wet.

"What's all this? Is this for Mrs. Price?" Ian gazed at the fast-growing crowd as more students ditched classes to be there.

"Yeah, man," said Sarah.

"Hey, bro!" Roland—another cross-country teammate—

bumped shoulders with Ian. "Thought you might be here."

The crowd of students had rapidly increased in size and was still growing.

The students crowd faced the small rock fountain at the center of Fountain Court, where a group of activist students representing the campus BLM chapter and African American Society led various chants.

"No Power, No Peace!"

"Stop the killing, end the shutoffs!"

Students took turns with a single bullhorn that they passed around, but it was hard to hear their words over the din.

After more inaudible shouts, the throng surged forward along Gullen Mall southeast toward downtown. Ian and his friends were swept along.

"Let's stick together," Roland yelled. "This is wild!"

Roland was getting into it. He grabbed Tina's hand and tried to get her pumped up as well.

"No power, no peace!" they chanted as they marched from Gullen Mall down the middle of Second Avenue, halting traffic. Roland pumped his fist in the air to emphasize each chant. Others slapped their hands on the hoods of stopped cars. A young couple in one car—probably fellow students— were clearly frightened as the crowd enveloped them. In another car, an elderly woman seemed to take it in stride, just watching and waiting for the crowd to pass by.

Ian recognized a few members of the university faculty marching right along with them, including the Dean of the

College of Liberal Arts, though he couldn't imagine any of them slapping cars or threatening drivers. He chuckled at the thought.

Residents, too, streamed in from side streets and joined the march. Their numbers continued to swell as they walked, and the crowds also filled Cass Avenue, a commercial corridor that paralleled Second Avenue, all the way to downtown. Ian and Roland emulated other marchers by jumping up and down to see how big the crowd was, but the march stretched as far as they could see in every direction.

"This is massive!" Roland shouted.

A helicopter with "POLICE" clearly marked on the tail boom made a low and loud pass, rose up, and hovered high over the growing march.

The noise was overwhelming. There was the helicopter above, sirens at various distances, protestors chanting, hands clapping, car horns honking, music playing, and people yelling to talk with each other over the racket. People all along the march had whistles—Ian wondered where they got them—and blew them spasmodically, adding to the incessant uproar.

Some kind of commotion seemed to be happening ahead and, as Ian and his friends marched on, they came upon a police car abandoned in the middle of the road with its siren still blaring and its headlights and emergency lights flashing. Its four doors were flung wide open. Its windshield was cracked and splintered, and two of the door windows were smashed.

Some of the marchers jumped on top of the police car. Two young guys stood on the hood and another on the car's roof as they kicked at and stomped on the emergency lights, trying to break them and strip them off.

The three protestors were forced to jump down as another, larger group of young men began rocking the police car. More people joined them, including Roland—against Tina's protestations—and the car was eventually tilted over onto its side, eliciting a raucous cheer from the crowd. And still the siren blared.

Chapter 3

Tony "JD" Wiggins, a twenty-nine-year veteran of the Detroit Police Department, had only recently become the city's chief of police. He had joined the force (or 'the Farce,' as the rank and file called it) after graduating from Cass Technical High School and, after three years on the job, he took night classes at Wayne County Community College. Fifteen years later, he even earned a law degree from Wayne State and passed the bar exam, and his fellow officers began calling him "JD" for his Juris Doctor. Soon thereafter, JD was promoted to major and assigned his own precinct.

That was fourteen years ago. And now he had just one year to go for a full thirty years of service and retirement with a full pension at the age of forty-eight. But first things first. Into the breach once again.

Although he was a firm believer in community policing—posting officers to districts in which they lived and encouraging them to be active members of their neighborhoods—Wiggins found it difficult to enact. The police department was too short-staffed and getting smaller each year, and the city too geographically dispersed to fully enact community policing. So he had to rely on "strategic policing" by which police assets were deployed from across the city to where they were needed most, which often changed from month to month, sometimes even day to day.

It was a game of Whac-a-Mole. Wiggins took a page out of the U.S. Army's playbook and "swarmed" crime hotspots with hundreds of police, sometimes nearly the entire on-duty police force from across the city. Car and foot patrols, even cops on horseback, would saturate the area for days on end until, naturally, they would be needed elsewhere in the city—often two, three, or four areas at the same time—when crime spiked as a result of the relative absence of police. Then police would redeploy and swarm to the new hot spots. And on it went.

~ ~ ~

The cross-country runners—Ian, Sarah, Tina, Roland, Dakota, and Trevor—didn't know where the march was going, except that it was headed for downtown. Ian imagined they were marching to City Hall. However, as they passed Cass Technical High School to their right, the twenty-five-story Great Lakes Energy Enterprises corporate tower, with the word "GLEE" emblazoned on the top astride its logo of a powerfully built man wielding a lightning bolt in one hand, and the sun in the other emerged directly in front of them, marking the entrance to Detroit's downtown. It was then clear to all where they were heading.

It took a little more than an hour for the head of the march to trek the two miles from Fountain Court, cross over Interstate 75, and enter downtown. As they crossed the interstate, the march melded into an even larger sea of protesters and pedestrians occupying the streets and sidewalks around the four-block long and two-block wide corporate complex.

As Ian and his runner friends entered downtown, they were stunned by the sheer size of the crowds. There was an excitement in the air, and Ian was struck by the kinds of people they encountered. There were people of all ages and all walks of life and, while the majority were black, the crowds were ethnically diverse.

The police helicopter that the runners had spotted earlier was hovering overhead, and two other helicopters circled the downtown. Ian read "WHWK Skyhawk" on the tail boom of one helicopter, with a cartoonish eye and beak painted on its front nose. He watched two more helicopters, one hovering far to the west and the other hovering to the south.

Ian pointed at the helicopters. "There must be more marches coming!" But no one could hear him.

~ ~ ~

Approximately three miles to the west of downtown, in Detroit's West Side, Michelle wrapped her arms around Aaron's narrow waist and rested her chin on his shoulder, causing Aaron to stutter-step as she clung snugly to him. AJ smiled and threw his arm over her shoulders, put his lips to her forehead and made a sucking sound. "Mmmm ... brains," he said in a zombie voice, "mo' brains." Michelle giggled and pulled away from him. Aaron "AJ" Jones and Michelle Gibbs walked with a crowd of nearly twenty others, mostly high school students who, like AJ and Michelle, had just gotten out of school for the day. Social media had buzzed all day about the fire the night before and about scores of people marching on downtown in protest. Some teachers were visibly upset by the news of the fire, and some had even abandoned their planned lectures for the day and instead talked about the GLEE shutoffs and Mrs. Price. As the school day wore on, social media reported large protests and sporadic rioting. All of the kids knew something big was happening, and they couldn't wait for school to let out.

After returning home from school, AJ and his friends met up and strolled south along North Campbell Street amid sparsely spaced single-family homes—most of which were abandoned and crumbling into ruins—to Michigan Avenue, which they found packed with protesters. A large crowd was milling around the intersection of Michigan and Livernois, so Aaron and his friends made their way there.

Several blocks ahead, flames danced from the window frames of a parked car, and thick black smoke billowed into the sky. More columns of smoke rose in the distance toward downtown. It seemed that the land itself—broken and burned houses, abandoned buildings, and the brown roots of overgrown vines and weeds—had shifted beneath their feet and somehow set fire to the random cars and buildings that had thus far escaped the rotten touch of neglect.

Car traffic was light; the few cars that did pass blew their horns. Many were packed with young people, some hanging out of the windows and flashing the "V" sign. Two GLEE vans heading south on Livernois came upon the intersection and found themselves under a barrage of rocks and bottles. They zigzagged through the intersection, ignoring a red light, passing through the gauntlet of flying projectiles.

There was anger among the crowd, especially among the older adults. But, for the teenagers and people in their 20s and 30s, the atmosphere was electric. They fed off of each other's excitement. They were experiencing a feeling they hadn't really known before, a feeling of being part of something important.

A police car speeding with its siren blaring and lights flashing, absorbed a barrage of assorted missiles before the driver slammed on the brakes. The car skidded to a halt. The crowd fearlessly swarmed in front of it and unleashed another, even more withering barrage of rocks and debris.

The police car reversed and peeled backward, its tires smoking. A Molotov cocktail was hurled against the vehicle, exploding on the hood. The driver threw the car into a 180-degree turn and fishtailed back in the direction from which he'd come, leaving a trail of smoke.

AJ and the crowd raised their fists and cheered in approval.

~ ~ ~

"Shit," muttered Assistant Chief (Field Operations) Elliott Wilson.

He was standing outside the Detroit PD's Mobile Command Center—known as "the beast" among the officers—which was parked in an empty lot behind a main intersection not far from Alter Road. He had just ended a call with the chief of police on his cell phone, and now it chimed with new text messages.

"Isolated unrest," he said, shaking his head. "There goes *that* theory."

"What's up?" asked his partner.

"Nothing. Downtown's erupting."

~ ~ ~

For Ian and his fellow runners, the atmosphere downtown was festive. Most participants had come with friends and family, and they chatted loudly to be heard over the clamor.

The demonstrations appeared largely spontaneous, but they organized quickly through social media and word of mouth. For most, it was a welcomed disruption of work and school—like a snow day. But it was also meaningful. They were doing something by protesting and hopefully making a difference.

Things were decidedly different, however, as they got closer to GLEE Tower. Police were lined up along the eastern perimeter of the corporate complex. They were decked out in full riot gear: shields, helmets, and batons. The northern perimeter was free of police. It was packed shoulder to shoulder with protestors, with more streaming in. Roland and Tina led the way, plotting a course to the front of the crowd.

"Roland," pleaded Tina, begging him to slow down.

As they pressed on, the crowd grew denser, packed inside the GLEE complex. There were four buildings to their left, including the company's main tower. To their right was the sprawling Grand Arnault Casino and Hotel complex. It seemed fitting to Ian that the power company would be co-located alongside a massive casino.

The crowd blocked the main entrance to the casino and hotel, where a group of burly men stood at the entrance to prevent protesters from entering the lobby. But the protesters were focused on the GLEE building, not the casino. With the large complexes on either side of the road, and Interstate 75 behind them, Ian and his friends felt hemmed in.

They appeared to have arrived at the center of it all—a small, nondescript street corner, right across from the main entrance to the Grand Arnault Casino & Hotel.

GLEE Plaza Drive divided the corporate complex, and was gated. It ran between the main tower of GLEE Tower and the GLEE parking garage, the bottom two levels of which comprised the executive parking lot.

Multiple television cameras were trained on various reporters in sports jackets, all of them with their backs to the GLEE Tower. It was the very corner was where Mrs. Louise Jackson led her daily morning vigils. And amid a small tightly-knit group of people of various ages, an older woman—looking distinguished and somber—was standing behind a young man with a bullhorn. It was Mrs. Jackson.

Sarah pointed her out to Ian.

The bullhorn was tinny and nearly inaudible amid the cacophony of whistles, voices, and competing chants. Nevertheless, the young man's voice carried over the racket.

"How many more needless deaths?" he shouted. *"No more!"* the crowd responded in a single thunderous voice. "How much longer do we wait?"

"No longer!" the crowd roared.

A block south of the epicenter of the protests and across the wide boulevards of Bagley and Michigan Avenues from the GLEE Tower and Grand Arnault Casino, sat a third sprawling complex of concrete and glass. This was the *former* temporary Grand Arnault Casino before its new location was built across the street. Now it was the Detroit Public Safety Headquarters, or DPSH, and housed nearly one-third of the city's 2,500-strong police force, the upper echelons of the city's fire department, and a number of other city departments and state offices.

Detroit's center for police and emergency response was located in the heart of the fast-growing and largest protest anyone could remember, with tens of thousands of protesters and demonstrators converging on a six-block radius surrounding the GLEE Tower.

~ ~ ~

A mile east of DPSH and GLEE Tower, Mayor André Murray simultaneously held a press conference. A podium was set up in front of the Woodward Avenue entrance of the Coleman A. Young Municipal Center, out near the sidewalk so that the towering Spirit of Detroit statue—a seated man, powerful and muscular, holding the sun in one hand and a family in the other—served as a backdrop.

André eulogized Mrs. Bernadette Price and her family. "Poverty is no crime," he said, concluding his remarks. "Enough of the shutoffs! We must put lives before profit."

"Tomorrow morning," he continued, "my administration is filing papers in court for an injunction against the GLEE Corporation to immediately halt all shutoffs in Detroit and restore power to those without it during this cold weather emergency. Further, I am requesting the state and federal governments to declare the City of Detroit a disaster zone in order to implement emergency procedures like this injunction and free up emergency funds to aid us in these extremely difficult times."

Chapter 4

The girls huddled together, which had the effect of bringing the boys in closer as well. They had been taking part in
the vigil and protest for more than three hours as different
speakers took their turns with the bullhorn. It was nearing
four o'clock, and the crowds had reached their zenith. Ian
had never seen such large crowds before in Detroit's downtown. The largest he had seen was before was on Sunday
afternoons before a Lions game.

It began to flurry again.

"I'm hungry," announced Dakota.

Trevor wrapped his arms around her. "This is history in the
making and you're hungry?"

"It's getting colder," Tina piped in.

"Yeah, let's go," offered Ian. "I'm hungry, too." Truth be told,
Ian had grown bored with the protest.

The runners attempted to navigate back the way they had
come, but the crowd had become too dense, so they instead
headed for the wide boulevards at the southern periphery
of the GLEE complex. The going in that direction was much
easier. They soon discovered why.

Throngs of police in full riot gear were lined up across the
boulevard. Behind them were even more police, countless

more, along with television and media trucks.

"What is that, police headquarters?" asked Roland. His question went unanswered because it was obviously so. It looked like a fortress from which police seemed to ooze.

~ ~ ~

Chief Wiggins stood on the steps of DPSH, gazing out over the masses of police methodically falling into muster. Beyond the police, protesters continued their chants as they maintained their still-growing siege of GLEE Tower. A young and militant few attempted to provoke a line of Detroit's finest who, by training, looked disinterested.

Wiggins imagined that the scene was not unlike watching opposing Civil War army camps gearing up for battle as they warily sized each other up across a wide bucolic field that both sides knew would soon be despoiled with the blood of wretched young soldiers.

He shook his head and dismissed the analogy; this was a protest in a free society, not combat. Not yet, anyway. But he had his orders. It was already after four o'clock, and hundreds of GLEE employees were trapped in their building. The casino, meanwhile, had been on lockdown since mid-morning, stranding guests.

After strategizing with his assistant chiefs and directors, and the mayor, Wiggins decided that Third Street was the obvious target for a spear-like thrust to clear out the protesters and end the siege.

"I know you want to give them space, JD," Mayor André Murray told Wiggins as they looked out on the mass of police gearing up. "But not *this* space." He swept his hand across Bagley and Michigan Avenues and, turning in a near circle, he enlarged the scope of his arm to encompass the whole of the downtown. "Understand?" Wiggins nodded reluctantly. "Don't go bleeding heart on me, Chief. I know you understand. So, tell me, why not this space?"

Wiggins silently glared at the mayor.

André asked again. "Why not this space?"

The chief removed his police cap and ran his hand over his bald head as he tried to keep his temper in check. "Investments," he said, finally, with a sigh. "Billions of dollars are invested here. And it's got to be protected."

"You're goddamn right." André turned and walked away.

Members of the police chief's executive team, including his assistant chief of administration, Harold Washington, stood a few steps away as Wiggins spoke with André. When the mayor left, Wiggins turned and nodded to them.

"Clear them out," he said, "and issue a Code Blue for the downtown."

Washington was confused. The downtown was so far peaceful. The unrest was still concentrated in the east near Alter Road.

"What about Jefferson/Mack—"

Wiggins cut him off.

"Just *do* it, man!"

~ ~ ~

The runners walked eastward among the thinner but still sizeable crowds along the southern periphery of GLEE Tower. They could see that the hectic activity of the police on the other side of Michigan Avenue was becoming somewhat organized; the police appeared to be coming together in purposeful groups, mobilizing.

"Wait," said Roland, stopping dead in his tracks. A block ahead of them, cops on horseback, backed by ranks of police in full riot gear, filled in across the boulevard, cutting off their path.

"Oh man, we have to go back," said Sarah, her voice marked by a sudden nervousness. The group looked around for a way to leave, but the only way out was back between GLEE Tower and the Grand Arnault Casino.

As they looked on, however, the masses of police slowly lined up on across the boulevard from them. Then they started to cross the street, forcing protesters to retreat. Demonstrators ran back into the packed crowds between the casino and GLEE Tower, or east toward the runners. But the police had already closed off that route behind them and were now walking directly toward the runners. They tapped their shields in sync with their steps. It was a well-practiced, graceful choreography. And it was terrifying. The runners' only way out was closed off.

"We have to go!" exclaimed Trevor. But their only way out was quickly being closed off.

The runners jogged back to the street between the casino and GLEE Tower, but it was jammed pack—and the police were methodically closing the distance.

Barely audible over the crowds and the police tapping their shields was a recording being played over multiple vehicle-mounted loud speakers: "CLEAR THE AREA... THIS IS AN UNLAWFUL ASSEMBLY... CLEAR THE AREA IMMEDIATELY OR YOU WILL BE ARRESTED."

The north-end of the crowd on Third Street, already packed shoulder to shoulder, pushed back against the protesters at the south end. The mass of people surged southward, pouring from Third Street onto Bagley.

The police lines did not move, and many protesters were pressed up against them by the surging crowd. Rocket-like projectiles were launched from behind the police lines. They flew high into the air before falling into the midst of the crowds on Third Street, leaving contrails behind them as they flew. White smoke billowed from the projectiles after they landed, forming clouds that hugged the ground and spread, sending the protesters scattering.

"Tear gas!" shouted Roland.

"Oh, man," exclaimed Trevor as a surge of protesters ran straight at them. The police slowly and methodically walked east on Bagley, tapping their shields in sync behind the scattering protesters. Another line of police slowly and methodically walked westward from First Street, also tapping their shields.

Ian's group and the other fleeing protesters were trapped. They had nowhere left to run. The police were closing in from both directions. They shuffled forward like zombies—*police zombies*, thought Ian—but still they came.

"CLEAR THE AREA... THIS IS AN UNLAWFUL ASSEMBLY... CLEAR THE AREA IMMEDIATELY OR YOU WILL BE ARRESTED."

"We're *trying*, dude!" shouted Roland.

"Come on!" yelled Ian. He gripped a wrought iron fence surrounding the GLEE complex, and hoisted himself over, avoiding the spear-like tips that topped the fence. The other runners followed suit, as did many fleeing protesters. They darted for the GLEE building itself. There was nowhere else to go.

Crowds poured into the executive parking lot on the ground floor of the GLEE corporate parking garage and began jumping on cars and smashing windows. Tear gas wafted in, further fueling their rage. Others threw rocks and whatever else they could find at the windows and locked doors of the executive entranceway. Inside, security guards could be seen hanging back, fear on their faces.

The runners were at this entranceway. Tear gas was thickening and the runners started gagging. Mucous streamed from their noses, and their eyes burned. Covering their faces with their arms and rubbing their eyes only made the burning even worse. The pain was excruciating.

Ian slumped to his knees. Trevor and Roland grabbed him under his armpits and dragged him along. Tina vomited.

Roland let go of Ian. He ran straight for the entranceway and drop-kicked the locked glass door. Others came with tire irons and car jacks lifted from the parked cars. The glass cracked and splintered into spider webs before a protester was finally able to kick through the glass.

An unknown protester, his face hidden behind a bandana, poured bottled water over Ian's face, then forcefully removed Ian's coat and T-shirt, despite the freezing cold. He soaked Ian's shirt with water and tied it around his face like a kerchief to protect against the tear gas, then wrapped the coat around Ian's shoulders.

Ian staggered to his feet with the help of Trevor, Sarah, and the protester, trying to regain his composure. He threw a brief hug of thanks around the protester, who then joined the crowd now swarming through the entrance to the GLEE building. Ian, Trevor, and Sarah followed, half-carrying Tina with them.

Inside, the runners and protesters found a brief respite from the tear gas but not the chaos. Protesters attended to each other, using bottled water to wash away the tear gas and mucous from their faces. Others began destroying the security counter, kicking and smashing it, ramming trash cans into the lobby walls, breaking through dry wall.

Protesters tried using the elevator, but it had been turned off. The stairway doors were locked. An authoritative voice boomed over an intercom. *"THIS IS GLEE SECURITY. RE-MAIN AT YOUR DESKS. A POLICE OPERATION IS UNDER WAY TO CLEAR THE BUILDING AND PROPERTY OF PRO-TESTERS."*

Roland crouched down to look at Ian, Sarah, and Tina. Ian had removed his shirt from around his face and was covering Tina's face with it, rubbing it as she hyperventilated. Mucous streamed out of her nose.

Roland paced. "We can't stay here." He was breathing heavily. His eyes were red and inflamed, and his face and hair was caked with mucous.

"Where are we going to go?" pleaded Sarah.

"We have to run. Just run—they can't catch us all."

Ian removed his shirt from Tina's face. "Can you run, Tina?" Her eyes were both inflamed, her right eye swollen shut.

Roland was incensed. "Holy *shit!* Motherfuckers!" Other protesters volunteered bottled water to pour over Tina's face and eyes.

Outside the lobby's south entrance, three cars—a silver Lexus LS, a black G-class Mercedes-Benz SUV, and a gunmetal gray Audi S8—were on fire. Thick black smoke filled the parking garage and wafted into the lobby. Protesters continued swarming into the garage, some of them taking time to jump on cars, pound on their hoods, or kick at them. Outside the north entrance, protesters jogged and walked at a less frenzied pace along GLEE Plaza Drive North.

The runners gathered themselves and prepared to enter the fray again, the boys dousing their T-shirts in water and wrapping them around their faces, the girls using their sweaters to shield their faces.

"Let's go!" shouted Roland, and the runners stormed out of the north entrance.

They found the going a bit easier along GLEE Plaza Drive North, but as they emerged from the GLEE complex at Grand River Avenue, what they saw shocked and frightened them. They had fled one war zone and entered another.

A running battle was raging between the crowds of protesters and riot police, including police on horseback, who charged at the protesters, forcing them to run, before pulling back to the relative safety of police lines.

Bricks, rocks, pebbles, glass bottles, cell phones—practically every projectile imaginable—was flying through the air toward groups of police. In turn, the police launched tear gas and fired bean bag bullets, punctuating the cacophony of breaking glass, car horns and sirens, shouts and screams, and the pitter-patter of raining bricks and stones with the booms of tear gas rifles and bean bag shotguns.

The three-by-five block area across from Grand River Avenue between I-75 and Bagley Avenue comprised mostly parking lots where buildings had once stood. The lots were unusually full of vehicles, most of which belonged to protesters, and there was a mad dash for the cars as protesters swarmed over the lots, running, opening doors, blowing horns, yelling.

Numerous cars along Grand River Avenue and side streets had been overturned. Cars lay on their sides or completely upside down. Police cars, a couple of GLEE work vans, a city car. A city bus was engulfed in flames. It was dusk now, and the flames burned brightly against the darkening sky.

Although the lots were almost empty of buildings, a few remained standing. They stood mostly at corners. They were either abandoned or served as extra storage space for some of the downtown businesses.

Now they burned.

Smoke poured from the ground floors of two buildings, and gently wafted from the upper windows of two more. One building, a six-story storage facility for GLEE, had flames thrusting out of every window. The building was three blocks away, but the runners could feel the heat.

They jogged north up Second Street and passed the one building, a church, that stood alone and unmolested. They crossed over I-75 and found themselves heading back the way they had come.

Once they had crossed over I-75, the crowds thinned out a little. Car traffic, however, was thick and slow-moving as they headed north out of the lots. Within the crowds, many people appeared distraught and even traumatized. That was certainly true of the runners. But there were no police here, and the runners and other pedestrians could relax a little.

As the crowds streamed northward and away from the chaos, others went toward the downtown. They were young people in their teens and twenties, nearly all male. A few menaced older people who stood in their way, some even throwing punches and then darting away. A woman was knocked to the ground and, when her husband dared intervene, he was set upon by multiple teenagers. They pummeled him with punches and kicks before continuing toward the downtown as if nothing out of the ordinary had happened.

Dakota was punched in the face by a passing teenager. It was a glancing blow, and Dakota wasn't really harmed, but she was shaken. The boy was long gone before the runners could give chase, and besides, what could they do?

As Ian looked back toward the city, watching the teenagers zigzag through the crowds, snagging purses and cell phones, and sparking some fights along the way, his eyes drifted to the city's skyline. He could see that several more fires had been set, casting dull orange hues amid the tall shadows of the buildings. Several helicopters circled the downtown with search lights shining downward, their boom and un-dercarriage lights blinking white and red as they moved.

It appeared that World War Three had descended on Detroit.

~ ~ ~

Some 270 miles to the north, across the Straits of Macki-nac between Lake Michigan and Lake Huron, on Michigan's heavily forested and sparsely-populated Upper Peninsula, forty-five-year-old Floyd Barksdale was sitting in his reclin-er in front of the television. The telephone rang.

"Who do you think it is?" his wife Gloria asked as she strug-gled out of the couch and waddled to the kitchen. Floyd only grunted as she picked up the phone.

"Ricky!" It was as if it had been years since she had spoken with Floyd's nephew. (It hadn't).

"Ricky boy!" shouted Floyd into the receiver after snatching it from his wife. "No, I don't got cable. Maybe it's on regular TV. Hey, honey, turn the news on!"

"I'm right here, for gosh sake!" She studied the TV before pushing the "Power On" button. The TV was very loud, a laugh track filling the interior of the trailer. "Oh, geez."

"We gonna miss it!" shouted Floyd.

Gloria switched to Channel 13.

"Sure you got the right channel?" demanded Floyd loudly over the high volume, but Gloria nodded emphatically and shushed him with a wave of her free hand as she studied the TV to find the volume button again to turn the darn thing down.

"Well I don't see nuthin' about no riot," said Floyd into the receiver, "but I'll keep it on."

Gloria moved to the couch and sank back into it with a deep grunt.

"Well, let's not get worked up just yet, boy," Floyd said into the phone. "We got a meet next Saturday anyways, so let's talk about it there. All right? Good, all right, then. See you then, Ricky."

Floyd Barksdale, "Colonel" in the Superior Volunteers militia group, held the phone out and waited for Gloria to work her way off the couch, take the receiver, and place it back into its holder in the kitchen.

~ ~ ~

In the WHWK Channel 13 news studio just north of the city, in Southfield, Wayne State University intern Josh Fink monitored relevant Twitter and other social media live. Two that proved to be particularly popular were the hashtag feeds *#EndTheShutoffs* and *#LivesBeforeProfit,* the latter slogan inspired by the mayor's afternoon press conference.

Before the reported fire on the east side that claimed Bernadette Price and her extended family, the #EndTheShutoffs hashtag feed typically had fifteen to twenty tweets daily, but it would spike to as many as a thousand following a reported house fire. Following the Price family home fire, however, the hashtag feed jumped to five hundred in the early morning hours, and soared to more than three hundred thousand before eleven o'clock a.m. Throughout the day, the number of tweets averaged more than one hundred every few seconds, with messages like "They're killing us!" "Shutoff GLEE!" "Shutoff Detroit!" and "March on GLEE!"

Facebook posts with these hashtags had also blossomed throughout the day, and cell phone videos of the protests at GLEE Tower were posted on YouTube and other social media outlets.

News of the Price fire, including articles about the lives of Mrs. Bernadette Price and her family, and news about the protests, whipped around the city and region through a range of social media outlets, including Twitter, Facebook, and Instagram. The explosion on social media was a story in its own right, and Josh was tasked with writing it—his first foray into professional journalism.

As the day drew to a close and the sun settled on the south-western horizon amid a fiery orange, red, pink and purple glow, a charged atmosphere descended over all of Metro Detroit and beyond.

Chapter 5

The overnight hours brought a semblance of peace to Detroit. Both in the downtown and across the city's neighborhoods, most of the protesters had returned home for the evening. Some teenagers and young adults had gone downtown in the early evening to partake in clashes with police (and anyone else, for that matter) as police maneuvered to clear protesters away from GLEE Tower. The Code Blue, however, had brought Detroit PD's full complement of 2,500 officers to the downtown and, by late evening, police in riot gear nearly outnumbered the roving bands of young miscreants.

The runners made it back to midtown without any more drama. They crashed at the apartment of roommates Tina and Dakota two blocks from campus. They did their best to treat each other's residual tear gas effects and the bruise on Dakota's face from the punch she took. Afterward, they stayed up for a while watching the news on television and surfing social media. They were wound up early in the evening, but exhausted by ten o'clock. The boys tried to stay up later, watching movies, but dozed off with the television still on.

Conditioned after more than a semester of early morning training, Ian awoke at precisely five-thirty the next morning. For a moment, he forgot where he was, and even forgot about the previous day's events, but a hushed conversation between Sarah and Dakota brought it all back.

He stumbled to the bathroom and, when he came out, Roland and Trevor were also awake.

Ian walked into the kitchen and peered into the fridge. He was intent on finding a can of Red Bull and, not seeing any, merely grunted. Closing the fridge door, he saw Sarah brewing some coffee. She stood with a hand on her hip and a *well?* expression on her face.

"Hey," he muttered, and walked back to the living room to pull on his jeans and mucous-stained T-shirt.

"Are we going to run today?" he asked out loud to anyone.

Within a few minutes, the guys were dressed and out the door. They returned to their dorms, changed, and started on their run. Rather than take a university shuttle to Belle Isle for their usual morning run, they opted to head down Woodward Avenue, a gentrified neighborhood that linked Wayne State University with midtown and downtown.

It was still dark, and traffic was light at six a.m. as they ran right down the Q-line track into downtown, jogging in a tight formation like sleek fighter jets. A caustic smell of smoke and chemicals assaulted their nostrils as they passed the Detroit Pistons' and Red Wings' Arena, crossed over I-94, and entered the downtown.

The downtown was busy despite the hour. A fire company stood watch over the rundown six-story GLEE storage facility that had burned overnight. Now it was just a charred shell. Its interior was gutted, and its roof and upper floors had collapsed into a blackened pile of smoldering debris.

A couple of smaller buildings that the runners had last seen burning were now simply gone, leaving piles of debris and smudges where they had once stood.

Police seemed to be everywhere.

The runners attempted to loop around GLEE Tower, but it was surrounded by all sorts of police and fire department vehicles, as well as police officers. Portable stadium lights were trained on GLEE Tower's executive entranceway, and they could see that the corporate parking garage's outer shell was stained by the oily smoke of burned cars and tires.

DPSH remained as busy as they had last seen it. Scores of police loitered about on the sprawling lawn in front, and dozens of tents had been set up. A mobile command center bus and several trailers were sitting in the parking lot. It appeared to Ian and the runners that the police were camped out at the DPSH, even sleeping there—an interesting if ominous development.

Roland shook his head. "What, the cops are the Army now?"

Third Street, the epicenter of the previous day's unrest, ran North-South for nearly a mile from Grand River to the Cobo Convention Center on the Detroit River. It passed in front of DPSH and between GLEE Tower and the Arnault Grand Casino. It was as if DPSH had grown across the street to now encompass all of Third Avenue, sprouting throngs of bored and cold police. It was closed to traffic, including pedestrians, preventing the three runners from getting any closer. So the runners headed south along First Street to the Cobo Convention Center, where they looped around the massive complex to the Riverwalk and continued their run northward for the almost three miles to their regular jaunt at Belle Isle.

As they trekked along the waterfront, they could see police on horseback and in riot gear. They were lining up in front of the gleaming seven-tower Renaissance Center, the city's crown jewel and the global headquarters of General Motors.

~ ~ ~

At five o'clock that same morning, Catherine Bowling rode in the passenger seat of a Detroit City Police car. It was thrilling for her, and she was surprised at how nice the car was. It was a new Ford Mustang with an updated paint scheme depicting the city skyline. "Can you drive with the lights and siren on?" she asked the uniformed driver like a little school girl.

The officer chuckled. "Sure, if you want me to." He flipped on the police lights and produced a loud WHAH WHA from the siren. He turned off the lights, however, as he turned onto Fiske Drive, a quiet residential street with nicely kept English Tudor homes. In another moment he turned into the driveway of Manoogian Mansion, the official residence of the mayor.

"That was fun," Catherine said as she opened the door. "Thanks for the lift, Officer... Thomas," she said, squinting to read his name plate.

"Anytime, Mrs. Bowling, so long as you don't have to ride back there," he said, nodding to the back seat.

"Been there, done that," she said with a twinkle in her eye, and closed the door.

"Welcome to Manoogian Mansion, Mrs. Bowling," said a young man dressed in a suit.

Catherine was ushered into the mansion's Ford Conference Room, where several city officials and various department heads stood about, drinking coffee and munching on an assortment of items from the full breakfast buffet. Catherine spotted the line of coffee urns at a table along the wall, but had to pass through a gauntlet of suits to get there. She took a deep breath and stepped forward, greeting the chief of police and exchanging pleasantries with the head of the Health Department, the head of Water and Sanitation, the director of Jobs and Economic Growth, and others, before reaching the coffee. *Victory.*

Mayor André Murray and his entourage soon filed into the room, and everyone headed for the long conference table at the center of the room. Catherine marched right up and took a seat while others fumbled about and deferred to one another.

"Thank you everyone for coming on such short notice, and at such an ungodly hour," André began. It was five-thirty sharp, Catherine noted, and the mayor and his staff commenced with briefing the department heads on the previous day's unrest. A police captain shared intelligence on what to expect later that day, noting that social media remained abuzz with highly elevated activity during the overnight hours. *#ShutoffDetroit* was a new social media hashtag that had gone viral.

Chief Wiggins laid out his strategy—the "Code Blue" for the downtown—for preventing a replay of protestors laying siege to the central business district. He also talked about coordinating with the State Police, who agreed to reposition assets to back up Detroit PD, and with the Governor's Office.

The Transportation director, himself a former career cop, identified the most important routes to be kept open and protected by police escorts, if possible. He shared his concerns for city buses and their drivers, and how the department might respond to reports of gathering crowds and unrest, which mostly entailed rerouting buses or shutting some routes down completely. Changes in routes and schedules would be announced via the department's website and through its mobile app.

André turned his attention to Catherine, and all heads turned in her direction. "I know it's getting late, Catherine," he said, nodding to a clock on the wall, "but..."

"I am of the mind to close the schools, sir," Catherine interjected.

Chief Wiggins whispered into the mayor's ear, and the two conferred in hushed tones. After a moment, Wiggins spoke. "We wish you wouldn't," he said. "If the schools close, we could have thousands of juveniles on the streets."

"You could have that anyway," responded Catherine.

"Yes, of course," said the mayor. "But, if we close the schools now, we would be broadcasting an expectation of unrest when, really, yesterday's events could very well be a one-off thing, despite the social media buzz. If our schools remain open, that would keep most kids off the streets and signal a continuation of normalcy."

"Lots of businesses stake their decision to close or not on whether the schools are open," contributed Dawn Lambert, the city's executive for Jobs and Economic Growth. "If the schools close, lots of businesses will close," she said.

"You see our dilemma," André told Catherine. "As superintendent of the school district, I know you're concerned about the safety of students; we all are. But I'm afraid we could be pouring fuel on the fire if we close the schools."

All eyes remained fixed on Catherine. They were waiting for her to respond, to give in to the mayor. He could just order her to keep the schools open. Why didn't he? Because this was a CYA moment. *The mayor doesn't want to give an order that could come back to bite him.*

Catherine cleared her throat. "If things were to deteriorate, how do you propose to ensure that our school children are returned to their homes safely and in an orderly manner?"

André seemed somehow physically relieved with Catherine's question, and turned his head to the police chief. Wiggins took his cue and launched into a description of how unrest, though often sporadic, tended to be centered at specific geographical points, and that police would coordinate with schools and buses to navigate around hotspots. He proposed using police escorts for school buses where necessary and allowing parents to pick up their children directly from the schools if possible.

The chief's plan wasn't at all convincing for Catherine, but the mayor now turned his attention to the chief director of operations, who laid out a plan to coordinate various city departments. After twenty minutes of administrative planning, the mayor and his entourage stood. "Thank you, everyone, for coming," he said. "We've got a long day ahead of us. Godspeed, everyone, and keep the lines of communication open."

And that was that.

Though Catherine never directly acquiesced, she tacitly gave the administration something to work with. And so, the schools remained open. *So that's why the mayor seemed relieved.* Catherine smiled to herself. *He's good.*

Outside, an assortment of cars and SUVs were lined up in the circular driveway. Catherine spotted the Ford Mustang police car where Officer Fred Thomas sat drinking a coffee and exploring his smart phone. He looked up and saw her, then raised his coffee cup to wave her in.

"How'd it go?" asked Fred, driving down Jefferson Avenue toward downtown.

"That mayor is a piece of work," Catherine noted.

Fred snorted. "Ain't that the truth."

Catherine looked out her window and saw the massive Renaissance Center up ahead. To their left, three college runners gracefully navigated through the leafless trees of MacArthur Bridge Park. Their presence projected a sense of calm. *Maybe things won't be so bad after all.*

~ ~ ~

Arturo Ayala broke out three neckties, one for himself and one for each of the boys. Jacqueline ushered them into the master bedroom, already donned in button-down collared shirts and blue jeans. Arturo handed them their ties and stood in front of the bathroom mirror. He began putting on his tie with slow and deliberate movements, the boys copying his steps.

"We're going in style," announced Arturo.

"My boys are so handsome," said Jacqueline, wrapping her arms around Artie's waist and resting her chin on his shoulder.

"Why we gotta dress up?" asked sixteen-year-old Frederick as he fumbled with his tie. "We ain't going to church."

"It's we aren't, and why do we have to," chastised Arturo.

"*¡Chale!*" said Frederick, making fourteen-year old Martín laugh, "*No somos quinqui.*"

"Besides," Arturo added, "it *is* church. It's *applied* church. We're standing up for what's right. We're standing up for people who can't stand up for themselves."

Jacqueline handed each of the boys a card and told them to put it in their pockets. She handed one to Arturo as well, and he looked it over, raising an eyebrow. It contained emergency contact and other information, like blood type and allergies.

"Just in case we get separated or anything bad happens," Jacqueline said.

"No, I get it," said Arturo, shaking his head. "It's smart. I'm just impressed that you thought ahead and printed these things up," he said, leaning forward to plant a kiss on her lips.

Jacqueline leaned back. "Impressed that I thought ahead?" she said, frowning.

"You know what I mean," said Arturo with a smile, pulling Jacqueline into a hug.

Within minutes, the young family was strapped into Jacqueline's Jeep Grand Cherokee and headed toward the East Pointe Park & Ride for the forty-minute rush hour trek into the city.

Chapter 6

Alexander Cooley was in his office at nine-twenty-five that morning, eating a bagel and mindlessly scrolling through his emails. It was the usual barrage of memorandums, policies, and meeting times, ninety percent of which didn't even pertain to him. *Delete.* He scanned the next email. *Delete.* After another half-dozen, he was all caught up and headed for the daily executive staff meeting.

"What's going on?" Alex asked Bobby, a kid right out of college.

"You didn't hear about the riots yesterday?" Bobby asked. Alex shook his head. "Yeah, man, there was a riot last night over by the casino. They were protesting a shooting or something." Alex only half heard him. He was checking his phone for the Piston's score before the meeting began.

Donnie Tillman, the bank's regional president, sat down at the head of the table, and everyone, including Alex, put away their phones.

"Hope no one had any trouble getting home last night," Donnie said with a chuckle. "I understand that there was some excitement downtown."

"What was it about?" asked Jim, the real estate point man thirty years' Alex's senior and, according to Alex, a total prick who didn't know how to operate a smart phone and was utterly clueless about apps, social media, and even the internet. How he remained a senior executive in good standing was beyond Alex. "Was it a police thing?"

"Something about a fire," Donnie said with a shrug.

And, with that, the meeting turned to status reports and updates on assets owned by the bank, the daily housing sales briefing, an update on commercial real estate sales and rents, and so on. The meeting was adjourned after an hour, and Alex was back in his office, staring at a spreadsheet. *It's just another day, another day on earth,* he sang in his head, a song with a dance beat that he had heard somewhere.

~ ~ ~

By the time Ian, Roland, and Trevor were back on the Wayne State campus, traffic had thickened with morning commuters. The day was getting on as usual and, for Ian, the events of the previous day seemed almost as if they hadn't happened.

Ian had a light Tuesday-Thursday class schedule: a Physical Geography class from 9:30 to 10:45, and a second class, World Civilization II, from 11:00 to 12:15. And then, except for assignments and studying, he was free for the day. Ian was a morning person, a rare bird among college students. It had become a running joke among his roommates and friends who would be half-asleep and easily agitated by the always cheery Ian in the early morning, and the roles would gradually reverse as the day wore on.

Geography class was a drag. Ian's cell phone vibrated incessantly. He stole glances at it when he could. Various student groups were calling for another march on downtown. Roland had texted Ian as well; he was eager to march again. As he scrolled his text messages, a new one came from Sarah. She, too, was back on Fountain Court where, apparently, even more people and students than the day before were gathering.

As his Geography class neared its end, Ian was fidgety. He would have fifteen minutes to get to his next class, but so many of his friends were joining what was turning out to be possibly an even bigger protest than the day before. He simply had to go.

I'll be there, he texted Sarah.

History could wait.

~ ~ ~

Five hours into her shift, Barbara Hinton navigated a fourth generation LF Series NovaBus, city bus line 34, from 9 Mile southbound for the approximately one-hour trip toward the Rosa Parks Transit Center in downtown Detroit. She'd already been back to the center twice since beginning her run there, and this would normally be her final run before lunch. It was the seventy-five or so bus stops in one direction along Gratiot Avenue that stretched what typically would be a twenty-five minute drive into an hour. Barbara was just ten stops in after turning around at the 9 Mile Park & Ride, the outer end of the line, and her bus was already beginning to fill.

On the radio, the two buses ahead of her had reported that they were already full and were now heading non-stop into the city. Barbara made it a few more stops before she, too, was full, having squeezed the last passengers that she could fit into the bus at 7 Mile. She radioed in that she was also loaded, changed the sign on the top front panel of the bus to read "Full," and drove right past the next stop where a large crowd waited.

It was nearly ten o'clock, an unusual time for city buses to be filling up, and the stops had become more crowded as the morning wore on. Barbara's route went more quickly because she couldn't make any more stops, and she did a mental calculation. She concluded that she would have to make another run, maybe two. *Shit.* She passed several more stops where large crowds waited.

As she neared the downtown, growing crowds of people snaked their way past the bus stops and toward the city, with many carrying makeshift signs. Barbara had heard about the previous day's protests, but her shift had ended just as the protesters had begun to descend on the downtown. Not so today. Today they were getting an early start.

On the bus, passengers were enthusiastic, even jubilant. Overlapping conversations produced such a din of voices that it was hard to pick out individual ones. Barbara tuned it out, humming an old Tina Turner song, What's Love Got to Do with It?

"Pretty crowded bus," said a soft voice audible just below the din. In her large rearview mirror, Barbara saw a nicely dressed and bespectacled young man in the first seat, nearly pressed into it by a standing crowd that towered over him. "This can't be normal," he said sheepishly.

"No," Barbara chuckled, "not even for a Pistons game. Are you all going to the protest?"

"Yes, ma'am," chimed in a tall, well-dressed bearded man with a nice trim standing a few feet back. "It's long past time for us to stand up. Our lives matter and we need to make our voices heard."

The bespectacled young man nodded.

"We have to stand up for those who can't stand up for themselves," said another well-dressed boy, and a fashionable, beautiful woman standing behind him patted him on the shoulder and smiled at Barbara—a young family, she guessed.

"Well, God bless you and you all be careful," she said, bringing the bus to a stop at the Rosa Parks Transit Center, just blocks from GLEE. "Final stop," she announced, gripping a microphone. "Follow the crowds for GLEE Tower," she said, opening the doors. "Give 'em hell," she added. Her voice over the intercom was barely audible with the clamor of multiple conversations, but many passengers laughed as they departed the bus.

"Right on, right on," said the bearded man, offering a raised fist and a smile as the family stepped off the bus.

~ ~ ~

Andrew Wilson navigated his NovaBus on Linwood Street south toward the city. His bus, too, was filling up, and traffic had thickened rapidly—both unusual happenings on this particular route, line 29—and it was well beyond the morning rush hour.

Pedestrian traffic on Linwood was also unusually thick. The bus reached capacity at Davidson Avenue, and could take no more passengers. Andy progressed along his route slowly but bypassed the crowded stops. The sidewalk was too narrow for the crowds of pedestrians, and many were walking along the side of the road. Andy was forced to slowly navigate into the left lane and. As he passed the crowds, some people waiting at a stop he bypassed gave him a thumbs-down sign, and others waved their hands in dismissal. Their body language suggested that it was mostly done in jest, and Andy offered a thumbs-up in return. It was a rough part of town, he knew, but the crowds seemed festive.

As the bus passed Joy Avenue, things took a more sinister turn. Groups of young people stood along the sidewalks on either side of Linwood, and some just wandered into the middle of the traffic to cross. One car was forced to stop as a teenager stepped in front of it. The driver blew his horn, and a gaggle of teenagers swarmed around the car, slapping their hands on the hood and trunk and cursing the driver. The driver—a large, muscular black man—got out of the car and, as he stood and stretched out, the kids scattered. Traffic was halted until the large man climbed back into his car and pulled forward.

Thick black smoke billowed a short distance ahead, where more crowds were gathered and more people walked amid the traffic. A boarded-up building on the corner of Hazelwood was apparently on fire; thick acrid smoke poured out of every opening and drifted across Linwood. People stood nonchalantly around the smoking building, even in the roadway. They parted to allow the bus to pass.

"Yeah, boy, it's getting real now," said a passenger.

"Burn, baby, burn!" someone shouted as Andy navigated the bus past the smoking building.

A tussle erupted at the back of bus. "Hey, hey, hey!" Andy yelled, stopping the bus and turning around. "What's going on back there?"

"They're throwing stuff at the bus," several passengers answered.

"Yeah, man, don't stop!" someone yelled from the back of the bus. Andy and the passengers felt a "thonk" against the side of the bus. He grabbed his radio microphone and spoke into it. "10-34 at Blaine Street" he said, using the police code for riot.

"Where's the po-po when you need 'em?" a passenger joked, eliciting laughter. But, come to think of it, Andy hadn't seen a single police car since starting his route.

A minute later, a voice came over the radio. "10-34 at Grand River and Livernois." Then, another voice: "10-34 at Michigan and Martin," followed by yet another, "10-34 at West Grand and Rosa Parks."

That last one was straight ahead on Andy's route. He approached West Grand Boulevard where he normally would turn left, then right onto Rosa Parks for the remaining two miles or so into the city. This time, however, he simply stopped halfway through the intersection to consider his options. Menacing crowds were all over West Grand to his left, some pelting passing cars with stones and debris. There were fewer people, however, to his right, between Linwood and the half-mile west to Interstate 96.

Andy put on his turn signal and slowly made a right turn from the left lane, keeping an eye on his right side mirror for traffic that he might be cutting off. He made the turn and cautiously made his way toward the interstate on-ramp. Mercifully, his bus wasn't targeted by the dozen young men walking back and forth across the road, intimidating drivers. And, as he merged into traffic on I-96, probably the fastest way into the city from West Grand, yet another voice came over the radio.

"All buses return to Transit Center immediately."

Chapter 7

Tony Wiggins' heart sank when he heard the first 10-34 from the bus driver on Linwood. He had the downtown area pretty much buttoned-up despite the gathering of more protestors, perhaps even more than the previous day's. Tens of thousands, potentially. With the exception of a few officers broken into teams to escort city and school buses outside of the CBD, if necessary, every single member of the Detroit Police Department was in the central business district. Wiggins was confident that they could manage any unrest there. It was the sprawling outlying areas that worried him. Perhaps if they could swarm an area quickly, they could nip any unrest in the bud.

A team of thirty officers remained on station from the day before, at Gratiot and Mack Avenue, along with a mobile command center. Those officers, patrolling the entire four-mile length of Mack Avenue from Gratiot to Alter Road, reported restive, growing crowds and several arrests.

Wiggins picked up his microphone to issue a Code Blue for Linwood Avenue when the second 10-34 came in, this one from Grand River. *Shit.* Then the third one came in.

He issued a Code Blue order for three separate teams, each assigned to one of the areas called in by the bus drivers. He knew there would be more, and he would have to send officers out from the downtown, something he was sure the mayor wouldn't allow.

Alex, while formatting a recommendation report on the twenty-five mortgages proposal to investors and working to get an amortization graph to center properly, heard people talking in hushed tones in the lobby. *There,* he thought, leaning back in his chair with his hands clasped behind his head as he surveyed the chart. It looked good.

He heard Bobby ask the two office administrators what was going on. This prompted Alex to poke his head into the hallway to listen to the conversation. Apparently, large crowds were gathering in the downtown again, according to the women. There were also rumors about a terrorist attack or shooting. Alex scoffed.

"In Detroit? I mean, why? Have they *seen* this place?" Bobby snorted.

Bobby and the two young women followed Alex into his office to look out his tenth-floor window. Alex was astonished. He hadn't heard a thing as he worked, yet the street was full of people, many of them holding homemade signs. They appeared to be heading toward the north side of downtown toward the stadiums—as if there were a daytime Detroit Tigers or Lions game. But it was out of season for both, and the Pistons were out of town. Still, the sidewalks were packed full; there had to be hundreds of people. Maybe a thousand.

Alex turned to the computer on his desk and surfed to the Detroit Free Press. "GLEE Protests Enter Second Day" read a breaking news headline, along with photos of the crowds and police gathering at GLEE Tower again.

Aaron and Michelle, along with Xavier and Devin, his neighborhood friends since forever, caught the school bus at 7:10 as usual for the ten-minute ride to school. Reggie, another childhood friend, hadn't shown up this morning. Actually, Aaron was surprised that anyone at all had shown up. They had stayed out late the night before, throwing stones at passing traffic, which consisted of only a few cars here and there.

Mostly they had walked along Michigan Avenue, meeting friends, talking excitedly, and wondering what would come next. It was a revolution, one kid from the neighborhood said with bravado. It did seem like something, with a ground-level orange glow casting dancing shadows on tall buildings downtown that they could see from their part of the city. A couple of parked cars also burned brightly nearby, the air acrid with smoke. It was exhilarating, the cold air, the crowds, his friends' animated bodies silhouetted against the glow of the flames from the burning cars.

But when he returned home a little after midnight, his mother apparently hadn't heard about any revolution, and didn't care. At 5:30 the next morning, she shook him awake, threatening to throw a glass of water on his face if he didn't get up and go to school.

"Schools ain't closed, so you get your ass up before I put my foot up in it!" she bellowed when he suggested that there probably wouldn't be any school today.

And she was right. School was open, as usual. *Some revolution.*

Once at school, though, things were different. Half—no, more than half—of the teachers, it seemed, had called in sick, and so he had a substitute teacher for his very first class of the day. It seemed as if half the students hadn't shown up either. The hallway was noticeably less crowded between classes. The buzz among students, and even teachers and administrators, was electric.

Aaron and his fellow students grew restless. At lunchtime, he met up with Michelle and his friends, like he always did, but this time, along with scores of fellow students, they headed for the exits.

They walked south along Vinewood Street for the mile from their high school to Michigan Avenue, a steady stream of euphoric high school students triumphantly ditching school.

The kids were excited, including Aaron. "It's like a revolution!"

"Yeah, *revolution!*" exclaimed Devin, dropping his skateboard at his feet and effortlessly hopping on. He raised a fist as he spun around, all in one graceful motion. *"Revolution's the solution,"* he sang in a nasal voice, and giggled as he coasted on his board.

~ ~ ~

The news, much of it rumor, had grown more alarming as the day progressed, and Donnie Tillman, president of the regional Apex Superior Bank, called an impromptu meeting of executives and announced that they were closing for the day. Other downtown businesses, even the behemoth General Motors, were said to be doing the same.

Alex met with Bobby and other young executives in the lobby to check things out. They stepped out onto Griswold Street and right into a crowd of police gathered in front of their building and all along the street, dozens of them. They were in full riot gear with helmets, shields, and batons, and a half-dozen or so were on horseback, the horses lazily clopping along the road.

Alex and his colleagues strolled a block down to Jefferson Avenue and watched as even more police on horseback and in full riot gear lined up along the wide boulevard, which paralleled the Detroit River that linked Lake St. Clair and Lake Erie. They lined up in front of GM's five-tower, futuristic glass-and-steel Renaissance Center headquarters ("hard to believe it was built in the 1970s," said Bobby, offhand), and all along the streets of the Financial District.

Alex and his friends picked their way through the police lines and some gathering protestors. Alex felt out of place in his suit; he and his colleagues stood out amid the uniformed police and casually dressed protesters, some stylishly urban, others grungy. As they passed, the stares of some of the protesters, particularly the young and hard-looking, revealed pure disdain for anything resembling authority, like police or white men in suits.

Emboldened by the presence of his co-workers and throngs of police, Alex straightened and returned a hard look back to the protestors.

One co-worker, an alum of Michigan State, who started at Apex Superior just a month or two before Alex, suggested that lunch and beer at the Top Hat, the posh revolving restaurant and bar atop the Renaissance Center, would be a cool place to drink and watch the protests unfold in the city below.

It wasn't far, and when they neared the "RenCen," they could see that it was crowded with GM employees and executives, workers from other nearby firms, and plenty of Financial District workers, all standing around watching the police and protestors.

~ ~ ~

Bernice Hamandawana, a graduate student in journalism at Wayne State University and freelance reporter for Motown Mirror, an independent online and live-streaming news site, was speaking into a camera held by fellow WSU journalism student Daniel Rush, a 20-year-old junior. Bernice was musing on the growing protests in the heart of downtown Detroit when a young man with dreadlocks approached.

"Look!" he said, sweeping his hand to encompass the throngs of police in riot gear, others on horseback, all gathered in front of the Renaissance Center. Daniel followed the young man's hand with his smartphone, filming.

The mayor and an entourage of city officials emerged, accompanied by a mob of journalists and reporters who moved briskly among them, speaking emphatically with what appeared to be the police chief and a number of corporate executives. A few immaculate-looking young men in suits—young executives, to be sure—stood in pockets behind the protective police barrier, looking festive and curious as they hung together and spoke in hushed tones among themselves.

"*Look,*" the dreadlocked man said again. "They're lining up together: the police, the mayor, the CEOs. The city is naked and everything is laid bare. They are lining up against us."

A toothy grin flashed across his face. He sang in a childlike, sing-song voice:

They're lining up against us
the mayors and the players
Lined up against thee

He erupted in a contagious, hearty laugh.

"Bee!" someone called, and Daniel swung his camera around to pick up another dreadlocked young man, this one a little older, spectacled and dressed in a tan sports coat and jeans. He embraced Bernice, then clasped hands and shoulder-bumped the smiling singer. "Lee-Ron, my man," he said.

"Yo, Walter," said the young singer, "how you been, man?"

"You know each other?" asked Bernice.

"Yeah, girl," answered Walter. "This is LeRon Gordon, artist extraordinaire, and 'The People's Mayor'." Then, to LeRon, "Doing good, my man. Whatchya working on these days?"

"Doing some writing, you know, got some projects going on," answered LeRon. With a knowing laugh, he tilted his head toward the throngs of police. "Sticking it to the man."

"Is that one of yours, out by the Kronk?" asked Walter.

"You know it, brother," answered LeRon. "That's the 'Hurricane of Love'," he said with a wide grin. It was an abandoned industrial warehouse near the famous Kronk Gymnasium, abandoned and crumbling like Roman ruins, that he was referring to, its remnants now covered with a dark but cartoonish mural depicting a harrowing storm whose rain was bullets, and whose puddles were blood, the streets below dotted with fallen, mostly black, denizens. The storm clouds, upon close examination, were police cars with uniformed police officers crouching behind them and firing their pistols on the world below.

It was a not-so-subtle dig at Governor Clifford Krueger who, when turning the city away from the state's coffers amid Michigan's ongoing budget crisis (after slashing taxes by billions of dollars), offered his justification: "It's not more money this city needs," he had thundered like a preacher from a pulpit. "It's love! It's *tough* love this city needs!"

~ ~ ~

Ian, Roland, Trevor, Sarah, Tina, and Dakota—the Wayne State cross country runners—had marched with an endless stream of students and faculty from Wayne State, and residents from surrounding neighborhoods, straight down Cass Avenue again toward GLEE Tower. Lines of police and physical barricades kept protestors far from the complex this time, however, and protesters instead filled in along the streets and side streets of downtown.

The protesters shouted as they marched, alternating between "No power, no peace!" and "Shut off Detroit!" The runners, along with Walter Clay and other WSU students and student leaders, followed the crowds to the Coleman Young Municipal Center on Jefferson Avenue, now familiar to Ian, Roland, and Trevor after their early morning run. Police lined up on both sides of the wide boulevard. They looked like an army camped out in Hart Plaza, the gleaming headquarters of General Motors.

Ian watched as the protestors milled about and chatted with relaxed deportment. On occasion, and with increasing frequency, a random young man or woman (usually a young man) would walk up to the line of cops and stand nose to nose with an impassive, stone-faced, officer. They would either glare menacingly at the cop, or scream, "No power, no peace!" or some other slogan, right in the officer's face.

Some screamed obscenities and threats. They even feigned

attack, trying to get the police to flinch. Ian watched intently. He didn't understand the action. The cops had nothing to do with GLEE shutting off electricity, so why scream in the face of the officers? Clearly it was meant to intimidate, but it seemed to Ian that it was akin to poking at a hornet's nest.

"Yeah, man!" bellowed Roland, just to Ian's right, as a protester spit into the faces of a line of officers. "Spit on the pigs!" the kid yelled with apparent amusement.

Now Ian eyed Roland blankly, and with alarm. Roland caught Ian's expression, lowered his voice and spoke under the cacophony of sounds. "Hey," he said, "it's a protest, man, just getting into it."

"We don't want any of that, young man," said a bearded older gentleman, talking directly to Roland. "We don't want any violence."

Just as he said that, a shirtless teenager ran straight up to the line of police and leaped into a wall of shields, sending officers and himself sprawling to the ground. A half dozen or so young men and teenagers raced into the melee, throwing punches and kicking at the officers struggling to get back on their feet.

The lines of police lurched forward and lost their linearity. The lines melded into the crowd and formed several pockets of baton-swinging, helmeted cops raining bone-crushing blows onto any unlucky protesters they surrounded.

The crowd surged forward.

"It's on!" shouted Roland, his face alight with excitement as the crowd surged toward the RenCen. The crowd parted, revealing a group of four helmeted and shield-carrying police working in sync, swinging their batons at anyone close.

Ian froze as he saw a college girl take a blow across her face. An arc of blood, momentarily suspended in mid-air, traced her descent to the ground.

"Let's go!" Roland shouted, tugging at Ian, who had turned to sprint in the opposite direction with his cross-country teammates. As they took their first step, a second circle of baton-wielding police emerged to their front and left. Roland was still focused on tugging at Ian and, as he turned, he ran straight into the circle of cops.

"Roland!" shouted Ian. Seeing the cops, he grasped at Roland's shoulder.

Roland saw the cops at the last moment and agilely stepped to his right to bypass them. But he never saw the baton that came crashing down across his temple.

~ ~ ~

For Ian, the world seemed to enter a strange new dimension where time slowed and nearly stopped. The cacophony around him went silent in an instant except for the crack of the baton across Roland's temple that now echoed ceaselessly in Ian's ears.

He watched as Roland gracefully took two more steps (maybe he wasn't hit after all, *but that sound...*) before crumpling to the pavement. He lay face up, his legs twisted beneath him, his face turned toward Ian, his eyes locking with Ian's.

Ian went to him but was slammed to the ground. He was forced into a fetal position to try to protect himself as he absorbed the striking batons on his ribs and back, even on the back of his hands that covered his head. Then the muffled pitter-patter of clubs on his body ended almost as quickly as it began as the circle of police moved on to the next protester.

Ian opened his eyes, and for a moment he was confused. All
he saw were legs running this way and that. Mostly, they
were the legs of uniformed police attacking and expanding
into an ever-widening perimeter.

"Ian!... Ian!" The sound of his name was muffled and far
away.

"Ian!" It was Trevor, crouching over him, tapping him lightly on the cheek. Trevor was saying something but it was too
muted to make out.

Ian sat up slowly, helped by Trevor. The world sped up now.
It took another moment for the sights and sounds to sort
themselves out, but his ears and head were assaulted by a
cacophony of sounds near and far, alternating between subdued and roaring.

Trevor turned away from Ian and moved out of sight. Ian
remained sitting, and Sarah's face, looking dirty and panicked, now filled his. She was saying something, and trying
to get him to his feet.

Ian acquiesced and stood. When he took a step—all sounds
now roaring again, but crisper—he was unsteady, and Sarah
gripped him tightly around his waist.

"Help him, for God's sake!"

Ian heard as the sounds in his ears popped into a penetrating roar. It was an awful, anguished-filled feminine voice
pitched to its limit, cracking. Ian looked over and saw that
it was Tina. She was being dragged backward by her curly
hair by a helmeted cop as she kicked out and twisted and

scratched at the cop's arms. She looked like a feral cat gone completely wild, and then it all came back.

Roland...

There, behind a wall of shielded, helmeted cops, was Roland lying in the road, on his side, his arms and legs stiffened and extended straight out, hands bent inward at the wrists, his upper body whiplashing. He was having a seizure and no one was helping him.

"Oh, no," Ian heard, not realizing it was his own voice, as it dawned on him that the side of Roland's head was slamming repeatedly into the pavement as he convulsed. *"Roland!"* he yelled, now pulling out of Sarah's arms and running straight toward the wall of shields standing between him and Roland.

"Get back, you little fuck," a smug cop warned, swinging his baton to keep Ian at bay.

"That's my friend!" Ian shouted, pointing to Roland. "He's *dying!"*

The officer smirked. *"Good!"*

Ian, filled with rage, dashed between two officers, very nearly breaking through the line. But he was quickly subdued and shoved to the ground facedown. Officers handcuffed him with plastic ties while driving their knees into his back and driving his chin into the pavement.

Ian had a hard time breathing with the officers on top of him. He lifted his head and saw that two officers knelt at Roland's side and were now preventing his head from further slamming into the asphalt. One officer held Roland's head in his hands as his shoulders continued to rock back and forth. Blood poured through the officer's fingers.

69

Chapter 8

Daniel Rush had his camera trained on Bernice Hamandawana, Walter Clay, and the charismatic, toothy LeRon Gordon, "The People's Mayor," when a roar emanated from the crowd just ahead of them on Jefferson Avenue in front of the Renaissance Center. Though the boulevard was wide, the crowd in which they were embedded was standing shoulder to shoulder and front to back, packed in between the Detroit River on their right and a forest of tall buildings to their left. The streets and side streets of downtown were also filled in. The crowds along Jefferson Avenue and the streets of downtown were becoming denser by the minute as throngs of protesters continued streaming into the downtown. They trekked in by bus and by foot from the Northwest Goldberg district to the west. Other groups walked or were bused in from the south, from districts like Delray, Melvindale, River Rouge, and Ecorse. Still others drove from the suburbs north and west of the city, like St. Claire Shores, Warren, Clawson, Southfield, and beyond, snarling city-bound traffic on Interstates 94 and 75 and the M-10 highway.

Daniel held his camera up as high as he could, but could not see over the crowd of people around him. He had no idea what was occurring beyond the two dozen people immediately around him. The same was true for Bernice and Walter. LeRon, however, had an idea, and sing-songed his conclusion.

The match is lit
Now we move to the groove or get hit

It seemed to Daniel that LeRon couldn't help but speak in rhymes.

The crowd lurched backward and Daniel's heart leapt in his chest. Don't fall down, he ordered himself. People up front screamed and Daniel was doubtless that people were falling down. He couldn't see anyone fall, but he sensed it with the swaying of the crowd, along with the screams. People were turning around to run away from something. The look of fear on their faces—including Bernice's and Walter's—sent a cold shiver down Daniel's spine. He also turned to run. And he knew that his face, too, wore a mask of fear.

But still he held up his camera, determined to film. He watched as the crowd behind him also began turning around, turning their backs to him, a wave of turning heads and bodies passing through the crowd like dominos.

He was pushed into a trot from behind. A visible wave passed from behind him to his front and away from him, a wave of people trotting, then running. They were scattering toward the Cobo convention center to his front and the downtown to his right.

Dropped cell phones, plastic bottles, bags, purses, sneakers, fast food wrappers, and the squirming bodies of people who had fallen down remained behind in their wake.

Still the wave reverberated outward, and there was a sonic wake of glass breaking, metal clanging on metal, screams, shouts, curses, and a loud sustained storm of sound like hail. Only this hail was composed of falling rocks and other debris, falling and bouncing across the pavement, everywhere.

The dense, peaceful crowds of people of all ages and backgrounds, entire families, broke apart as they fled the onslaught of baton-wielding police officers. The crowds along Jefferson Avenue and nearby streets had broken into total disarray, a wave of chaos spreading outward across the downtown, with people calling out in panic for their loved ones as individuals became separated from their groups.

Bands of angry and scared individuals organically and swiftly organized into units that clicked together. These groups blended together, broke apart, and blended together again. Small cliques working in unison, a storm being born.

They descended on police cars and news vans, swarming them, smashing them, overturning them, the furious bands of protesters passing around Daniel in a visible wave that spread outward. Two vehicles flipped and rolled away from Daniel as the protestors tore ahead of him, leaving behind smashed and overturned vehicles just coming to rest as Daniel followed close on their heels. If anyone present had been through a tornado, the sights and sounds of things breaking all at once were familiar.

As Daniel ran, now separated from Bernice, Walter, and LeRon, but still filming with his camera, a prominent building had its lobby-floor windows smashed, and along the street several parked cars were set ablaze. Others were rolled over into the middle of the boulevard. Broken glass and debris littered the entire canyon between buildings as far as Daniel could see.

~ ~ ~

For Jacqueline Ayala, her worst fears were realized. Arturo never even considered the possibility, but now, as he scrambled to get back to his feet before he was trampled to death, he thanked God for Jacqueline's foresight in printing out the emergency cards. The cards even had a rendezvous point on Brush Street across from the Renaissance Center, which could be seen from nearly any point in Detroit.

Which was where they were when the crowds surged and turned into a panicked, running free-for-all.

Arturo got on his feet, but was nearly knocked back down when he tried to walk against the surging tide of the crowd. Instead, he was shoved forward.

"Jackie!" he yelled, running to keep pace with the crowd while looking all about. "Jackie! Martín! Frederick!" he yelled, his head swiveling as he searched for his family.

"Artie!" He caught a glimpse of Jacqueline jumping and waving her arms, but then she was gone, the crowd pushing them apart.

"Jackie!" he yelled again, trying to fight his way to where he last saw her, but it was impossible. They were being pushed farther apart.

At last, Arturo went with the crowd and prayed that she and the kids would do the same. They could all double back through the side streets of downtown to the rendezvous point.

Arturo jogged up Woodward Avenue with the crowd and broke north at Cadillac Park to Randolph Street, just a block away from Brush Street, but his way to Brush Street and the Renaissance Center was blocked. Crowds streamed up Randolph Street as well, away from the Renaissance Center. Police in riot gear—and now donning gas masks—walked in unison, tapping their shields with their batons as a vanguard of cops waged war out ahead of them, chasing protestors and violently lashing out with their batons.

Arturo heard the distinctive sound of tear gas canisters being fired, and Randolph Street was soon engulfed in the white gas, which clung low to the ground as it drifted outward.

Although the bluish-white smoke was still a block ahead of him, Arturo's nose and eyes burned, and he was forced to turn back toward Woodward. That, too, he saw, was also now enveloped in tear gas, forcing Arturo to run north. Each time he tried to double back, he was met with the stinging gas and throngs of people running from the center of downtown.

Arturo eventually found himself between Comerica Park, home of the Detroit Tigers, and Ford Field, home of the Detroit Lions—Brush Street!—and he ducked into a gate overhang at Comerica Park, and waited. He couldn't head south into downtown to the Renaissance Center; the crowd was thick and still moving in the opposite direction, away from downtown. Still, he hoped that Jacqueline and the boys would find their way to Brush Street as he had done and, if they were pushed along, he might find them.

He now had time to pull out his cell phone. He had five missed calls, four from Jackie, one from Frederick. He dialed Jacqueline's and the boys' phones, but no one answered. He frantically texted his location to each.

His phone buzzed in his hand as he texted his youngest son. It was Jackie. "Baby!" he answered, but she was cut off. He called her back and the same thing happened.

He texted again and waited eagerly for her reply. Within minutes, Arturo, Jackie, and Frederick hugged tightly. They had seen his texts and found their way to Comerica Park. Jackie and Frederick looked awful; their eyes and noses were red and inflamed, and mucus coated their jackets.

"We can't find Martín!" Frederick said before Artie could ask. "He fell, and then he was gone!" said Frederick. "I tried to reach him but we got pushed!"

"I know, I know," said Arturo, hugging his wife and son. "We'll find him."

~ ~ ~

A mile to the northwest of the city line, in Southfield, WHWK Channel 13 news reporter Ernie Brown climbed into the station's "SkyHawk 13" Robinson R44 news chopper. The helicopter's engine was already revved up, its rotor blades on full spin. It was a few minutes before three o'clock in the afternoon, right about the time for the regular traffic report. Typically, Peter Schmies, the SkyHawk 13 pilot, would fly over the city solo and give the report himself directly through his headset. The station's various police scanners picked up reports of unrest in the downtown and beyond, however, so this time Peter was accompanied by a cameraman and by Ernie, who would give live reports from the helicopter.

With Ernie and the cameraman safely buckled in and wearing their headsets, Peter lifted off. As they neared the downtown, the scale of the protests became apparent. Lines of black dots snaked their way from major arterial roadways and secondary streets into the downtown like tentacles, thickening to cover the entire breadth and width of the downtown streets. From a distance, Washington Boulevard to Jefferson Avenue appeared to be the spine of protests, with no discernible gaps among the protesters packed along the length and width of the avenues.

As the SkyHawk helicopter approached closer overhead, however, the thick lines of protesters along both Washington Boulevard and Jefferson Avenue dissolved into gaps—like Swiss cheese that opened and closed—and the lines themselves pulsated as protesters moved in either direction and into side streets.

They were running.

Washington Boulevard in particular seemed to drain off protesters as they streamed *en masse* onto each side street, leaving some groups behind, including individual protesters who had fallen amid the chaos. Some now moved as stragglers and joined the exits to the side streets.

Ernie recorded his report of the protests turning violent as the cameraman zoomed in on police wielding batons and swarming aggressive protesters. Peter steered the helicopter in a circle over the city, and the cameraman panned out and focused on various clusters of protesters away from the police lines. Various bands of protesters attacked parked cars and building lobbies, threw debris, and kicked at cars and windows.

It was a full-scale riot down there.

Peter circled to the west side of downtown over GLEE Tower. It was once again under siege, but this time it was by police. They swarmed out of DPSH and enveloped the combined complexes of DPSH, GLEE, and the Grand Arnault Casino.

However, it was Grand River Avenue, across Interstate 75 from downtown and the DPSH-GLEE-Grand Arnault complexes, that caught Ernie's attention. The avenue was one of those tentacles full of protestors that appeared to be marching into downtown. However, as Peter steered the helicopter northwest over Grand River Avenue and out over the Woodbridge, North Corktown, and Core City residential districts, it was apparent that these were not people marching into the downtown. Instead, these were neighborhood locals who had gathered along Grand River Avenue itself, with the crowds gathered primarily at major intersections.

Vehicle traffic was heavy and slow along Grand River Avenue. The intersection of Grand River and Fourteenth Street was particularly thick with traffic as large groups of people meandered into and out of traffic, forcing cars to crawl at a snail's pace. One car crept forward as a group of young people walked in front of it, and that apparently angered some of them. They turned on the car and swarmed over it. They slapped on its hood and roof and tried to break the windows. The driver nudged the car through the crowd more forcefully as it became a target, and then sped away. A gauntlet of rocks and bottles followed the car as it headed southeast.

Ernie spoke into his headset with the station manager in Southfield. "We have to go live," Ernie said. "I am watching a crowd attack cars on Grand River."

Chapter 9

At age fifty-five, Forrest Avery ("Fave" to family and associates) was not your typical gangster. No longer the crazy-eyed, fly-off-the-handle young psychopath—an image he cultivated in his twenties, but now looked back on as foolhardy and he counted himself lucky to have survived that period—he was now a sort of elder statesman. He was deemed "the Boss," but only because his 57-year-old brother William "Pops" Avery kept an extremely low profile. All business and communication was done through Fave. He also worked as a mentor and advisor to his 35-year-old nephew Jayson, who was cool-headed like "Pops," his father.

Today, however, Forrest felt it was necessary to act as boss in his brother's stead. With a late morning errand to Woodward Avenue near Wayne State University, just over a mile from his house, Forrest cursed under his breath at the unusual amount of traffic of both vehicles and pedestrians. The way home, usually ten minutes at most, dragged into thirty.

As he sat in traffic, he asked a teenager walking past with his young crew what was happening.

"There's a riot going on, man." Forrest chuckled. *My only weapon is my pen, and the frame of mind I'm in.* The boy looked confused.

Forrest had heard about the previous day's unrest, but only snippets, and he didn't pay it any mind. But now things seemed to be getting real. He flipped the radio dial until a news station came on, but it was talk radio. Nothing about a riot.

As he snaked his way home through the traffic, horns honked and people held up the "V" for victory sign. When he crossed Grand River Avenue back to his side of the tracks, crowds of hard-looking kids were gathered at each inter-section. A few nodded knowingly at him with respect when they made eye contact.

He made it home and saw his nephew Jayson's black Cadil-lac Escalade EXT parked on the curb. Fave's wife Greta was on the front lawn talking with Viola, Jayson's elegant young wife. Her bright eyes brimmed with intelligence, as her two boys squealed and played in the front yard.

"Hi, Forrest, how are you?" asked Viola as Forrest stepped out of his Cadillac, a black sedan.

"Viola," he said, and gave her a hug. "Boys inside?"

"Yes. They're watching the news. It's awful," she said, then nodded to a helicopter hovering high over the city a mile or so away.

Forrest looked quizzically at the two kids. "Jayson didn't want us at home by ourselves with all that's going on," she said, reading the concern etched on Forrest's face.

"Can't blame him," he said. "I'll see you in a few."

Jayson stood in the kitchen and helped himself to green tea in the cabinet while two of his boyhood friends—now body-guards and enforcers—Elijah Freeman and Darrell Alonso, sat at the kitchen table. Darrell browsed his smartphone and Elijah stared intently into the living room where the HD television played live news of the unrest unfolding downtown and elsewhere across the city.

Elijah and Darrell stood as Forrest walked in the front door. The three greeted and hugged when he entered the kitchen. He took a seat at the tiny kitchen table and the rest followed, filling each of the four kitchen chairs.

"Glad you're safe, Fave." Jayson nodded to the back door. "With all that's going on."

Fave grunted, and Jayson studied him. His uncle's head was lowered in thought, his eyes squinted. Jayson remembered when his uncle was a gold-toothed beast with a big smile that was more crazy than genuine. Jayson feared his uncle when he was a little kid, and he was protective of his younger cousins Raymond and Charles. They seemed oblivious to their father's reputation as dangerously unpredictable. But when they were killed as teenagers, Raymond in a drive-by shooting, and Charles shot dead in a separate incident, each within a few months of each other, Jayson saw a total transformation in his uncle. He went from that larger-than-life, brooding-eyed hustler with a streak of paranoia to the quiet, slightly stooped, soulful man he was today.

Fave straightened. "I'd like us to keep a low profile." The others listened intently as Fave paused and deliberated the words for his thoughts. "This," he said with a nod to the TV, "will pass."

"With previous unrest—Baltimore, Ferguson, Los Angeles—a lot of that stuff was picked up on camera. Shit," he scoffed, "idiots even filmed themselves, putting it on the internet. It's all fine and good in the moment, but when it passes—and it always does—the police, the feds, they've got all the time in the world to review all that shit. They rolled up a lot of that business consequently."

The younger men nodded and grunted.

"I want our boys off the street." Fave spoke with authority. "Let the Gees do whatever the fuck they'll do, 'cause you know they'll cock up things epic, bring the muthafucking UN down on their shit."

Elijah and Darrell snickered.

"Catch my drift?" Fave stooped his head and squinted again, and Jayson felt a palpable and familiar sense of primordial danger emanating from his uncle. Elijah and Darrell even drew back a little. Jayson smiled. *Uncle's still got it.*

Elijah and Darrell nodded with severity etched on their faces. "Get the word out. Pronto."

Elijah and Darrell departed, giving Jayson a hug on their way out.

And then all hell broke loose.

~ ~ ~

The *pop pop pop* of gunfire was unmistakable. Jayson had just leaned on the kitchen counter and eyed his uncle, who leapt to his feet and pushed past him. Jayson was startled by Fave's sudden movement, and it was only when he was chasing after him that he registered the sound of gunfire.

They ran through the living room as bullets tore through the windows, shattering a lamp and destroying a picture on the wall, knocking it to the floor. Small bullet holes appeared in the front door as wood splintered inward, then a bullet came through the window on the left of the door, striking the wall and ricocheting.

Fave and Jayson dashed through the front door. Darrell lay in the middle of the walkway in front of the house, gurgling and gasping for air, his hands wrapped around his throat. Elijah was kneeling beside him, his hands also pressed against Darrell's throat in an effort to stop blood that spurted between his fingers.

A low-riding blue Honda squealed away, with a young man sitting up on the passenger door frame, still firing a pistol. The car was quickly gone, but Jayson had his pistol out and fired multiple shots in its general direction, and scanned the street for any other threats.

Then he heard the screaming.

Viola...

Greta and Viola were lying on the ground by the bushes in front of the house, Greta on top of Viola, who scrambled out from beneath her, screaming for her children.

JJ and Tino...

The toddlers, running on the front lawn, stopped wide-eyed. Both started crying at the sudden commotion.

Viola and Jayson whisked the kids into their arms and checked them for injuries. But the bullets had all gone high, aimed at the house, and the boys didn't have a scratch.

Viola squeezed Tino and burst into tears.

Fave was on his knees alongside Greta, an arm draped over her shoulders. "Baby, are you hurt?" he asked repeatedly, but Greta didn't answer right away. She was in shock and didn't know if she'd been hit.

"Viola and the babies!" she screamed after a moment, scrambling to get up.

"Baby, they're fine, they're fine!" soothed Fave, pressing his hands against Greta's body, looking for a wound. There were none.

"Are you okay, Baby?" Fave asked again.

"Oh, Fave!" exclaimed Greta, and buried her face in his chest.

"Shhh, it's okay," soothed Fave. "It's okay."

"We gotta get him to a hospital!" shouted Elijah. He hovered over Darrell, his hands pressed against the wounded man's neck.

~ ~ ~

Aaron Jones and his friends Xavier and Devin practiced skateboarding in an open parking lot behind a long-ago abandoned garage and storefront on Warren Avenue, across McGraw Street from the once-famous and long-abandoned Kronk Gymnasium, where several world champion boxers had trained, including Milton McCrory, Thomas "The Hitman" Hearns, Mark Breland, and Oba Carr, among others. The boys did jumps and ollies on their skateboards but also kept an eye out as Nathan Brody and Dwayne Evans, both older teens. The sixteen-year-olds worked in front of the remains of a garage and storefront a block from the intersection where McGraw crossed over Warren in an "X" intersection.

The garage was Nathan's normal spot while Dwayne stood between the twin stone columns at the entrance of an abandoned bank the next block over. Typically, a car would slow down in front of the bank, and Dwayne would take the money; the car would proceed to the boarded-up garage, and Nathan would hand off the tiny bags. The transactions were done so gracefully and nonchalantly that customers in their cars barely had to slow down. And, if one wasn't paying close attention, the whole thing was practically invisible.

Kids acted as lookouts for police or any other sign of trouble, and would alert Nathan and Dwayne with whistles and hand signals.

Groups of people stood all along McGraw Street, especially at the "X" intersection. Whenever a car came down the street, the crowds jeered and pummeled it with rocks and bottles. They left Nathan and Dwayne to their work—they were armed, after all, and you didn't want to mess with them. With the unrest, there was little business to be had by car, but there were no police around, and the streets pulsated with hundreds of people. They could do business right in the open, and customers lined up on foot.

But the boys had to be sharp—even sharper than usual. A skinny man tried to sneak up on Nathan and steal a bag, but Dwayne saw him. The skinny dude didn't see Dwayne, who sprinted from behind him and pistol-whipped him in the back of the head just as he tried to snag a bag from Nathan's hand.

The man went straight down, face first, stiffened, and rolled onto his back, his arms outstretched and his eyes rolling up in his head, blood pouring from the back of it. He was knocked out cold. No matter. Dwayne and Nathan punched and kicked the prone man, then turned on another guy who got too close, watching. He stumbled away after absorbing several lightning punches to the face and head, only to be set upon by a group of teenagers who knocked him to the ground and kicked him repeatedly while laughing maniacally. When their attention turned to an approaching car, the man staggered to his feet and stumbled away.

The approaching car came slowly, blowing its horn. Teenagers sat on the passenger door frames, holding handguns aloft in one hand, and flashing a "V" for victory with their other hand. Many in the crowd hooted and jumped up and down, also holding their hands up in "V" signs. A bunch of happy Nixons.

The boys gawked at the car as the crowd parted before it. Children ran alongside the vehicle, giving high-fives to the teenagers.

Xavier recognized one of the young men and whistled, but Nathan and Dwayne couldn't hear him amid the crowds.

"Yo, Nathan!" Xavier yelled.

Then Aaron and Devin saw it, too. These were River Gees.

Nathan looked over and saw the three boys waving their arms frantically and pointing. Nathan looked back to the car and made eye contact with the driver. Recognition filled both their eyes, and the car leapt forward toward him, clipping two guys in the street and sending them flying end over end like bowling pins.

Nathan turned and ran. "Run, Dwayne, run!" he yelled as he ran.

But it was too late.

The car stopped, and six River Gees scrambled out and took chase, shooting their handguns.

The crowds scattered.

Dwayne cartwheeled backward as several bullets slammed into him. The momentum sent his body head over heels into an awkward roll before he stopped, face down in a clump of weeds.

"Dwa-!" shouted Nathan, but a bullet slammed into his back, clipping him in full stride and sending him tumbling forward, his body limp before he hit the ground. He rolled limply, like a ragdoll, before landing face up.

The six River Gees caught up with him and started stomping and kicking him. But Nathan was dead. His eyes and mouth hung open, revealing silver braces on his teeth, his head lolling with each kick.

"This is our street now!" yelled the driver, shooting his pistol into the air.

His name was Dmitri Johnson. The other boys followed suit, shooting their pistols in the air.

Aaron, Xavier, and Devin had fled when the gunfire started. They abandoned their boards and headed straight for the Kronk Gym. Each expected bullets to tear into their backs, but Aaron stole a look behind him and saw Nathan go down. One of the Gees looked his way, so Aaron turned and fled for his life.

Chapter 10

Most of the crowd on Warren Avenue, which scattered when the River Gees opened fire, ran east a couple of blocks and descended on Interstate 94. Drivers slowed as dozens of people appeared on the side of the highway, and traffic quickly came to a standstill. Someone shouted "Stop the Traffic," and an impromptu protest began. Pedestrians marched through the stopped vehicles and repeated the chant, "Stop the Traffic!" The Channel 13 news helicopter, SkyHawk 13, passed overhead, describing the unrest below.

"Protestors have entered Interstate 94," said reporter Ernie Brown. "By golly, that's dangerous," he said as oncoming cars braked hard to avoid crashing into stopped traffic and groups of pedestrians. One car swerved into another lane to avoid slamming into the back of a stopped car, and nearly ran over a protester.

Traffic soon came to a complete standstill all along I-94. Young people walked and ran between the lanes, slapping the hoods and roofs of the cars and menacing their occupants.

One driver panicked and tried to maneuver through the crowd, nudging several protesters and knocking three of them to the ground. Someone smashed a brick or rock through the driver's side window and the car lurched forward. Three protesters were upended, their bodies tossed into the air like rag dolls, before the car stopped. The driver and a passenger were pulled from the car, which then drifted driverless into more protesters.

"Oh, no," said Ernie Brown as the cameraman continued to broadcast live, "I think we just witnessed some people getting killed... Several protesters are down, run over. Oh, man, now the crowd is beating someone, a couple of people."

More cars tried to pass, but there was nowhere for them to go, and any movement drew the ire of angry protesters. Rocks, bottles, and debris rained down from an overpass onto the stopped traffic below.

Ernie was silent now as several drivers got of their cars and fought with protesters. Others simply abandoned their cars and ran away along the backed- up traffic.

One driver pulled out a pistol and opened fire on the crowd as they surrounded him. People scattered and dove to the ground.

"My God," said Ernie, "there are no words."

Protesters on the Livernois Avenue overpass also rained rocks and bottles onto the vehicles below, and many descended onto the highway to join the melee. Abandoned cars were attacked, their windows smashed, their doors ripped off their frames. Several cars and a tractor trailer were set ablaze. Other news helicopters joined SkyHawk 13 to film the chaos from above.

Across town, mobs descended on the M-10 freeway as well, near Calvert Avenue, and traffic was forced to stop there, too, as protestors ran out onto the highway. Several people were dragged from their cars and beaten. Likewise, others abandoned their vehicles and fled on foot.

The WLKE TV Channel 45 helicopter, Copter Lake 45, was

covering a large crowd in the streets at the intersection of Grand River Avenue and Oakman Boulevard when they learned of the M-10 freeway violence from their police scanner. They circled over the intersection one last time, then banked east toward the M-10. A sound of metallic *tings* filled the cockpit. News reporter Darrell Williams and the pilot exchanged looks, but before either could react, the copter's engine sputtered and the controls stiffened in the pilot's hands. Alarms on the pilot's console went off at once.

"Hang on, buddy," said the pilot. The helicopter jerked hard to the right and dropped more than 100 feet. "Mayday, we're going in," the pilot reported in an impossibly calm voice. The helicopter spiraled sharply to the right and lost more altitude, leaving a looping trail of smoke in its wake. The engine shut down with an ear-piercing whine.

Copter Lake 45 landed hard in the residential intersection of Webb and Holmur Streets, a usually quiet street where hardly any occupied homes remained. The helicopter slammed hard into a vacant lot at the corner of the intersection, breaking its pilot-side landing skid and tipping over. Its blades smashed into the grass and dirt and exploded into shrapnel. The tail snapped in half and the tail rotor churned up more dirt and grass before it, too, broke into pieces.

The helicopter body came to rest on its side.

~ ~ ~

The pilot of Detroit News Channel 10's helicopter "City 10" heard the "mayday" and emphatically pointed out the disabled helicopter to his camera man, who trained his lens on the chopper. The videographer captured the helicopter as it spun out of control and crash-landed in the residential neighborhood.

"Dear God!" shouted City 10 reporter Luis Sanchez, "Copter 45 just went down east of Grand River! Repeat: Copter 45 has gone down and we are over the crash site!"

The City 10 crew watched helplessly. "We're going to stay on site until help arrives for Copter 45, which may have been shot down," Luis said. "Jesus, they just shot down a helicopter!"

Various people headed for the downed helicopter as two people climbed out of the wreckage. A red pickup truck with men in the bed wielding rifles and shotguns came onto the scene. The Copter 45 crew climbed into the truck bed and waved an okay at the helicopter circling above.

The truck slowly pulled away. The City 10 helicopter circled above and filmed the truck's movement for nearly twenty minutes through residential streets. Luis remained silent throughout. Only when the truck pulled into Henry Ford Hospital did he breathe an audible sigh of relief and commend the armed citizens below for aiding the crew.

~ ~ ~

The Grand River Gs, or Gees—the G stood for "gangstas"—transected the neighborhoods of Northwest Goldberg to the south and Petosky-Otsego to the north of Grand River Boulevard.

With a rate of 155 violent crimes per 100,000 people, the neighborhoods were two of the most violent in the entire United States. The unemployment rate was nearly twenty-five percent, and as much as sixty-five percent of the population—which numbered just over 10,000 combined—weren't even counted as being in the labor force.

The area was once the territory of BMF, the Black Mafia

Family, headed by the Flenory Brothers: Demetrius ("Big Meech") and Terry ("Southwest T"). They had built a drug empire that stretched all the way to California and to the Deep South. The brothers even relocated to Los Angeles and Atlanta, respectively, to oversee their network's operations and growth.

The whole thing came crashing down two years ago with the brothers' arrest and conviction for multiple murders, racketeering, and a slew of drug trafficking charges. They were both sent to prison for life. Their entire organization, in Detroit and elsewhere, descended into civil war as different factions sought to inherit the kingdom, so to speak.

In Detroit, the Flenory Brothers' veteran lieutenants were divided. Each sought to consolidate his own power to the detriment of the others, and the civil war that ensued reduced their number in short order. The last of the lieutenants would be done in by the up-and-coming kids.

It was kids, literally, that eventually took over the former territory of the BMF in Detroit. They were mostly teenagers, though some "enforcers" were as young as twelve. The kids were brutal and disorganized in their efforts to seize control. They were quick to kill, and totally disregarded every tradition and norm, such as they were. And they quickly descended into all-out war among themselves.

This was the opening that allowed the older and more disciplined Avery Organization—and the multiple military veterans they employed—to grow their territory at the expense of the old BMF areas.

The Avery Organization grew to encompass much of the West Side, west of Interstate 96. In turn, the Northwest Goldberg and Petosky-Otsego areas to the east of I-96 were consolidated by two depraved young men, Caleb Sessions

and his drug-crazed boyhood friend Dmitri Johnson. Together, they lorded over the vicious youth gang known as
the Grand River Gees.

Caleb was the more strategic of the two. He thought it was a
good idea to attack on all fronts while the police were not a
factor. Caleb decided that the "old guys," the Avery Organization that flanked their west, offered the best opportunity
for expansion.

But what Caleb didn't account for was the likelihood that his
managing partner, the enforcer, would get swept up in the
moment. Dmitri and his crew attacked and annexed the first
major intersection west of I-96, killing the Avery Organization's two dealers. In their euphoria, they followed the irate
crowd, sliding down the grassy slope from the neighborhood
and right onto the I-96. Thus a whole contingent of riled-
up young men and women high on adrenaline, (and, quite
possibly, crystal meth), swarmed the road, unmindful of
the dangers of walking onto a high-speed interstate. When
the cars stopped, there were mostly white suburbanites in
them. They looked fearful, and some appeared indignant,
blowing their horns and snarling at the young protestors.

Snarling at Dmitri and his crew? You didn't get away with
that.

Dmitri's crew pried open the door of a Ford Fiesta, pushing
and bending it beyond its frame until it nearly came off.
Dmitri reached into the car.

"Get the fuck out, nigga!" Logan, one of Dmitri's gang,
yelled as a panicked white man, soft and slick with sweat,
desperately fended off Dmitri's punches and grabs. The guy
wouldn't come out of his seat until someone had the good
sense to release the seatbelt. Then he came out, covering his
head with his hands to protect it from the punches. But the

gang's attention turned to the car itself. Three gang members got lodged in the open door frame as they each tried to scratch and claw their way into the driver's seat.

Dmitri turned his attention to the white man, who tried pulling away, all the while whimpering and crying. It was the glasses and the button-down collared shirt. It was the khaki pants and paunchy belly. It was the slickness of the sweaty, double chin, the parted hair, the boyish thirty-something smugness. Most of all, it was the fear in the young man's eyes that revolted Dmitri and fed an empowering sensation of pure rage.

Dmitri picked up a brick among several that had been thrown at the stopped cars. Most of them had broken into bits, but not this one. This one was fully intact and weighty. It fit his hand perfectly and, as he raised it up, the white man ducked, blindly waving his arms out to block what was coming.

Dmitri brought the brick down and, just before it struck home, the white man turned his head. The brick connected solidly with the side of his face. Dmitri felt the brick make contact with something hard—something that instantly splintered into a million tiny cracks—before continuing into a mushy interior.

"Whoa!" Dmitri bellowed in a high-pitched roar as he recovered his balance. The white man crumpled onto the pavement.

"Ye-eah, boyee!" Dmitri shouted again. He pumped his chest and raised the bloody remnants of the brick over his head. "Look at that!" he yelled as he circled the man's prone body, sliding through a pool of blood growing beneath the head.

A helicopter circled above.

"Check that shit!" Dmitri shouted again, tossing the bloody brick pieces onto the motionless body. Then he jerked his arms over his head and held two middle fingers high in the air, taunting the helicopter.

Logan took a step back from the car and looked at Dmitri. Despite the noise generated by the crowd, the sickening sound of a brick striking home cut right through the cacophony. That sound, and the sight of Dmitri prancing around the dead man—Logan just couldn't get that out of his head.

~ ~ ~

It had been a long day for everyone. For the protestors, for everyday people, for victims caught in the riots, for the police, for firefighters, for school teachers and administrators, for business owners, for the mayor and cabinet officials, and for news reporters. Like Ernie Brown.

As the protests grew bigger by the hour, the station's three younger reporters set up at different locations to record stock video, then live broadcasts, of masses of protestors marching or driving to downtown. Ernie took to the sky at three o'clock to provide more comprehensive coverage from above. SkyHawk 13 allowed the news channel to cover more ground, reporting from areas that were either inaccessible or unsafe.

The sun was setting, and Ernie checked his phone for the time. It was a few minutes after six p.m. He had been in the air for three hours straight, save for a brief refueling stop back at the station. *Only three hours.* It had seemed like an eternity.

From his mobile perch in the sky, Ernie watched as protestors fled from police lines, and riot control vehicles massed on Jefferson Avenue between the Renaissance Center, the Coleman A. Young Municipal Building, and the Cobo Convention Center. A police fortress centered on the area around DPSH, GLEE Tower, and the Grand Arnault Casino.

Police had cleared the four-block financial district between DPSH and the Renaissance Center, and now worked to clear protestors and rioters from the areas around Ford Field and Comerica Stadium. Interstate 75 separated the relatively new Pistons Arena from the two stadiums on the downtown side of the freeway, but the Woodward Avenue bridge linking Pistons Arena with the other two stadium complexes was a bridge too far. Police parked a riot control vehicle right on the bridge, and its wall-like extensions on either side encompassed the width of the bridge, preventing protestors from crossing back into downtown.

But the Pistons Arena was outside the consolidated police zone, and from Ernie's perspective, it was geographically indefensible, not unless the police were to give up ground elsewhere in the downtown.

The police apparently had the same idea. The arena was being systematically looted as police stood their ground on the other side of the freeway.

Outside the central business district, the sprawling metropolis appeared to have erupted in flames.

Plumes of black smoke rose across the landscape, and their number seemed to have doubled, then doubled again. There were maybe fifty plumes, some more vigorous than others, and they seemed to grow in numbers still, with columns stretching to the western horizon, itself alight with the setting sun.

Daylight was flickering out.

SkyHawk 13 headed back to the station at Farmington Hills for another round of refueling. As the ground passed beneath them, Ernie noted countless glowing orange pyres. From his height, they looked like the burning ends of cigarettes—flaring brighter than the dull hue of city street lights, pockmarking the darkening land below.

It was going to be a long night.

Chapter 11

At the Channel 13 news studio in Southfield, Ernie's live report from Skyhawk 13 had given way to live feeds from reporters on the ground spliced with stock footage recorded throughout the day. An exhausted Josh Fink, the young Wayne State intern, stood just outside the news desk's camera shot.

Reporter Wally Mickiewicz, host of the daily morning news program *Morning, Motown!*, was currently on duty. It was all hands on deck for the news station. "What do you have?" he asked Josh curtly. He kept an eye on the director, who indicated ten seconds before going live from the desk.

Josh handed his note to Wally, who quickly scanned it. "What is that? An 's'?"

Before Josh could answer, Wally was speaking to the camera. "Thank you for that report, Austin. Stay safe out there.

"Meanwhile," Wally continued, "our staff here at News 13 has been monitoring police scanners and reports all day, and our young intern Josh Fink has counted more than 500 separate reports of fires. Many of the fires appear to have been set in abandoned homes and structures, as Ernie Banks in Skyhawk 13 has reported. Unfortunately, there is no shortage of abandoned buildings in Detroit. The city has lost two-thirds of its population since its peak of almost two million in the 1950s, leaving more than seventy-five thousand abandoned structures and thirty-five thousand abandoned homes around metro Detroit. And, well, that's a lot of kindling."

Turning slightly to face a different camera, Wally changed gears. "We are getting word that unrest has spread beyond metro Detroit and across Michigan. We have colleagues from WFLN in Flint and WAAM in Ann Arbor standing by. Helen in Ann Arbor, are you there? Very good. What can you tell us?"

The "on air" light dimmed as Helen in Ann Arbor gave her report, and Wally waved Josh over.

"Good stuff, Josh. Thanks for getting me those numbers," he said. Wally lowered his head and added, with a grim expression, "Now, I need for you to do something *really* important."

Josh stepped up expectantly, ready to be a soldier.
Wally pulled out his wallet, withdrew a ten-dollar bill, and held it out for Josh to take. "Coffee run," he said, his face softening into something of a smile.

~ ~ ~

Alex and his fellow young executives at Apex Superior Bank made it to the 72nd floor of the RenCen and entered the Top Hat Bar & Grille. They found it overflowing and uproarious despite the relatively early hour. They ordered beers and chatted about the GLEE shutoffs, the possibility of riots, off-season trades by the Detroit Tigers, and a co-worker's new Harley sportster. From their station atop the RenCen, they watched as the crowds below on Jefferson Avenue grew so thick that there were no open spaces among them. They butted right up against lines of police decked out in riot gear.

A roaring wall of sound wafted up to the Top Hat from the street below. Patrons of the restaurant erupted with a cheer each time the police were able to corral and arrest a protester. For executives and revelers, it was like watching a football game.

But things got crazy.

A pitched battle raged beneath them, with tear gas canisters launched into the crowd, which surged forward and scattered in all directions. The din among the executives and partygoers in the Top Hat audibly dipped, and a hushed murmur spread through the restaurant. They feared that protestors might break through the police lines and storm the lobby below.

Their fears eased as a sea of helmeted police pushed out from spaces below their line of sight. To their relief, practically all of Jefferson Avenue was quickly abandoned by protestors. The police were on the offensive.

Although fears of being overrun by protestors proved unwarranted, a new concern soon emerged: how to get home. As night descended on Detroit, partygoers could see the orange glow of multiple fires burning like flares in the gathering darkness.

And, on the multiple, high-definition flat-screen television sets adorning the walls of the Top Hat, local stations abandoned regularly scheduled programs to cover the unrest live. Helicopter footage—some live, some from earlier in the day—showed crowds swarming onto the freeways, where they attacked drivers and passengers. Vehicles stood at a standstill far into the distance as the helicopter cameras zoomed out to capture the impact of the protests on interstate traffic. Nearly all of the executives and partygoers at the Top Hat commuted from the outer suburbs, affluent places like the Grosse Pointes, Orchard Lake, Bloomfield Hills, or communities like New Baltimore on Lake St. Claire. Their way home appeared to have been closed off by the violence.

On one television, the news channel replayed the downing of Copter Lake 45. On another, young protestors with bandanas covering their faces battled helmeted police. But this scene wasn't in Detroit. This was the university district in East Lansing, home of Michigan State University, and the protestors were presumably university students. Another cut-in showed riot police lined up in Benton Harbor, a small city in far western Michigan on the shores of Lake Michigan. A ticker below reported that protests, in solidarity with demonstrations in Detroit, had spread to cities throughout Michigan's Lower Peninsula, including Flint, Pontiac, Battle Creek, Grand Rapids, Saginaw, Buena Vista, Freeland, Ypsilanti, and Muskegon, and that some of the demonstrations had grown violent as day gave way to night.

~ ~ ~

Just off of West Jefferson Avenue in Delray, abutting the industrial zone along the Detroit River immediately south of downtown Detroit, Maria Aznar—a twenty-eight-year-old, part-time nurse assistant at a downtown nursing home—lay wide awake in her bedroom. Her five-year old son Miguel Joaquin, "MJ," and her seven-year-old daughter, Isabella, lay beside her, also wide awake and snuggled tightly with Maria. All three stared wide-eyed at the ceiling. Maria hummed softly while stroking MJ's hair with her right hand, her left arm wrapped around Isabella. Antonio, a six-month-old infant, was asleep in his crib next to the bed. Outside, it was like the Fourth of July, except it wasn't fireworks they were hearing. It was mostly gunfire, people shooting at ... Maria didn't want to contemplate what they could be shooting at.

"I smell smoke," whispered MJ, his eyes as big as saucers.

"Me, too," added Isabella.

Maria got out of bed and walked into the narrow hallway. The apartment was definitely smoky. She spotted a vent on the wall from which heavy smoke poured in.

"MJ, Maria, grab some clothes!" she commanded, rushing back to her bedroom. "We've got to go!" she said as she scooped up Antonio, who cried loudly.

Maria grabbed MJ with her free hand and headed for the door. "Isabella, come! Let's go!"

Just then, someone pounded on the front door and shouted, "Fire!"

"But my clothes, momma!" Isabella whined.

"Forget that, we have to go *now!*"

As they rushed out the door, Maria saw that a small crowd had gathered outside, mostly residents dressed in night gowns and T-shirts despite the frigid temperatures. Heavy smoke poured from the two units at the east end of the row. An orange lick of flame momentarily appeared in the window of the farthest apartment.

Maria loaded her children into her battered twelve-year-old Kia Soul. She heard the window of the farthest unit break and looked over. A whoosh of flames pirouetted out of the window, followed by swatches of burning curtain. Maria climbed into the driver's seat and drove down Jefferson Avenue without looking back. She didn't give any thought to where they were going. It was automatic. Her parents lived nearby, on Vernor Highway, just across I-75, and she naturally headed there. She couldn't find her cell phone and decided she'd left it at the apartment during her panicked exit. She couldn't call to tell them she was coming.

She followed Jefferson Avenue toward Grand River, but traffic was very heavy, despite the late hour. Semi-trucks and cars converged on Grand River, and Maria slowly maneuvered into the stream of vehicles.

Two lanes of traffic converged into one. Maria's view was blocked by semi-trucks on her left, and she was forced to make a sharp right turn with the traffic. Thirty minutes passed before she realized that she was on the entrance ramp to the Ambassador Bridge into Canada. There was no getting off. She couldn't turn around amid the heavy traffic. Eventually, when she reached the middle of the Ambassador Bridge, the stop-and-go traffic came to a complete halt.

Maria and her children sat in the unmoving traffic, with the car's heater blowing at full blast and the fuel gauge in the red.

Maria's gas ran out after an hour of sitting in the middle of the bridge. She kept the ignition key turned on to keep the heater going, but it didn't take long for the Kia's battery to drain.

Traffic hadn't moved an inch since they had stopped, and now the sun was setting. People got out of their cars and walked to find some vantage point to see what was going on. It was windy on the bridge, and the river below was frozen solid. With the sun setting, the already cold temperatures would soon plummet further.

Maria had no time to grab coats or blankets when she fled the apartment and, with the gas having run out, her situation was becoming desperate. She popped the trunk and got out of the car to look through it, hoping to find a blanket or towel. She found an extra baby blanket in the trunk in addition to the one already covering Antonio.

She bundled up Antonio and MJ, and commanded Isabella to grab onto her night gown. Together they walked briskly toward Canada with their heads bowed against the frigid wind.

~ ~ ~

Matthew Pitt sat in his Willoughby International Trucking rig about two-thirds of the way across the old Ambassador Bridge, working the radio with fellow truckers to learn what was happening.

After nearly a decade of driving his own rig, Matthew had seen it all: horrible car wrecks, police chases, tornadoes, wild fires, you name it. But being stuck in traffic at a border crossing in sub-freezing temperatures—because of a riot— was something new.

Movement in his side view mirror caught his eye, and he did a double-take. He saw a young woman in a night gown with two small children struggling against the freezing wind. *What the hell,* he thought. *What the hell is she thinking?*

Matthew opened his driver side door as they approached. "Get in!" he shouted against the wind. "Get in!" he shouted again as they got closer, and the woman led her small daughter to the truck cab. Matthew reached down and effortlessly lifted her into the cab, then did the same with a small boy. He got out and helped the young woman up as well. He was shocked to see that she was holding a baby wrapped in blankets.

He shut the door behind her and ran around the front of

the truck to the passenger side and climbed in. The woman and the two children were shivering uncontrollably, and the baby was ominously silent. Without words, Matthew lifted the boy and the girl into the sleeper behind the front seats, and wrapped two blankets around them both.

He checked on the baby, who looked up at him with large and curious eyes. The baby seemed just fine. "Let me," he said softly as he took the blanket-wrapped baby from the young woman and placed it softly on the bed next to the two children, who stared out from the blankets as they shivered.

"Oh, my God, thank you so much," said the young woman, her teeth chattering as she furiously rubbed her hands together. Matthew placed his hands over hers to help them warm up faster. He couldn't believe how cold her hands were.

"Are you okay?" he asked. "Is anyone else with you?"

She shook her head no.

Chapter 12

News and footage of the unrest in Detroit, including the downing of the news helicopter and some of the most harrowing incidents, spread rapidly across the country and the world. Much of it was broadcast live through CNN, Fox News, and other national and international television outlets, as well as online media. The magnitude of the unrest in Detroit and the speed with which it happened was shocking. The largest riots and civil unrest in the USA since the Rodney King verdict in 1992 was clearly underway ... and spreading.

Amid the reports of violence and increasing chaos, Mayor André Murray held another hastily organized press conference in the early evening, along with various community and neighborhood leaders, to plead for calm. The mayor and other leaders offered assurances that investigations into the Bernadette Price fire and GLEE's shutoff policies would ensue.

The mayor announced a city-wide curfew from dusk to dawn, and requested activation of the Michigan National Guard. After the mayor concluded his press conference, Governor Clifford Krueger held a press conference in Lansing, and announced the activation and deployment of the National Guard to both Detroit and Flint.

The *Motown Mirror* website featured a series of filmed on-the-ground reports by Bernice Hamandawana and her cameraman, Daniel Rush. Bernice and Daniel's reports showcased a disproportional police response to a few belligerent demonstrators, with police launching a full-scale frontal attack on mostly peaceful demonstrators at the first hint of aggression.

The panicked stampede that ensued, the fear on people's faces, the utter chaos as police advanced—swinging batons with total abandon, striking flesh and producing cringe-worthy *thwacks* that sounded like breaking bones, and the horrors of pepper spray and tear gas—was riveting footage. No other footage captured the on-the-scene thrill of people from all walks of life protesting together in one moment, singing songs and standing peaceably for justice, and then experiencing sheer terror in the next. It was reportage from the perspective of the protestors, not the spin of the mayor, police chief, or corporate media. The videos and reports were raw and potent. Each video went viral within minutes.

Included among the filmed reports for *Motown Mirror* was Bernice and Daniel's brief encounter with the playfully charismatic artist, LeRon Gordon, "The People's Mayor." His catchy turns of a phrase would inspire multiple online video memes, turning his words and rhymes into songs replete with beats and instrumentation. "The People's Mayor" would, literally overnight, become a minor celebrity. And it wasn't just his rhymes that endeared him to his sudden fans. His words and delivery presented a witty intellect, and he pulled no punches.

"Why are you called 'The People's Mayor'?" Bernice asked at one point.

"Because I'm a gainsayer, a truth sayer," he answered with his toothy grin before launching into an on-the-spot rhyme (on the dime, in real time, no less):

> The mayor's a player

~ ~ ~

Major Bradley Davis, commander of Alpha Company, 1st Battalion, 125th Infantry Regiment, U.S. Army National Guard, and an executive at the Detroit-based payday loan company Cash-in-a-Flash (which charged annual interest rates averaging 500%), left his home early in Grosse Pointe Shores for the twenty-minute drive to the Detroit Olympia Armory. He had watched the governor's announcement that he was mobilizing the Michigan Army National Guard and, though he had yet to receive official notice, he had ordered his 150-fifty-man company to report by 6:00 a.m. As the commander of Alpha Company, he wanted to be there at least an hour earlier than his men, so it was 4:30 a.m. and still dark when he climbed into his Mercedes G550 SUV.

He *still* hadn't received official word that the National Guard was being mobilized, even though more than eight hours had passed since the governor's announcement (bureaucracy, he mused), but Bradley had taken the initiative. Alpha Company, 1st Battalion, 125th Infantry Regiment, was the designated Michigan Rapid Reaction Force that was slated to deploy within seventy-two hours anywhere in the state once activated. Olympia Armory, west of downtown Detroit, was the regiment's home base and rally point.

Normally Bradley would take Interstate 94 right to the armory at the junction of I-94 and I-96. But the news from the night before reported that I-94 was closed because of the previous day's unrest, with many cars set on fire and abandoned. So Bradley took Lake Shore Drive, which paralleled the shore of Lake St. Claire and became Jefferson Avenue at the Grosse Pointe line.

Before he even crossed into Detroit at Alter Road, it was like entering a war zone. Hundreds of police from the various Grosse Pointes' police departments, and also police from Warren, Troy, and other towns to the north, as well as sheriffs' deputies from Oakland and Macomb Counties, were lined up all along the city-county line and decked out in full riot gear. All traffic into Detroit was blocked.

Although Brad was dressed in army fatigues, the police at first refused him entry into the city. After he presented his credentials, he was allowed to proceed, but only after sitting through a stern warning that he was completely on his own from that point forward.

He crossed the border at Alter Road. On any given day—thanks to the many empty lots and burnt-out buildings—this area already resembled a war zone. But now, several buildings were either smoldering or burning outright, with no fire trucks or police in sight. Amid dancing shadows projected by the glow of a burning storefront two blocks ahead, Brad saw the movement of people in the street.

He stopped his SUV at the intersection of Chalmers Avenue. He had obviously been spotted, and he could see shadowy figures running toward him. He sat there and watched them come, unafraid. The quiet, comfortable interior of his Mercedes provided a false sense of impregnability.

The first rain of rocks that bounced off his hood, windshield, and roof snapped him out of this delusion. An angry, sneering crowd was suddenly upon him.

Bradley threw the SUV into reverse and gunned it. Other

shadowy figures emerged from the side streets around him that he didn't see until now. He clipped one figure, then a second, and a third—nameless, faceless, even shapeless. He never actually saw them, just felt the impact on his vehicle as he backed into Marlborough Street. He threw the SUV into drive and floored it, leaving a trail of smoke behind, but not before a rock shattered the rear window.

Brad's heart raced as he crossed back into Grosse Pointe Park and behind the lines of police. He wondered if he had just hurt somebody, or worse. Then he wondered how in the hell was he going to make it to the armory.

~ ~ ~

The previous day was hell for Jayson Avery and his family. He still couldn't believe that Darrell was gone. They had grown up together, and now he was dead.

Fave's house was now a fortress. Jayson, Darrell, and Elijah's crews were all camped there, with cots and sleeping bags laid out on nearly every uncovered surface on the first floor.

Even Pops himself came over. It was war.

Young men came and went all night. The attack on Fave's house was just one among several. They counted ten separate attacks in total as the Grand River Gees targeted multiple corners run by the Avery Organization, and even some of their lieutenants' homes. Jayson's house a few blocks over was shot up in a drive-by as well, though he and his family were at Fave's.

Two of their dealers were dead, along with a lookout—just kids. The dealers were teenagers, both sixteen. The lookout, attacked at a different corner, was just twelve.

This was total war, and it came out of the blue.

Pops, Fave, and Jayson took over the kitchen. Pops and Fave sat quietly at the small kitchen table as Jayson made coffee. The news played silently on the kitchen's small flat-screen TV on the counter. It played the scene of the I-94 murder over and over again, freezing on the young man as he looked up at the helicopter and flipped it a two-handed bird.

More than ten minutes of silence passed as Jayson worked. The only sound in the house was of Jayson scraping mugs, opening the coffee bag, setting up the coffee maker as others awakened throughout the house.

He poured Pops and Fave a cup of coffee, then one for himself. Taking a chair, he and the other two men silently blew on their coffees and took a sip.

Fave tilted his head, his eyes resting on the kitchen cabinets, but squinting. He was in thought mode.

"These Gees," said Fave, leaning back and stroking his chin. "They're exploiting this situation expeditiously."

After another moment of silence, Pops added, "Without a fucking doubt."

"We gotta game this shit out," said Fave after more silence.

Jayson remained silent. Clearly, Fave was going over some deep shit. This is what made Fave so effective. He was *never* irrational. Even when he was the gold-toothed, crazy-eyed son-of-a-bitch in his youth, he must have been calculating. He certainly was now, and that kind of thing didn't just happen. Jayson focused on Fave's right index finger, which lightly tapped on the kitchen table, keeping time to Fave's thoughts.

Fave's finger stopped tapping. His eyes drifted to the small TV, which again froze on the blurry image of the I-94 murderer.

A shadow of a smile crept up his face. "End times," said Fave.

Fave looked at Jayson and squinted.

"Get your Army crew together," Fave ordered. This was the handful of military veterans in Jayson's employ. Jayson himself had served in Iraq with the Marine Corps after high school.

"We've got a lot of work to do," Fave said. "In the meantime, you and me," he said to Pops, "got some phone calls to make."

~ ~ ~

Detroit Police wearing gas masks marched up Brush Street, tapping their riot shields with their batons.

Arturo, Jackie, and Frederick heard them before they saw them. Then came the tear gas canisters, which forced the family across I-75 to the Detroit Pistons' Arena.

Arturo twice tried to approach the police to seek their help in finding Martín, but there was no reasoning with them in full riot mode. They aimed shotguns and fired tear gas in his direction on both occasions.

They had stayed at the arena until after sunset, hoping to either find or hear from Martín, or find a police officer or another first responder to whom they could report that their fourteen-year-old son was missing. There were none, and after dark, the arena was set upon by rioters all around them. They were forced to continue their trek north along Brush Street and, in some kind of ominous omen, Brush Street ended at the Children's Hospital of Michigan.

Thankfully, their son had not been admitted, but the family was stuck there. They spent the night in the family waiting room.

~ ~ ~

On the Ambassador Bridge linking the cities of Detroit, U.S.A., and Windsor, Canada, the dawning sky was marked with hues of purple, pink, and orange. The situation for Matt, Maria and her children, however, remained desperate. Matt had only a few bottles of water and some bags of chips, and they were mostly gone now. He sure didn't have any milk or baby food. Maria had only one bottle of milk for baby Antonio, which she used sparingly, and that was it. Worse, the truck's fuel gage was now on empty. Despite the warmth and cozy comfort of the truck cabin, it was clear they could no longer stay.

After discussing the situation, Matt and Maria agreed to brave the cold and join the throngs of bundled-up, shivering people trekking across the nearly mile-and-a-half long bridge to the border post on the Windsor side. Matt collected his paperwork, including his international commercial driver's license, bill of lading, passport, and other documents. It was time to go.

When they stepped out of the cabin, the bitter wind cut to the bone. *Holy shit, this is crazy,* thought Matt. But they had no choice. Matt hoisted Isabella in one arm and MJ in the other as Maria carried Antonio, and they huddled together against the cold wind, walking as swiftly as they could.

Crosswinds on the bridge were absolutely brutal, sending the wind chill plunging to as low as twenty degrees below zero. They didn't have far to go but, if they didn't get inside somewhere soon, their very lives would be endangered, particularly the kids'.

As they passed vehicle after vehicle, Maria saw that most of them were empty; their occupants had already abandoned them and walked into Canada. Some of the empty cars were full of clothes and even furnishings. Several vehicles had broken windows and looked as though they had been looted.

It was just over a tenth of a mile before the bridge reached land and the crosswind subsided, but it was the longest tenth of a mile that Matt or Maria had ever walked. The Ambassador Bridge, however, remained elevated for another half-mile inland, and they trudged on.

Chapter 13

Twenty-year old Brian Worthington learned of the Michigan National Guard call-up through social media. Then he got a text on his smart phone from his company commander. He was excited. It was the first time he had been called to duty. He tried to temper his enthusiasm because he wasn't sure it was appropriate to be excited about quelling a riot, but it shook things up and that was definitely something to be excited about. He called the day manager at the Southtown Crossing Shopping Center Walmart in Southgate to inform them that he wouldn't be able to come to work the following morning.

He called 19-year-old Daniel Alvarez, his best friend in Alpha Company. Daniel lived about twenty minutes away in Dearborn where he worked with his dad and two brothers as a drywall contractor. The two guardsmen decided to ride together to the Olympia Armory.

After picking up Alvarez, Brian turned onto Michigan Avenue, the most direct route into Detroit from Dearborn, but Daniel had reservations.

"I don't know…" said Daniel, his voice trailing off. "I think Michigan Avenue might be one of the places hard hit by the riots."

"I heard Grand River," said Brian, "but I think it was pretty much all over the place, right? Still, how else are we going to get there? And Grand River runs right by the armory."

They soon encountered a Michigan State Police checkpoint blocking the road into Detroit. As they approached, Brian rolled down his window. "We're with the National Guard," he said to the state trooper. The young trooper peered inside and saw that they were in their grayish combat uniforms. Brian and Danny both held up their military IDs. An older trooper came over and peered in through the passenger's window.

"All right, be careful, guys," said the older trooper, waving them through. "Whatever you do, don't stop."

Brian drove on, and soon the scenery changed into something out of a horror movie. Trash and debris lay scattered all across the street and surrounding lots. They passed a couple of burned-out cars laying on their sides, and several burned buildings were still smoldering. Nearly every single building along Michigan Avenue—garages, convenience stores, barber shops—had been burned or was still burning. It was mostly dark, despite the growing dawn, but several burning fires lit the road ahead. Brian drove slowly as the two took in all the damage. The scale of it was truly unbelievable.

Out of nowhere, a rock smashed into the windshield, leaving a large spider-web pattern of cracks. Brian instinctively stomped on the brakes, stopping quickly.

"Drive, man, drive!" urged Danny, and Brian floored the gas pedal.

Another rock smashed through the driver side window and into Brian's left cheek.

"*Oh, fuck!*" yelled Danny as the truck lurched to the right and slammed into the brick façade of a half-burned, boarded-up storefront.

~ ~ ~

Matt and his little group finally neared the end of the Ambassador Bridge, where the two-lane structure fanned out into the broad, twenty-three lane Canadian Border Services tollbooth plaza. Every single one of the booths was besieged by a line of vehicles that just sat there. Hundreds of people, maybe thousands, desperately pressed against the tollbooth plaza in the front.

The crowd was raucous, hollering and hissing, begging to be let through. On the other side of the tollbooths were throngs of Canadian Border Services Agency officers sporting helmets, shields, batons, and other riot gear. They physically blocked passage into Canada. And behind the border officers were City of Windsor Police and Ontario Provincial Police. Several Canadian police and news helicopters circled above.

A car near the center lane was enveloped by flames. Matt looked closer at the burning car. It faced the wrong way and sat at an awkward angle, and it was clear that all the other cars had navigated around it. It was a Canadian Border Services Agency police car.

Matt stopped and gawked. A realization settled over him that left him sputtering. *These people are Americans.*

He felt MJ go heavy in his right arm, so he gently bounced the boy. MJ was falling asleep. His eyes were listless.

"You all right, buddy?" Matt asked.

MJ was silent. Maria and then Matt felt his forehead. The child was hot.

"How do you feel, honey?" asked Maria, deeply concerned.

A watery tear ran down MJ's cheek.

"Come on," said Matt. "We need to get him out of the cold."

Matt led Maria and the children through a more subdued section of the crowd toward the northeast corner of the lanes, where an entrance ramp took drivers from Windsor onto the east-bound lane of the Ambassador Bridge to Detroit.

The on-ramp was also blocked with stalled traffic and several police, but Matt walked as though he knew where he was going. When a Windsor police officer approached them, he and Maria ran.

"Hey, hey, *hey!*" shouted the policeman, who then spoke into his radio to alert more officers. Matt and Maria darted between cars until, to their surprise, they ran smack into hundreds of local Canadian residents and Windsor University students. They were protesting the Border Agency's refusal to let them bring food and blankets to the desperate Americans refugees. The Canadians surrounded Matt's group and shielded them from the police.

"My boy is sick!" cried Maria, as they were led north by what Matt would later describe as an "old hippie couple." Within minutes, they arrived at the couple's home on Askin Avenue in downtown Windsor.

~ ~ ~

In Washington, D.C., President Cynthia Belle and members of her national security team met in the White House Situation Room at 9:00 a.m. Along with the President, others present included Vice President George Wartmann, the Secretary of Defense Lynn Benjamin, each of the joint chiefs of staff, National Security Advisor Oscar Schwartz, the attorney general, and an assortment of support advisors and staff. Also present via video conference were the governor of Michigan, the adjutant general of the Michigan National Guard, the mayor of Detroit, and the mayor of Flint.

Mayor André Murray briefed the President and her team with the latest updates on the situation in Detroit, and was followed by the mayor of Flint. Governor Krueger gave a briefing of his own following the two mayors. He outlined his order to deploy the Michigan National Guard to both Detroit and Flint, as well as his order for the Michigan State Police to reposition assets from around the state to Detroit and Flint.

The Michigan National Guard's designated Rapid Reaction Force was currently being activated, reported Major General John Veazey, the adjutant general of the Michigan National Guard. A full deployment of Alpha Company to Detroit was expected by late afternoon or early evening, and a deployment to Flint was expected during the overnight hours.

At the Pentagon in Washington, military planners ran through various contingencies in the event that the Michigan National Guard and state police were unable to pacify the cities. They determined that the 10th Mountain Division based in Fort Drum, New York, and commanded by Major General Lance McIntyre, was the active duty unit best positioned to deploy to Detroit.

With the President's blessing, the division was put on alert.

~ ~ ~

It was just after five p.m. and, while the days were getting longer, it was still early February. Twilight was approaching.

Ian shivered as he sat Indian-style on the floor, along with at least 100 others, in a large conference room of the Cobo Convention Center, named for 1950s-era Mayor Albert Cobo. Like Ian, each person had their hands cuffed behind their backs with plastic zip ties. Tina sat beside Ian, her head buried in his shoulder. His whole body throbbed with a dull pain that sharpened whenever he moved or shifted his weight.

The police were entirely indifferent. Another fifty or so officers from a variety of law enforcement agencies, as well as paramedics, stood watch over the detainees. They spoke loudly and incessantly to each other, and barked orders to the steady stream of arriving prisoners.

It was a circus.

With Ian and Tina sat fourteen-year old Martín Ayala. Tina had spotted the boy sitting alone, his back to a sturdy conference room divider. It looked like he had been crying. Only when she and Ian approached did she see the mucus on his jacket and recognize the effects of tear gas. But he'd also been crying.

"I'm Tina," she said. sitting beside him, "and this is Ian."

The boy was quiet and apprehensive. Tina told him they were students at Wayne State, and how they had ended up in custody. She asked how he'd gotten here and, after a moment, the boy opened up. He told her and Ian that he had gotten separated from his family and had lost his phone. He started crying.

"Nuh, Nuh, Nuh-guy-guy-yen," a fat corrections officer read from a list, his voice booming across the room. Another officer spotted Ian and poked his baton into Ian's back to force him forward. "Here he is," said the officer, reading a name tag taped to Ian's back. He poked Ian harder. "Answer when your name is called!"

~ ~ ~

Two pickup trucks carrying men armed with semi-automatic rifles in the beds slowly pulled up to the fenced and chained junkyard on Southern Avenue. They were greeted by a rusty sign that read "Jimmy's Garage & Auto Parts." Another sign read "Jimmy Towing Service." The trucks rolled to a stop.

"Want me to blow the horn?" asked Elijah.

"Just wait," said Fave softly.

"You see what I see?" Elijah nodded toward the roof of a building that peeked over the other side of the fence and dead-looking shrubbery. Two men were on the roof, armed with rifles aimed straight at the trucks. Both had long-range sights.

A young man with an AR-15 semi-automatic rifle slung over his shoulder stepped from behind some aluminum siding along the fence near a wheeled gate.

"Can I help you?" he asked.

"Fave Avery to see Mr. Auletta," said Fave. All of his men remained silent and bored-looking.

The young man looked to somebody else who, apparently, was behind the aluminum siding, waiting. After a couple of minutes, he removed a ring of keys from his pocket, unlocked the gate, and wheeled it partially open, just enough to walk through.

"Just you," said the boy, pointing at Fave.

Fave got out of the truck cab, stepped through the gate, then waited for the kid to close it behind him and lock it.

Fave looked around and counted fifteen armed men, each of whom watched him stoically. One of them, a lit cigarette dangling from his lips, stepped up. "Follow me," he said.

Fave recognized the man as Freddie, Frank's slightly younger brother.

Freddie led Fave to an L-shaped building with four large garage bays and a maintenance office. Junked and smashed cars piled on top of each other filled the junkyard compound.

Fave was led into the maintenance office. Frank Auletta was a thick-nosed guy with slicked-back hair. A fifty-something Italian, he sat behind a metal desk spilling over with papers.

"Hey, if it isn't Flava Fave!" he said loudly as he stood, his delivery reminding Fave of Rodney Dangerfield, but not funny. But Fave never thought Rodney Dangerfield was all that funny, either. Four other men sat in the maintenance office. Freddie took up a position against the wall behind Fave.

"He's clean," Freddie said.

Frank nodded. He ordered everyone to leave, except for Freddie.

Frank sat down and eyed Fave. "What can we do you for?"

Fave laid out his proposal, and then sat with his head tilted and eyes squinted.

Frank looked to his brother, who was standing in the back, lighting a cigarette. He took a drag on the cigarette, held it, then blew smoke in a long exhale as he thought. After a while, he simply nodded.

Rubbing his head, Frank shifted in his seat. He leaned back in the chair and eyed Fave. "What's in it for us?" he asked.

"You get the guns ..."

"We've got guns," Frank interrupted, but Fave continued, "and that heavy shit. You can move it. That's money in your pocket."

Frank and Fave stared at each other, each thinking in silence.

"Your boy was a Marine," Frank said. Fave nodded slowly.

~ ~ ~

After seeing to it that their guests were properly fed with a breakfast of eggs, bacon and toast, and Gerber's baby food for Antonio, Maxwell and Linda Levine sat at the kitchen table sipping coffee with their guests. All three of Maria's children were fast asleep in one of Max and Linda's two extra bedrooms, rooms that had once been their own children's before they had moved out a decade before.

Max and Linda were both sixty-plus-year-old retirees of the University of Windsor. Max had taught Physics for more than thirty years, and now he taught part-time, primarily for the enjoyment of it. His wife Linda was a Mathematics professor and college dean before she, too, retired.

The two had taken their usual early morning stroll down

to Sculpture Park on the city's waterfront across from Detroit and astride the Ambassador Bridge. Multiple helicopters circled over both Detroit and Windsor, and they heard a lot of sirens from police and emergency vehicles as they walked. Detroit had erupted the day before, and from the look and sound of things, it was still ongoing.

It was all so surreal, and Linda admitted there was an element of the forbidden to continuing with their daily trek to the riverfront. Amid the acrid smoke wafting across from Detroit and enveloping Windsor, and even with the distant sound of gunfire, Windsor remained idyllic. Taking a stroll to the park across from everything that was happening... It was morbid fascination is what it was, Linda mused.

But it wasn't just Maxwell and Linda. Scores of people had gathered at the waterfront park since the unrest had begun, eying in disbelief the heavy plumes of smoke and the circling helicopters.

Max had thought of zombies as he watched the long lines of people shuffling along, framed by an apocalyptic skyline behind them. *It's like a zombie apocalypse.* "They're fleeing Detroit. They're *refugees,* Linda. Honest to goodness *American* refugees. Whoever would have thought such a thing?"

All of the police activity and sirens on the Windsor side of the border now made sense.

The couple walked back up Askin Avenue past their own house to Wyandotte Street. Just three blocks to the west on Wyandotte was a secondary Canadian entrance to the Ambassador Bridge northbound to Detroit.

What they saw astounded them. Multiple police officers—some on foot and horseback, even more in riot gear—were attempting to cordon off the Wyandotte Street entrance to the Ambassador Bridge. Even more astounding was that throngs of people were running at the police from two sides. People on the bridge side of the line were trying to break through, and several did. But when police tried to subdue them, the crowd on the Canadian side surged forth to shield them.

Max and Linda saw a young man with two young children in his arms and a young woman with a baby in hers.

"My boy is sick!" sobbed the young woman. That's when Linda marched right up to her and the young man, leaving Max wondering what in God's name she was up to. "Come with us," Linda said.

~ ~ ~

At the intersection of Michigan and Livernois Avenues in Detroit, Aaron and Michelle walked among the crowds, which were growing despite the early hour. Schools were closed, and the atmosphere was electric. Aaron bumped fists with friends and neighbors that he and Michelle encountered.

"Yo, this is *craayzee,* man," said his friend Devin excitedly as the crowd spontaneously erupted into a chant of *"No power, no peace!"*

A huge fire burned vigorously a few blocks to the west, with a large crowd of protesters bustling around. Aaron and Michelle, along with Devin and two other friends Xavier and Reggie, jogged toward the fire. As they approached, they could feel the heat as flames leapt high into the air from two rows of old brick storefronts. The thick black smoke darkened the morning sky. The four boys removed their coats, took off their T-shirts despite the cold, and wrapped the T-shirts around their mouths to protect against the smoke before putting their coats back on. Michelle buried her face in her coat.

Xavier had just tied his shirt around his face when he tripped over something. He stopped his fall and looked down, and then did a double-take. *What's a mannequin doing in the middle of the street?*

He recoiled in shock.

The mannequin was actually the body of a Latino kid. It was shirtless, pale, and unnaturally still amid the chaos. The guy's eyes were open, like a mannequin's, and flames danced in their reflection.

Michelle, seeing the body, screamed and ran back in the direction they had come. She shook her hands and shuffled her feet in a wave of panic. Aaron wrapped his arms around her, and she screamed again before burying her face in his chest. "Oh, my God, Oh, my God," she wailed.

"It's a soldier," said Reggie. "There's another one over there." He pointed farther up the road.

"Soldiers?" Aaron slowly shook his head. "Man, this shit's for real now."

~ ~ ~

By late afternoon, the mayor of Windsor had declared a state of emergency and appealed to Ontario's lieutenant governor to deploy the Canadian Forces Reserves to help police the growing crisis at the Ambassador Bridge. Police and city officials warned Windsor residents to stay indoors and to keep their doors locked. Newscasters repeated the call shrilly and often.

The images coming out of Detroit and Windsor were reported globally. The United Nations general secretary weighed in, calling the Canadian prime minister and the U.S. President and demanding that both countries restore order and care for the refugees. Seeing the UN general secretary on TV admonishing the U.S. and Canada, and talking about Detroit and Windsor as if they were a Third World war zone, was crazy.

~ ~ ~

Approximately four miles from Maxwell and Linda Levine's house in Windsor, Canada, protesters gathered for a third day at the intersection of Grand River Avenue and West Grand Boulevard in Detroit. They also gathered along West Grand Boulevard to the M-10 freeway, including the intersection of West Grand Boulevard and 12th Street, which was ground zero for the 1967 riots. Multiple businesses and parked cars were set ablaze, and traffic was pelted with rocks and bottles all along West Grand Boulevard.

Right in the thick of the violent unrest along West Grand Boulevard and Grand River Avenue was the site of the former Detroit Olympia Arena. Parochially known as the "Old Red Barn," the arena was the one-time home of the NBA's Detroit Pistons and the NHL's Detroit Red Wings before it was demolished in 1987. The site was now occupied by the Michigan National Guard's Olympia Armory.

As many as fifteen soldiers worked at the armory full time. They maintained the property and equipment, worked as recruiters, and performed administrative duties for the various commands housed there. Four of the full-time soldiers managed to make it into work when this third, more intense day of unrest began, and each of them had a cracked windshield or other vehicle damage to show for their effort. The armory itself was largely left alone by the rioters, but the four soldiers stuck inside were anxious. They watched the news on a television set and kept an eye on the CCTV screens that monitored the property. Each soldier kept an M-4 rifle at the ready.

"Something's up, Sarge," reported Corporal Tony "Flaco" Alvarez, his eyes glued to the security screen. Four cars, each stuffed with armed men, pulled up outside the east-side property fence on McGraw Street. Several more cars, also carrying armed men, pulled up on the west side of the fence.

Chapter 14

Of the four soldiers at the Olympia Armory, twenty-eight-year-old Sergeant Willie Jackson was the most senior. After being laid off during one of the multiple rounds of job cuts at GM's Hamtramck Assembly Plant, he counted his lucky stars for landing a Title 32 full-time job as a recruiter for the National Guard, with whom he had already put in six years as a cook.

He watched the CCTV screens intently along with his three fellow soldiers: twenty-five-year-old, newly minted Sergeant Barry Washington, who was also a recruiter; twenty-two-year-old Corporal Tony Alvarez, a logistics specialist; and twenty-year-old Private First Class Andrew Stevens, a mechanic and the only member of Alpha Company to have made it in after the supposed call-up.

The two groups of armed young men outside the property fence on opposite sides of the building seemed to be hanging around, just waiting for something. Several U-Haul trucks and vans pulled up to the group on McGraw Avenue, across from the garage bays, and stopped. Several men piled out and joined the group already waiting. So, it wasn't the U-Haul trucks they were waiting for. Or, not *only* the U-Haul trucks.

What are you doing? Maybe they aren't interested in the Armory after all.

As if on cue, a truck with a trailer, which appeared to be

hauling construction equipment—a Caterpillar 323F excavator, to be precise—pulled alongside the other vehicles. After some exchanges among the young men, the trailer's tracks were extended to the street. A man hopped into the Caterpillar and started it. He carefully backed it off the trailer, turned the Caterpillar to face the fence, and raised its boom. He then brought the boom down on the fence, tearing away a large section. Security alarms blared inside the complex.

The armed men—Jackson estimated twenty or so—gleefully jogged through the hole and swarmed onto the property.

"Shit, they're coming in, Sarge!" announced Flaco, his voice nervous and high-pitched.

On the west side of the building, the other group of armed men clamored over the fence. One by one, each of the four CCTV screens covering the four sides of the building went dark.

When the last of CCTV cameras was shot out, Jackson and his fellow soldiers took shelter in an office near the main lobby of the Armory. Except for administrative offices lining the east-west hallway of the Grand River Avenue side of the building, the Armory had no windows. The soldiers were essentially blind, so they took turns ducking into an office to steal glances out the windows.

It wasn't long, maybe two or three minutes, before the Caterpillar swung around the corner, roared into view, and drove to the front of the building. The operator, a bearded African-American about thirty years old, raised the boom high above the one-story building, and then brought it down onto the roof.

The entire building shook with a *boom*, and dust rained from the ceiling, followed by a very loud, metallic rattling.

That was the sound of the Caterpillar shaking as the operator raised the boom in a jerky fashion.

The soldiers heard another *BOOM!* and this time a few tiles fell from the ceiling, followed by a fluorescent light fixture that exploded in a blue flash.

Jackson and his men had no time to think as the Caterpillar raised and dropped its boom yet again, and this time tore away the entire front office and crushed part of the ceiling.

"Let's go!" ordered Jackson, and the four soldiers retreated into the interior of the building. As the Caterpillar tore away a whole section at the front of the building, armed men poured into the building.

~ ~ ~

Jackson and his men ducked into a corridor office. Flaco Alvarez dropped to a knee and fired a volley down the hallway at the intruders before following suit.

The intruders took turns laying down covering fire as individual members advanced from room to room. "They're organized," whispered Washington. "They're working as a fire team," he said.

The building grew silent. The soldiers tensed up and readied their weapons. Jackson took deep, slow, calming breaths. The silence endured.

A soothing baritone voice called out. "G.I. Joe, we got no beef with you. We're here for what's in the vault. Just give us the keys and we'll be on our way."

Alvarez automatically touched the key chain draped across his neck. "You know we can't do that," answered Sergeant

Jackson in an equally calm voice. "You're trespassing on a U.S. Army facility."

"Sure you can, son," said the baritone voice. "You're out-manned and outgunned. Ain't nobody coming, either. Those boys with you—you're responsible for them, right? Nobody will blame you for looking out for your men. We ain't gonna hurt you. What would be the point of that?"

"They'll kill us for sure," whispered Washington, his eyes wide.

"What kind of assurance can you give us?" asked Jackson as he motioned to each of his fellow soldiers, ordering them into specific positions. If they were going down, they were going down with a fight.

There was a momentary pause as Jayson Avery considered the question. "I'm coming up empty, Brother G.I.," said the voice. Then a "hmmm," as Jayson looked over at Bobby "Bones" (for 'Skin n' Bones') Bailey, the youngest member of the day's crew at twenty. He was a goofy, happy-go-lucky kid. But Jayson liked having him around. He kept things light. But another role just revealed itself to him.

"Tell you what," said the voice, "I'm going to send my boy Bones here unarmed in there to demonstrate my sincerity. If you shoot Brother Bones, then you will have made your bed and that of your mates. Are you hearing me, Brother G.I.?"

A muffled argument ensued. "Bones" apparently objected to this plan.

"Nigga, *pleez!* Get your ass down there!" boomed the baritone voice.

A skinny, dreadlocked kid ducked his head inside their office, his eyes wide. Then, just as quickly, he moved behind the wall outside.

"Show me your hands!" bellowed Jackson, sending shivers of fear down Bones' spine. "Show me your hands or I will shoot you dead right there!"

Bones stepped inside, his arms raised. "H-h-hello," he said nervously.

~ ~ ~

Overnight, Jackson and his men—and Avery and his crew, for that matter—faced a conundrum: 1) stay and fight against twenty armed tangos, whose numbers seemed to be growing by the minute; 2) surrender; or 3) leave.

He didn't have a lot of time to think, but Jackson was certain of two things: he and his men were not giving up their weapons and they weren't going down without a fight.

For Jayson Avery's part, did he really want four dead U.S. soldiers on his hands? That would bring the Hammer of God—in the form of the U.S. government, anyway, which pretty much meant the same thing—down on him and the whole Avery Organization. Robbing a National Guard Armory wasn't a small crime, of course, but killing U.S. soldiers was a whole other thing. They had the keys to the vault, and having them would certainly make things easier, but he had an excavator, for crying out loud, and he was getting into the vault with or without the soldiers' keys.

They soon came to a mutual agreement: option number 3. "In case you didn't know it, there's a riot going on," protested Jackson. But, really, what was the alternative? Jackson agreed to depart the building, but he wasn't giving up the keys. And, surprisingly, Avery didn't ask for them again.

That was six hours ago, and it was now the dead of night. Jackson and his men had decided to make their way down Grand River Avenue to downtown, which was reportedly fortified and locked down. That's where all of the Detroit P.D. was hunkered down, protecting many of the city's major landmarks and corporate headquarters.

Fortress Downtown was two-and-a-half miles down Grand River Avenue, with a lot of hostile territory in between. But they had nowhere else to go. And, worse, they had to go by foot. A vehicle drew too much attention. Also, there was a lot of debris blocking the streets, including burning tires, dumpsters, and abandoned vehicles.

They operated as a fire team, individually sprinting from whatever cover they could find to the next while their teammates scanned for threats with their rifles. The first mile was uneventful, though they had to stay low as they navigated through pockets of protestors. They pointed their M-4 rifles directly at people multiple times as they moved, but the civilians merely stared back at them, the glow of flames reflected in their eyes. Nobody threw anything at them. But, man, did those stares chill Jackson and his men.

They had crossed over the M-10 freeway and entered perhaps the most dangerous final stretch, less than a half-mile to the bridge over I-75 into downtown, when a massive explosion shook the entire city. Jackson and his men dropped to the ground and took cover, feeling the searing heat of a massive fireball on their backs and then their faces. When they looked up, they saw a giant, fiery mushroom cloud rising over the city almost directly over their heads.

"Stay down!" shouted Jackson, as *zips* and *pings* were heard all around them. Bullets and shrapnel ripped through the air. Debris fell from the sky.

It was the arms cache at the Armory.

The mushroom cloud quickly dissipated, blending into the night sky. The flaming air cooled as it rose, but flashes from smaller explosions intermittently lit up the streets. Each explosion momentarily cast light on the ugly mushroom cloud as it drifted over the Detroit River toward Windsor, Canada.

~ ~ ~

It had been a restless night for Maxwell and Linda Levine, and their guests. Police aggressively patrolled the streets of Windsor all night long. Patrol cars passed Max and Linda's house at least ten times during the night, aiming search lights into the darkened interior every time they passed, flooding each room with bright light in their search for fugitive American refugees.

As if that wasn't enough to unsettle the residents of Windsor, the massive explosion at the Olympia Armory in Detroit punctuated the uneasy night with a low rumble, triggering what felt like a minor earthquake. Starting at about 2:30 a.m., windows rattled in their frames, followed by another rumble every few minutes. This continued for several hours.

Overnight, the Essex and Kent Scottish, a reserve regiment of the Royal Canadian Infantry Corps, was ordered to mobilize, and every mile of their trek was captured by news helicopters and broadcast live on television.

Chapter 15

All of the 250-man-strong Foxtrot Company, 1st Battalion, 125th Infantry Regiment, were mustered into formation at 7:00 a.m. at the National Guard Armory in Bay City, Michigan. While not part of Michigan's designated rapid reaction force, the geographical extent of unrest across Metropolitan Detroit and beyond made it clear that the entire 125th Infantry Regiment would be needed. The adjutant general ordered all companies to deploy as soon as possible.

After three hours of assembling equipment, assessing intelligence reports (gleaned entirely from the news on television and the internet), and coordinating with other companies, the first convoy of five AM General M35 troop transport trucks—two carrying twenty-five soldiers each while the remaining three were purposefully empty—departed the Bay City Armory and entered Interstate 75, which the small base abutted. Twenty-five minutes later, the small convoy pulled into the armory in Saginaw, Michigan, where Bravo Company was assembled and ready to board the three empty trucks. More convoys were to follow throughout the day.

~ ~ ~

Colonel Floyd Barksdale, along with his twenty-four-year-old nephew Rickey—an actual corporal in the Michigan National Guard, but a captain in the Superior Volunteers Militia—and other Superior Volunteers sat, stood, and otherwise hovered nearby. Many were watching a twenty-four-inch computer screen perched on Floyd's desk in the command trailer, which was parked in the woods just off Port Inland Road between McDonald Lake and the Seul Choix Bay limestone quarry in the Upper Peninsula.

They watched with rapt alarm as reporters in helicopters and stationed throughout Metropolitan Detroit spoke rapidly and with astonishment, reporting that the National Guard was nowhere to be seen. And yet, in Canada, the Essex and Kent Scottish of the Royal Canadian Infantry Corps had deployed in the pre-dawn hours. They had secured the entire perimeter of the Ambassador Bridge border station and, by midday, had set up a small tent city. There were sleeping tents, a mess tent, a medical tent, and a processing center to care for (and identify) all the refugees.

Floyd's heart raced. He had talked about the need to prepare for a breakdown of society—an EMP attack from North Korea, perhaps, or an invasion by China, even an Islamic takeover of North America, like what had happened over there in Europe, according to the internet. But what he mostly anticipated was a breakdown engineered by the socialist elites on the coasts, who controlled the federal government, so they could, once and for all, round up true patriots, confiscate their guns, and implement their globalist world order.

And. Now. It. Was. Happening.

No matter that the President was a Republican. Nope, they were *all* implicated and, for goodness sake, the President had been a hedge fund manager on Wall Street before taking office.

Colonel Charlie Pike, who ran his own forty-man unit in Iron River near the Wisconsin border, and was commander of the entire 200-strong Superior Volunteers, all based in the Upper Peninsula, had put all units on alert two days earlier.

But, in the early morning, Colonel Pike ordered all units to duty and called all unit commanders for an emergency teleconference via the encrypted WhatsApp program. Volunteers streamed into camp throughout the day as they got word. There were other militia groups, too, some of them really out there, according to Floyd. These people believed in all kinds of crazy conspiracies—like aliens and lizard people. They, too, were mobilizing.

Floyd's Volunteers unit numbered about thirty. They were just about at full contingent, and some members had brought their families, making the camp swell to nearly sixty people. Despite the cold, it was like a big family gathering and picnic. Many had brought sandwiches, and they gathered around in various cliques.

The news reported that unrest had spread to Ann Arbor, Flint, Pontiac, Battle Creek, Benton Harbor, Grand Rapids, Saginaw, Buena Vista, Freeland, Ypsilanti, and Muskegon. The entire Lower Peninsula appeared to be blowing up.

Rumor had it that all of Michigan's State Police had been ordered south to Detroit and other cities, and many town and county sheriffs across the state had also deployed to Detroit and other Lower Michigan cities. Streams of refugees, rioters, and anarchists, meanwhile, were said to be on the prowl. Some were even heading north, and the Upper Peninsula was totally unprotected.

It was up to them, the Superior Volunteers, to defend the Upper Peninsula.

As the 'soldiers' huddled about, some using the downtime to practice shooting on the range, Floyd and other commanders strategized via WhatsApp. *Operation Superior*, they would call it.

On the television, pundits debated the failure of the Michigan National Guard to deploy while the Canadian Forces Reserves did so swiftly. Then came searing images of what appeared to be the bodies of two young soldiers sprawled in the middle of the road on Michigan Avenue on the west side near Dearborn. They were laying astride the smoldering shell of a pickup truck, with burning buildings on either side of the road.

It was time to act.

CHAPTER 16

"Let me be clear. The tragedy that has befallen the family of Mrs. Bernadette Price and so many others is felt by all of us. We are all deeply hurt by the tragic and senseless loss of life to fires that were wholly preventable..."

Floyd clicked the "X" on his browser in the middle of the U.S. President's speech and was off the internet. *Things are happening fast now.* He stepped out of his command trailer. He was dressed in full army combat uniform camouflage, and wore brown combat boots and the green oak leaf of a major on the center of his chest. In the place of "U.S. Army," the words "Superior Volunteers" were stitched above his left breast. In place of the U.S. flag on the right shoulder, he sported a camouflaged version of the famed Gadsden flag of the American Revolution, which depicted a coiled rattlesnake and the words "DON'T TREAD ON ME."

A sea of pickup trucks and cars filled the lot between the command trailer and the picnic area. The bustle and din of men in uniform subsided.

Floyd looked out at his men and their trucks. They looked back at him with eagerness and fear. *I should say something profound.*

"Men," he said in a squeak. He cleared his throat with a phlegmy *ahem* followed by a rattling smoker's cough. "Men," he continued, "tonight we take our country back. Godspeed!"

A "woot!" from someone in the crowd elicited some laughs. But they still stood there, waiting for an order, and Floyd stared back, somewhat befuddled.

"Go," he finally said, wondering why they hadn't started up their cars yet. "Go!" he said louder. "The mission is a go!" He waved his hands forward from his hips, motioning them to ... *go*.

"Yeah, boy!" someone shouted with a raised fist as the first truck roared to life. "Yee-ha!" another hooted.

The trucks roared to life, and men climbed into their cabs and beds.

Operation Superior was underway.

~ ~ ~

In Sault Sainte Marie, a small idyllic city in Michigan's Upper Peninsula, Sergeant Eric Andrews of the Michigan Army National Guard left his home for the local armory at 4:45 a.m. Eric was an active duty Personnel Services Specialist, and he needed to arrive early to prepare to process the soldiers who would be reporting for duty because of the official call-up. There was a lot of paperwork to do.

He turned onto the riverfront East Portage Road, and came across soldiers in the road just before the armory. A soldier held up his hand as Eric approached, and he came to a stop. *Looks like some guys made it in early.* But ... *Why they are stopping traffic?*

He rolled down his window as the soldier approached. "Road's closed," said the soldier. "Go back." An M-4 was slung over his shoulder.

"I'm headed to the Armory," Eric said, fumbling for his military ID card. He was wearing civilian clothes because he normally changed into uniform on site. "I'm Sergeant Andrews," he added as he pulled out his ID.

"Armory's closed," said the soldier again.

Eric was confused. And there was something off about the soldier's uniform. "But I'm—"

"Road's closed, Armory's closed, go home."

Four other soldiers now flanked the first soldier, each pointing their M-4s at Eric. It was only then that Eric saw the words "Superior Volunteers" on their battle dress uniforms."

"Okay, okay," said Eric, showing his hands. "Thank you." He felt a burst of adrenaline in his chest as he put the truck into reverse.

What do I do now?

After arriving home, he sat in his driveway for a moment, trying to calm down and collect his thoughts. He picked up his cell phone and dialed 911.

~ ~ ~

Meanwhile, far to the south in Adrian, a few miles from the Ohio border, Army Signal Corps Captain Adam Coffey was the first to arrive at the Adrian National Guard Armory. After letting himself into the building and making his way to his office, he paused in the hallway. Something didn't seem right. He looked around but didn't see anything out of the ordinary.

He walked down the hallway and turned on light switches. When he turned back toward his office, something caught the corner of his eye. He looked back down the hall and saw it. The hair on his arms stood up. The door to the vault was open.

Adam cautiously made his way to the vault, peeked inside, and turned on the lights. The vault—or "the cage" as the soldiers called it, because it was, essentially, an open-air cage—was wide open.

The cage had been stripped of most of the M-4s. Only four remained. Papers were strewn about the office portion of the room, and the desk drawers were open.

Did the battalion deploy without me?

That couldn't be. The cage wouldn't be open, and the room wouldn't be such a mess.

Adam's heart raced as the realization set in. The armory had been raided.

A couple of hours before sunrise, a convoy of ten vehicles, a mix of pickup trucks and work vans, crossed the Mackinac Bridge from the Upper to the Lower Peninsula and into Mackinaw City. They turned east onto Central Avenue, which ended at a marina. The marina was the small-town heart of downtown Mackinaw City. And, just before the marina, to the right, was the municipal building that housed the city's government, including its tiny police department.

Mackinaw City's Police Department comprised seven full-time officers. Three officers worked the day shift, three worked the night shift, and one worked the overnight shift.

That lone overnight officer, Barry Schneider, sat in the cramped office, his head buried in his arms on his desk. He had tried to stay awake, but it was always a losing battle. At twenty-one, Barry was the youngest of the police officers and most junior. And so, after a couple of months of daytime training and supervision, he was stuck on the midnight shift.

Barry heard the front office door open and was startled awake. Hardly anyone came in during the overnight hours. Actually, no one ever had. He sat up, a little embarrassed at being caught sleeping, but the scruffy-looking man didn't notice him right away.

"May I help you?" Barry asked. The man looked around at the office walls, as two other men entered.

The first man, bearded and wearing army camouflage—in fact, all of them wore camouflage—looked at Barry with steely eyes.

"Yes, you may," said the man. "You are relieved." The two

other men raised their M-4s and pointed them at Barry. That was the first time Barry noticed the weapons.

Barry gulped. "Um, okay," he said.

Once they were satisfied that Barry was unarmed—his service pistol, and those of his fellow officers, were locked in the department's safe—the soldiers escorted Barry outside. He was free to leave.

Unsure of where to go, Barry climbed into his Ford F-150 pickup truck. Chief Ralph Wendowski lived a few miles south of town, on Carp Lake. That's where Barry decided to go.

En route, Barry could see that soldiers (*not* soldiers, he reminded himself, not *real* soldiers) had the Nicolet Street entranceway onto I-75 blocked off and were manning what looked like a checkpoint.

Barry navigated to Mackinaw Highway heading south out of town. At the Mackinaw Highway entrance to I-75, Barry saw five or six cars stopped, their taillights glowing. He pulled into the parking lot of the Southside Liquors minimart and watched. He guessed that another checkpoint blocked off I-75. He decided to double back and take the long way south and out of town, wondering if that route, too, was closed off. If so, all routes into town would be blocked.

It's like Red Dawn. Except they weren't Chinese or Russian invaders taking over. They were armed American militiamen.

~ ~ ~

Ralph Wendowski was an early riser. The older he got, the truer that was. Today, he was wide awake by 4:30. He lay staring at the ceiling for a few minutes as he thought about the day's tasks, then slipped out of bed without waking Mary, his wife of forty years.

He was in the kitchen drinking coffee and surfing the morning news and sports on his laptop when his cell phone vibrated. *That can't be good.* He stole a glance at the clock before reaching for the phone.

It was Barry. Ralph was slightly relieved on the one hand and irritated on the other. The kid probably wanted some guidance on something he should be capable of handling himself.

"What's up, Barry?" he asked. "You're *where?*" Just then, headlights briefly filled the kitchen windows as a car pulled into the driveway.

"Who did you say they were?" asked Ralph after he let Barry in.

"Their unis said 'Superior Volunteers'," replied Barry.

Ralph pecked away on his computer, googling the group. "Here we go," he muttered. The Superior Volunteers had their own website. Ralph clicked on it. Definitely a militia group. There were photos of men in army fatigues, pictures of men at target practice with rifles, pictures of family picnics and, in all of the pictures, the men and boys were always dressed in camouflage. The 'who we are' link led to a manifesto of sorts, outlining the Second Amendment right to bear arms and to form "well-regulated" militias.

Naturally.

Ralph clicked on their X link, and there it was: their latest tweets:

@SuperiorVolunteers: In this time of need, the Volunteers are stepping up. We are maintaining peace & stability in the UP. Protecting our communities!

@SuperiorVolunteers: The Superior Volunteers are mobilizing! Join the effort! Yoopers, defend the UP!

Ralph leaned back in his kitchen chair and sighed. "You did the right thing coming here."

"Good morning, Barry" said Mary as she entered the kitchen clad in an ankle-length robe. "What brings you over so early in the morning?"

Ralph let Barry tell his story as Mary put on coffee. Ralph, meanwhile, called his second most senior officer, fifty-eight-year old Frank Carrol, and ordered him to come to his home ASAP. "Take the back roads, Frank, you hear? I mean it. Take the back roads."

Ralph called the remaining officers and ordered them, without explanation, not to report for work, but instead wait for further instructions. He called the village President, Mackinaw City's equivalent of a mayor.

"What do I do?" asked Barry as Ralph finished speaking with the village President.

"You're going to eat breakfast," said Mary, retrieving a carton of eggs from the refrigerator. "And then you're going to stay in the guest room."

A new pair of headlights flooded the kitchen as Frank pulled into the lot, just as Mary was serving scrambled eggs, bacon, and toast.

Fed to satiety and fueled by coffee, Ralph and Frank—both dressed in their police uniforms, armed with personal rifles, and riding in Ralph's F-150—pulled into the public boat ramp parking lot astride Conkling Heritage Park, which was across the street from the Mackinaw City Municipal Building. Village President Bob Mollen climbed from his car and waved.

"Are those necessary?" he asked, nodding to the rifles.

"I hope not," answered Frank.

Ralph, Frank, and Bob walked to the front entrance on Main Street, where two militiamen stood guard outside the door. When they saw the two police officers with rifles slung over their shoulders, they straightened with alarm. One "soldier" brought up his rifle.

"Do you see me pointing my rifle at you, son?" barked Ralph in a stern voice.

The young "soldier"—he looked to be a teenager—let his AR-15 rifle dangle at his side, but kept his finger on the trigger.

"I want to speak to the man in charge of ..." Ralph said, his voice trailing off before finding the words, "whatever this is. Who would that be?" He turned toward the second "soldier," who was even younger than the first.

"Colonel Jenkins," the second boy replied nervously.

"But you'll have to wait here," said the first kid. "Who are you?" he asked.

"Chief of Police, son," answered Ralph, and nodding to Bob,

"and this is the village president."

"The what?"

"The mayor, son, the mayor."

"Oh," the boy said, then nodded to the second one, presumably his younger brother. The second boy went inside the municipal building while the first stood silently, his eyes glued to the mayor and the two policemen.

The second boy appeared in the doorway. "You can come in," he said, and held the door open.

Ralph, Frank, and Bob walked inside and the boy led them down the hallway to the village president's office.

Five armed men occupied the small office, and they were all in uniform.

"I'm Colonel Jenkins. I've been expecting you," said a hard-looking man in his forties, sitting in the president's chair. "Not this early," he said, nodding to the clock, "but expecting you, nonetheless."

"What are you doing here?" demanded Bob.

"You've all seen the news, I'm sure," answered the colonel. "The Lower Peninsula is going up in flames as we speak, and so we—the Superior Volunteers Militia—we're doing our duty.

"Gubmint's gone to shit, fellas," Jenkins continued. "Those liberals down there have finally taken the cake. We can't let those people and all of that bullshit come up this way. So we closed the bridge. *We're* the government now, in the U.P."

Ralph was about to speak when Bob held up his hand, silencing him.

"How about we coexist?" said Bob. "Let us continue to do our jobs, and we'll stay out of your way. You've closed the bridge. Fine. But life goes on. Old folks need their medications. People need to grocery shop. Cats get caught in trees. Children got to go to school. People got to go to work."

Typical politician.

"You need us," continued Bob, "to do our jobs and keep people from panicking. Shoot, ninety percent of 'em probably agree with you. But keep them from earning their keep, even for a day, and they'll turn on you."

"And these boys," Bob said, nodding to Ralph and Frank, "are familiar to the public here. They're part of the community. You are not. Let them do their work keeping the peace. You'll *want* them to. I mean, for goodness sake, what are you going to do when Miss Gulley complains to you about the Sinclairs' poodle pooping on her lawn? You going to shoot her? Or shoot the Sinclairs? Or what if that truant Sawyer kid steals a canteen or something. You going to shoot him, a teenager? Or send him to jail somewhere, a jail that you don't have? What about—"

"Okay, already!" interrupted Jenkins.

"Also," added Frank, "the Northern Militia boys are going to be mightily displeased when they find one of our towns is occupied by Yoopers. If you stick to keeping the bridge closed, it should all work out."

Frank and Jenkins stared sharply at each other.

"We can handle those amateurs," spit Jenkins.

"Uh huh," nodded a dubious Frank.

"Gentlemen, gentlemen," interrupted Bob, "I believe we are in agreement." He turned to Ralph and Frank. "Call your deputies," he ordered, "and bring them up to speed. And I don't want that kid on the night shift alone. See if you can switch him with a couple of your more seasoned officers."

Then, turning to the colonel, he added, "One more thing, Mr. Jenkins. Can I have my office back? Chief Wendowski here can set you up in the Police offices. In fact, it would be good for people to see that you folks are working right alongside our police."

Jenkins tried to maintain a poker face as he absorbed the village president's reasoning. He looked at his men standing silently against the wall. They offered no clues to what they might be thinking. Colonel Jenkins took a deep breath and nodded his agreement.

Ralph was impressed. *Well, I'll be damned. Bob Mollen, furniture store extraordinaire, knows how to take charge.*

Chapter 17

The excitement was palpable as Zach rode in the back of an army transport truck with twenty-four other soldiers from his unit. News of the riots, the cancellation of classes, and the call-up by his unit—it was all kind of surreal, even now as they neared Detroit. They couldn't see anything from the back of the canvassed truck, but the police sirens were non-stop as they barreled down the highway with a state police escort.

Zach, like his fellow soldiers, bounced his legs and tapped his rifle as his adrenaline flowed. It was only five months since he graduated high school and made the fateful decision to join the Army. His mother and stepfather had called him into the living room where they usually sat watching television. When the TV was turned off, Zach knew this would be a "serious" conversation What the fuck, when did they ever want a serious conversation? Now that he was graduating, now that he was eighteen, he knew it was about getting a job, about moving out or paying rent, or something like that.

Sure enough, it was.

"Zach, have you thought about what comes next?" asked his stepdad.

"What do you mean?" Zach replied, trying not to sound defensive but failing.

"You're eighteen now," his stepdad said. "It's time to think about getting a full-time job."

"I want to go to college," Zach said.

"That's great, honey," his mother said way too soon, obviously expecting him to say that, "but we just can't afford college tuition. All our money is tied up in the garage, and things haven't been good for a long time now."

Zach could feel his face turning red with anger, but he already knew that they wouldn't pony up for his tuition. His older brother Aaron worked part-time at Kmart during the day and at Burger King at night, all while trying to go to community college and keep his heavy metal band going. Meanwhile, their stepdad watched soap operas on TV all day while his garage turned to shit. Their mom worked ten to twelve hours a day processing the paperwork of repossessed cars for the Ford Motor Credit Company in Dearborn.

"I thought about joining the Army," Zach said with a sigh, looking down at his feet. He really *had* thought about it over the past few months, but he really just wanted this conversation to end before he was overcome with spitefulness.

"I think that's a great idea" his mom said.

"An excellent idea, Zach," his stepdad agreed.

Zach felt the mood in the room lighten as his parents beamed about how smart and courageous he was. His parents really were happy, elated even, and somehow that elation was contagious. Zach felt like a burden had just been lifted off his shoulders. He promised to follow the advice of his stepfather, that was, to not sign anything right away and to think about getting a job as a supply specialist.

And here I am, he sighed.

The truck shuddered to a halt. Sgt. Harrison stood and leapt from the vehicle. "Lewis and Arnold!" he barked, and Zach's stomach tightened with nervousness and excitement. He clamored out of his seat, jumped off the truck, and stumbled into the arms of Sgt. Harrison.

"Sorry, Sarge," he muttered as he straightened up and tugged on his uniform and backpack. He slung his rifle over his shoulder and looked around.

~ ~ ~

In Lansing, Governor Krueger and Major General John Veazey, the adjutant general of the Michigan National Guard, held a press conference. The first questions pertained to what was widely perceived as the painfully slow deployment of the National Guard in light of the fact that Canada had already actively and visibly deployed the Kent and Essex Scottish. The governor deferred to his adjutant general.

"The National Guard is being deployed as we speak," Veazey said. "First Battalion, 125th Infantry Regiment, is tasked with deploying within seventy-two hours of activation. It has been a little over sixteen hours. Alpha Company is the unit based in Detroit, out of the Olympia Armory, which has been compromised by the unrest. We have, therefore, redirected the deployment of Alpha Company to other bases.

"To that end, soldiers are mustering with Bravo Company in Saginaw, Charlie Company in Wyoming City, Delta Company in Big Rapids, and the supporting Foxtrot Company in Bay City. That's more than a thousand soldiers. We expect convoys to start entering the downtown within the next few hours."

Even as Major General Veazey spoke, the first convoy of National Guard trucks closed in on downtown as it traveled down I-75. With three miles to go, however, the traffic came to a complete stop, despite a state police escort. Two miles ahead, demonstrators from the adjacent North End neighborhood had entered the freeway and sat down, blocking traffic.

Lieutenant Marco Gordon requested Staff Sergeant Harris, with Specialist Zach Arnold and Corporal Jamal Lewis, both Detroit-area locals, to accompany him in his Humvee to help scout an alternative route into downtown.

They slowly turned the Humvee around and exited the freeway by going the wrong way up an entrance lane to Clay Street. They turned left on Oakland Avenue, and two blocks later, they stopped at the intersection of Oakland Avenue and East Grand Boulevard.

"Back that way is a big Ford plant," said Zach, pointing east.

"That's a GM plant," Jamal corrected. "My dad worked there."

"Whatever," said Zach. "Woodward Avenue is just up here," he said, pointing to his right. "It'll take us right into downtown."

"Great," said Lieutenant Gordon, "but how do we get from here to there," he said, more to himself than to anyone else. Huge crowds meandered all over East Grand River, actively looting storefronts and otherwise just hanging around like it was a big block party. The shells of burned out cars lay scattered and overturned in the middle of the boulevard. To their left, a pile of burning tires blocked the overpass to the GM plant.

"There's a road over there that parallels the plant. It'll take you in close on the North Side," said Jamal. "But I don't know if we can get past *that*," he added, pointing in across the interstate to where a massive complex burned out of control. The road that Jamal pointed out seemed to go right through the inferno.

"All right," said Lieutenant Gordon, his mind apparently made up. "Let's see what Woodward looks like."

Heads turned in their direction as they drove slowly up East Grand River Boulevard. People seemed dumbstruck by the sight of an army Humvee appearing on the road in the middle of a riot. The lieutenant made eye contact with an older man, about thirty-five years old, wearing an old desert camouflage army jacket, who gazed stoically at the Humvee.

Thirty-seven-year-old Jackson Mills saw the desert-camouflaged army Humvee turn onto Grand River, and he just stared at it with a strange sense of nostalgia. It was the same vehicle that he had worked on in the Army and in Iraq. He knew the Humvee like the back of his hand. He loved his job as an Army mechanic, and he was proud to have made it through basic training and to wear the uniform. The Army promised job skills and a way out of Motown, and he was appreciative. He served in Iraq, where the work was non-stop, hot, and dirty. It was in Iraq that he had come to know the Humvee so well because they took such a beating. But then came the drawdown, and he was out of the Army with no money saved and nothing to show for his time in the service. Certainly no job waited for him, at least nothing as steady as the Army. And here was the Army again, but it wasn't his Army anymore. With no steady job and a battle every three months or so with GLEE to keep his power on or get it back, it was clear to him that he was the enemy.

He was an Iraqi now, an insurgent.

Jackson nonchalantly picked up a chunk of debris, a piece of a rock in a pothole, and hurled it at the Humvee. That one rock turned into a hailstorm of rocks and other detritus as others took their cue and threw whatever they could find at the Humvee.

But it wasn't the bricks and rocks the soldiers were concerned about. Zachary pointed to a sizeable group of people standing over a collection of glass bottles glistening in the sun and organized in neat rows in the parking lot of a gasoline station, each being stuffed with oily rags.

"Uh, guys," is all Zach had to say when he pointed out the group and their collection of bottles.

"Get us the fuck out of here *now*, El Tee!" Harris commanded, and Lieutenant Gordon gunned the vehicle while swerving to avoid a protester.

But it was too late. Their movement caught the eyes of the crowd and, thinking they were police, one of them set a rolled-up newspaper on fire and ignited the oily rags. Others picked up the lighted cocktails, and threw them hard at the Humvee.

The lieutenant did his best to weave between raining Molotov cocktails, but at least four found their mark, engulfing the outer body of the Humvee in flames. He continued driving, but with flames on the hood blinding him and smoke filling the cabin, he stopped the vehicle and ordered his men out.

Staff Sergeant Harris unlatched the safety of his M-4 as he scrambled out the door, and ran from the burning vehicle. He then dropped to his knee and opened fire on a group poised to launch yet more Molotov cocktails. The deafening jackhammer sputter of the M-4 echoed off the boulevard's buildings, and three teenagers fell where they stood. Flames erupted alongside their bodies where they dropped their flaming cocktails. Demonstrators up and down East Grand River ran for cover, clearing the entire length of the boulevard.

Zach stood wide-eyed in the middle of the road, staring at the three fallen teenagers, flames licking at their unmoving bodies.

"Move your ass!" commanded Sgt. Harris, but Zach only stood there. "Move it, Private!" barked Harris, tugging at the kid until his feet moved. Harris scanned the abandoned and boarded-up storefronts with his rifle. The four soldiers moved as a fire team, spreading out to give each other cover, but with Harris keeping the young private close. They began to make the half-mile trek back to the interstate, taking cover amid the burning and smoldering buildings as they pressed forward. Their abandoned Humvee was now an inferno.

Behind them, they heard wailing as family members discovered the three fallen teenagers. Several people opened fire with handguns, shooting wildly at the retreating soldiers, even stepping into the middle of the boulevard for better aim.

The soldiers ducked into the alleyway behind the storefronts, and continued to beat their retreat through the neighborhood. They followed the alley north before turning east on what Lieutenant Gordon read as Custard Avenue.

Well that's just great.

When the men turned onto Custer, they were met with

nearly half of their entire 125-person company. They had all climbed from the freeway on foot after hearing the gunfire, and were taking up positions on Custer Avenue and all along the service road parallel to the interstate.

Lieutenant Gordon and Sergeant Harris briefed Major Stanley Payne ("Major Pain," naturally) on what had just happened: one of the soldiers on the knoll had fired warning shots at a group of young people—gang members, most likely.

"Goddammit," muttered Major Payne as a bullet zipped past. "Cease fire!"

"We've got armed tangos coming down from the hood, sir," protested an excited young corporal.

The major ignored him, snarling as he stroked his beardless chin and assessed the situation.

His trucks were wedged in by traffic that was backed up all the way to downtown, which was about three miles. The northbound lanes were entirely empty, but a series of concrete Jersey barriers the length of the freeway separated the north and southbound lanes.

Perhaps with a chain they could pull apart two or three of the Jersey barriers to create a space wide enough to get the trucks through. "Harris, do we have a chain?" he barked.

"Yes, sir." said Sergeant Harris. They had at least two chains.

Another *pop, zing* and a metallic *tink* as a bullet bounced off a car in front of the convoy. Which made Major Payne think, *What if there are rioters in their path? What then? Engage them? Kill them?* He hadn't received any orders that extreme—at least not yet.

"Listen up, men!" he yelled. He'd reached a decision.

~ ~ ~

Araminta was in the middle of doing the dishes and just stopped, listening intently. She was no stranger to the sound of gunfire. But this was different, and a sense of dread came over her. It sounded...*industrial.* That was the word that came to mind. Its echoes were as loud as the initial barrage.

Brandon...

Araminta dropped the partially washed plate into the sink and was through the living room and out the front door in an instant. She walked-ran around the block south to Grand River Boulevard; she was certain that was where the gunfire had come from.

She heard a scream, a primordial scream that made her shudder. When she came around the corner at Brush Street, she saw the Humvee in the middle of the boulevard, engulfed in flames.

People came out from buildings and from behind them, coming out from taking shelter and checking if it was safe to do so; heads were turned toward the east, and she looked, too. The next block over was that gas station and garage run by Darius, that old mute, and in its lot lay three young men sprawled on the pavement, not moving, and they were the center of everyone's attention.

Brandon...

Oh God, don't let it be Brandon. As she approached the scene, she saw a lake of blood between the fallen boys.

Sheila, the mother of Brandon's friend Dominic, came bolting into view. Her legs turned wobbly and she fell to her knees. A large woman, just crumbling to the pavement in the middle of the road. "Dominic!" she screamed, then crawled toward the unnaturally still bodies.

It was Sheila's voice that Araminta realized had made that awful scream a moment before. "Oh, *Gawd!*" she screamed now, tears streaming down her face.

Araminta could see them now. Dominic, Brandon's friend, so sweet, lay sprawled on his back, his tall skinny body stretched out and draped backward over the outstretched leg of Shawn, another of Brandon's friends, arching his back. Dominic's jacket was splayed open and his t-shirt was crumpled up to mid-torso, his tender navel pointing skyward. The teenager's eyes were open, gazing skyward, vacant, his mouth gaping. But it was his bare stomach that burned in Araminta's mind as she pried her eyes away and looked to the third body.

Chad was the name the came to her. Chad. Not Brandon. Not Brandon.

She took a deep breath and exhaled haltingly. Her hands, at her chest, were shaking. And then she saw him. He emerged from the crowd, his eyes glued to Dominic's outstretched body, gawking. His face was passive, his eyes distant. Araminta continued her walk-run, walking straight up to Brandon, and she threw her arms around him. She buried her face into the nape of his neck.

Brandon still stared at the bodies of his friends. He said nothing. Nor did Araminta.

Araminta composed herself, grabbed Brandon's hand, and pulled him along. Tears streamed freely down her face as she walked briskly, her back to the bodies, Brandon being pulled along, his face still turned back.

~ ~ ~

In Coldwater, in the far south of central Michigan, a stream of thirty pickup trucks, cars, and SUVs—some sporting U.S. flags, others Confederate Battle flags, and still others Gadsden flags—converged during the early morning hours at an open field.

At precisely 9:00 a.m., the convoy departed the field and meandered onto West Chicago Boulevard, heading east toward town.

The convoy drove through the center of town, traveling at a parade-like pace. Indeed, the convoy was very much a parade, with its multiple flags flying amid the vehicles, the truck beds full of camouflaged men, women, and boys sporting an assortment of automatic and semi-automatic rifles. People in other cars and on the sidewalks gawked at the procession. Heads turned in the local Arby's and McDonald's.

A Coldwater Police cruiser sped out of the McDonald's parking lot after the convoy passed. It raced east and, as it caught up to the convoy, it turned on its emergency lights and raced ahead of it.

As the convoy continued to the eastern side of town, several police cars stopped traffic ahead, allowing it to pass through intersections unmolested. Drivers in the convoy tooted their horns in appreciation as they passed.

The convoy reached Interstate 69, the eastern terminus of Coldwater, and turned left onto the northbound ramp. With no Michigan State troopers to worry about—they had all been sent to Detroit and other cities—the convoy drove north for nine miles to the county line. There, the procession slowed to a halt at a small turnabout, and everyone disembarked.

Within minutes, the festive group of men and women had stopped traffic in both directions. They set up orange cones and plastic Jersey barriers to funnel traffic into a single lane.

Checkpoints on each side of the highway were quickly established. Armed men stood alongside the checkpoints. Each vehicle would be inspected, each driver and passenger questioned.

"Where are you coming from?"

"Where are you heading, and why?"

The South Michigan Militia of Branch County had arrived.

If the state couldn't protect them from those diseased zombies in the cities—if the state couldn't prevent the violent anti-Trump globalists of the past from pouring into God's country—the good people of the South Michigan Militia would.

In Branch County, Cass County, Hillsdale County, the South Michigan Militia spread into each of the counties bordering Indiana and Ohio to set up checkpoints and control traffic into and out of the southern counties. The Superior Volunteers had effectively seized control of the Upper Peninsula.

Chapter 18

Governor Krueger and the adjutant general were huddling with their staffs at the Governor's Mansion in Lansing, watching hard-to-stomach images on a large screen TV.

The contrast between the two armies—one seemingly competent and professional, the other unresponsive, ineffectual, and in retreat—set off alarms in Washington, DC, and in capitals around the world.

"An unmitigated disaster," national pundits decried.

More bad news filtered in from beyond Detroit. Massive crowds had overrun police lines in Ann Arbor, setting parked cars ablaze and smashing storefront windows in the downtown. In Flint, the city hall was reportedly on fire.

The governor and the adjutant general ordered the entirety of the Michigan National Guard, all remaining units, to duty, but it would take at least three days for them to deploy. And now it appeared that they would have to fight their way into Detroit and possibly Flint and Ann Arbor, a task for which the National Guard was not designed.

Reports filtered in from the north and south that various armed militia groups were setting up illegal checkpoints on federal interstates and state highways.

The whole damned state was in rebellion.

The governor, adjutant general, and their staffs now agreed that mobilizing the Michigan National Guard wouldn't be enough.

"Get the President on the phone," ordered Governor Krueger.

~ ~ ~

Brandon's mind was empty, but raced at the same time. It was full of images, of Dominic lying sprawled out on the ground, surely dead, right? He just laid there, he and Shawn and Chad. Dead. That Humvee on fire. Soldiers, too. There were soldiers. A crowd.

Dominic was dead?

Araminta's mind raced, too. Everything, all at once. She had to protect Brandon. Brandon was quiet, too quiet, his eyes still distant.

She didn't let go of Brandon's hand, and he didn't try to pull away. He was still back *there*, gawking at the bodies. They walked through the front door, into the living room. There they were, her car keys. On the lamp table next to the sofa. She grabbed them.

Clothes. Forget about them, just go. Shoes? No, just go. Just go.

They turned around and walked back out the front door and to the Jetta. Araminta opened the passenger door.

"Get in," she said, no *ordered,* and Brandon climbed in, still distant, still utterly silent. Araminta closed the door and held her breath as she went around the front of the Volkswagon to the driver side, certain that Brandon would bolt. She was no longer holding his hand.

She climbed in and started the car. Brandon stayed put, staring out the windshield.

Araminta put the car in drive, and down to Grand River Boulevard she drove, and then onto the interstate.

Brandon turned his head and looked at her. "Where are we going, Momma?" he asked.

~ ~ ~

At the National Military Command Center in the Pentagon, known colloquially as the "War Room," a lively debate ensued among military commanders and analysts. And, as evening approached, it became increasingly obvious that a full deployment of the 10th Mountain Division would be needed to quell the violence in Detroit and perhaps beyond.

Major General Lance McIntyre and staff had flown in from New York in the morning and briefed the men in the room on the preparations and readiness of the 10th Mountain Division. He presented a detailed battle plan, including timelines and logistical needs.

After a series of technical questions about the logistics of deploying U.S. troops to Detroit, discussion turned to the political ramifications. Stephen Wright, the undersecretary of homeland security for intelligence and analysis, spoke up.

Gentlemen," he said, "the images of bodies of National Guard troops lying in the streets, retreating National Guard vehicles, the Olympia Armory burned to the ground, American refugees fleeing to Canada, etc., have been pretty shocking and, to civilians, potentially destructive. The government's legitimacy is severely undermined when its army is seen as ineffectual. Think Iraq after the U.S. withdrawal."

General Hank Scranton, U.S. director of intelligence, bristled. "Let's not over-estimate the situation," he scoffed. "America isn't Iraq."

"Hey," said Wright, throwing up his hands in mock defense. "Don't shoot the messenger. I'm just saying that we need to be prepared for any contingency, as remote as some may seem."

"Violence has spread to Flint and Ann Arbor," added Brigadier General Aaron Palmer, U.S. Marine Corps, "and now to Plymouth. There are also protests in Washington, New York, Chicago, and even Rust Belt cities like Cleveland. I agree with Secretary Wright. We must go in full-force; no monkeying around. Set an example. Shock and awe."

"Exactly," said Wright. "I heard something about militia groups gearing up as well. What we need to do, if I may be so blunt, is reestablish a monopoly of violence. And we need to restore confidence in our military."

"I am going to need the full might of the U.S. armed forces at my disposal," said Lt. Gen. McIntyre. He folded his arms across his chest and waited for questions.

"What do you need?" asked Admiral Erik Sorenson, chairman of the Joint Chiefs of Staff.

"The full package," replied McIntyre. "A tank company and close-in air support, for starters."

~ ~ ~

Araminta drove west on Grand Boulevard. Brandon's question, *Where we going, Momma?* still hung in the air, unanswered. Brandon went back to looking out the window.

Araminta kept looking to the eastern horizon, waiting for those familiar steel towers of the Ambassador Bridge, the bridge to Canada, to emerge.

Araminta grew up just west of downtown, across the street from Stanton Park. Looking north from her house stood the abandoned and hauntingly beautiful Michigan Central Station. In the opposite direction loomed the two steel towers of the bridge to Canada, as she'd always known it. Many times as a little girl, she would gaze at those towers and wonder. *Canada,* she would think. What was it like over there? It seemed to hold some kind of promise.

All her life those steel towers loomed in the distance, and she would catch herself staring off at them as if in a trance, just like when she was a little girl, and think, *the bridge to Canada.*

Alas, a bridge too far.

The car was hit with several glass bottles along the way, but mostly they drove unmolested. Araminta was fearful when they came upon crowds in the road, but they would part as she slowly approached and weaved through the crowds and avoided burning piles of debris. Some peered at her with deranged, angry eyes, but they only stared and didn't attack.

Maybe because we're black.

A sudden splintering of her windshield into large spider-web cracks dispelled that notion.

Araminta and Brandon made it through the two-and-a-half miles to Interstate 96, where she entered the southbound lane. Traffic was light but, after just over a mile, the traffic came to a standstill. It was a parking lot; there was no movement at all. After waiting for just about two minutes, two minutes that felt like at least ten, Araminta opened her car door. "Let's go," she said, and climbed out.

Brandon got out, too, a quizzical look on his still, too-stoic face. Araminta grabbed his hand and began walking, steeling herself against the cold, straight down the middle of the freeway between lanes of idle cars. It was a brisk twenty-five minute walk when it became clear to Brandon that the large steel bridge towering not too far in the distance was the destination.

The bridge to Canada.

~ ~ ~

At 6:00 p.m., Cynthia Belle, multibillionaire founder of the Los Angeles-based global property developer and venture capital conglomerate Business Geography International (BGI), and currently President of the United States, addressed the country on television.

"Good evening," she said, solemnly. "Earlier tonight I spoke with Michigan Governor Clifford Krueger and Detroit Mayor André Murray. They told me that the already frightful situation in Detroit and elsewhere in Michigan has deteriorated further. Particularly in Detroit, incidents of random terror and lawlessness continue unabated: More than 20,000 fires, untold damage to private property, attacks on interstate highways, hundreds of injuries, and the senseless deaths of more than fifty people, including two National Guardsmen.

"Following the first day of unrest this past Tuesday, I spoke with Michigan Governor Clifford Krueger and Detroit Mayor André Murray. They reported then that there are two thousand police on duty in the city of Detroit, and up to two thousand more law enforcement officers from across the state who are ready to augment Detroit's police forces. One thousand National Guard troops also stand ready.

"These forces were mobilized within the past twenty-four hours but, given the dispersed nature of unrest, their deployment has met with great difficulties.

"To supplement state and local efforts, as President I have taken several additional actions. First, this morning I ordered the Departments of Justice and Homeland Security to dispatch 1,000 federal law enforcement officials to help restore order in Detroit, beginning tonight. These officials include FBI SWAT teams, special riot control units of the U.S. Marshals Service, the Border Patrol, and other federal law enforcement agencies. Second, another 1,000 federal law enforcement officials are on standby alert. Third, earlier today I directed 5,000 members of the 10th Mountain Division to stand by at Fort Drum in upstate New York.

"Tonight, at the request of the governor and the mayor, I have ordered the 10th Mountain Division to immediately deploy to Detroit and other cities in Michigan, and to use whatever force is deemed necessary to preserve life and liberty. I am also federalizing the Michigan National Guard, and have instructed Major General Lance McIntyre, commander of the 10th Mountain Division, to assume authority of these forces under his command ..."

As the President spoke, the first C-17 Globemaster III transport aircraft, carrying soldiers and equipment of the 10th Mountain Division, took off from Fort Drum in Upstate New York. The President had personally secured passage earlier in the day for military flights across Canadian airspace, since the shortest flight route from Fort Drum to the Detroit area takes aircraft over southern Ontario. This plan would ensure that the first, and subsequent, C-17 aircraft arrived at the Selfridge Air National Guard base, twenty miles north of Detroit, about one hour after take-off.

At Selfridge, the just-federalized Michigan Air National Guard scrambled to accommodate the hordes of media personnel, trucks, and communications equipment that descended upon the base. Even though it was already nighttime, once it became known that Selfridge would be the primary staging area for arriving troops, reporters and camera people rushed to the base to record the arrival of the first aircraft and troops.

Some pundits expressed amazement at the rapid transformation of the Selfridge Air Base from sleepy air strip to bustling forward base within just a few hours. The efficiency of it all—particularly after the inability of the National Guard to deploy—was both gratifying and humbling to outside observers. It was quite a contrast with what was happening elsewhere in the state.

Chapter 19

The following morning, Selfridge Air Base was buzzing with activity. Aircraft continued to arrive every few minutes, bringing more soldiers and equipment. News broadcasts showed an impressive array of aircraft and helicopters parked on the over-crowded flight line, which included four C-5M Galaxy cargo aircraft, the largest aircraft in service in the United States, several C-17 Globemasters and C-130 Hercules cargo planes, four business class C-21A transport aircraft, more than two dozen Black Hawk and Apache attack helicopters, and four Kiowa Warrior observation helicopters. A stealthy U.S. Air Force Avenger drone was also parked on the tarmac.

Each of the Galaxies had ferried two M1A2 Abrams tanks of the 1st Armored Division based out of Fort Bliss, Texas, along with support personnel. The tanks, and several Army bulldozers, cranes, and other heavy equipment, occupied their own row on the flight line.

~ ~ ~

Mohammed "Moe" Ibn Adil was an imposing figure. He stood six foot three inches tall and weighed around 225 pounds. He was dark-skinned and gruff-looking, but professional in appearance. His experiences growing up as the elder son of Nigerian immigrants, combined with his twenty-five years in the U.S. Army, had bequeathed him intelligent but world-weary eyes. He was stylishly dressed in a charcoal overcoat, tie, dark plaid winter English cap, black leather gloves, and blue jeans, as he entered his office at the U.S. Army Criminal Investigation Command, or CID (the "D" a holdout from the original Criminal Investigation *Division*, established after World War I), in the Russell-Knox Building on Quantico Marine Corps Air Base in Quantico, Virginia.

He was just taking off his coat when the commanding general of CID, Major General Theodore Rose, stepped in.

"Don't get comfortable," the general said. "Multiple National Guard armories, including the Olympia Armory in Detroit, were raided last night in Michigan, possibly by militia groups. Get your team ready. You're going to Motown."

~ ~ ~

At 10:00 a.m., four low-flying Marine Corps F-35B Lightning II joint strike fighters roared over metropolitan Detroit in tight formation. The fifth generation stealth fighter planes were sleek and breathtakingly graceful as they sliced through the air. The four jets first made their appearance by flying low and extremely fast, so fast, in fact, that they startled anyone who happened to catch a glimpse of them as they flew by—*silently*—causing many people to duck instinctively. Then came the sound—a heart-thumping, ground-rumbling *BOOM*—causing nearly everyone, including those who had seen them, to jump in alarm. Minutes later, the jets returned, flying much slower but still in tight formation, flying in a full circle over the sprawling city as their engines roared, rattling windows in their frames. After the jets completed two full circles over the city, their engines lit up momentarily as they gained altitude and disappeared over the northern horizon.

As short-lived as the flyover was, it accomplished its primary mission: rioters, spectators, residents, pedestrians, and even automobile traffic throughout Metropolitan Detroit paused momentarily as people gawked at the awesome fighter planes above. More importantly, the jets announced that the U.S. military was close at hand, and that the firepower and resources under their command was far more imposing than anything displayed by the Detroit police or Michigan National Guard.

PART TWO:

BATTLE OF DETROIT

Chapter 20

Not announced as part of the emergency build-up of the 10th Mountain Division at Selfridge was the deployment of a platoon of the U.S. Navy's SEAL Team 2, based out of Norfolk, Virginia. In support of SEAL Team 2, several Blackhawk helicopters on the flight line were part of a detachment of the U.S. Army's 160th Special Operations Aviation Regiment (Airborne), known as the Night Stalkers, based out of Fort Campbell, Kentucky. The Night Stalkers typically transported and supplied Army and other special forces in support of their missions. They were instrumental in the U.S. Navy SEAL raid in Pakistan that killed Osama Bin Laden in 2011.

Though the SEALs and the Night Stalkers didn't expect to encounter the kind of resistance that an enemy state could muster, the deployment to Detroit at least offered real-life training against urban-based non-state actors.

In addition, and perhaps more to the point, McIntyre felt the country could use a feel-good story—one in which the power and strength of the U.S. armed forces overcame the disaster unfolding in Detroit. And so, embedded with the Night Stalkers and SEALs, were a couple of U.S. Army Public Affairs Broadcast Specialists.

In the pre-dawn hours, the Night Stalkers lifted off from Selfridge Air Base in four MH-60 Blackhawk helicopters. They ferried two squads of SEAL commandos and a broadcast specialist to the Ambassador Bridge, and transported two squads and a broadcast specialist to the Coleman A. Young International Airport.

At the Ambassador Bridge, the two Blackhawks hovered as SEAL commandos fast-rappelled onto the suspended roadway. The SEALs swept across the bridge in both directions, startling refugees hunkered down in vehicles. There was no resistance, and nearly everyone welcomed the commandos. Food and water would be delivered later in the morning, the commandos promised.

The Coleman A. Young International Airport was located nine miles to the northeast of downtown, right off of Gratiot Avenue. Once the major international airport serving Metropolitan Detroit (before the Detroit Metropolitan Wayne County Airport was expanded and modernized in 1947), it was now primarily a cargo airport.

SEAL commandos fast-rappelled onto the tarmac, and stormed the airport's small terminal and main hangar where, in each case, they encountered not a single soul. After the airport was secured, multiple helicopters and other aircraft were cleared to relocate from the overcrowded Selfridge Air Base.

During the overnight hours, meanwhile, Humvees and army trucks, including flatbeds with D9 armored bulldozers on top, and several large M88 recovery vehicles, formed three long single-file convoy lines at the Selfridge Air Base. Five M1A2 Abrams tanks, painted in desert tan, formed the middle of the lengthening convoys. Starting around 5:00 a.m., throngs of young soldiers in full combat gear mustered near the convoys. By 5:45, all of the Humvees, trucks, and tanks had their engines revved and ready to roll, and soldiers climbed aboard.

At precisely 6:00 a.m., a little more than an hour before the sun broke over the horizon, the lead Humvee carrying General McIntyre, sporting two large U.S. flags perched atop each of its side-view mirrors, crept forward and then sped up. The line of Humvees, trucks, and tanks behind it followed close behind.

Two souped-up blue Dodge Chargers with Michigan State Trooper markings sped ahead of the general's Humvee with their lights flashing and sirens blaring.

In the sky above, a Kiowa Warrior-class observation helicopter with its distinctive, ball-like camera system perched above its rotors, monitored the convoy's path for any threats. The ball—known as a mass-mounted sight, or MMS—contained an array of sensors, including a high-definition television camera with long-distance zooming capability, a thermal imaging sensor, a laser system for target acquisitioning, and navigational tools.

The convoy moved rather slowly—about forty-five miles per hour—and slowed down even further whenever the Kiowa helicopter spotted something it deemed threatening. News helicopters flew at a minimum distance of ten miles from the convoy.

Nearly forty-five minutes after departing Selfridge, the convoy passed under the Alter Road overpass and entered Detroit proper. Despite the early hour and freezing temperatures, a considerable crowd stood atop the Alter Road bridge. They had tied a large U.S. flag to the pedestrian fence, and they cheered loudly as the convoy passed beneath them. To the delight of the crowd, General McIntyre's

Humvee honked its horn as it went by.

Entering the heart of police-fortified downtown Detroit, the convoy slowed to a crawl. It turned right onto Broadway Street, and left onto East Grand River Avenue. From there, it entered the sea of parking lots across East Grand River Avenue from GLEE Tower, which was now designated "New Fort Detroit." The site was just five blocks north of the original Fort Pontchartrain du Détroit, the isolated French outpost built in 1701 as a defense against British incursions into the North American interior.

The second and third convoys, each composed primarily of AM General M35 troop transport trucks, fifty in total, with each truck carrying twenty-five soldiers, closely followed the first one. However, rather than turning into the parking lots of New Fort Detroit, one convoy continued northwestward on Grand River Avenue in full force. Accompanying it were the five M1A2 Abrams tanks, a flatbed truck transporting a D9 armored bulldozer, and an M88 recovery vehicle.

The third convoy snaked left on Washington Boulevard, and then right onto Michigan Avenue.

The Grand River Avenue convoy, which included the five Abrams tanks, separated into thirds. The tanks took the lead as the first section traveled straight up Grand River, smashing through or flattening the burned-out hulks of cars, pyres of burning tires, and other debris. The tanks took up positions on all sides of the Olympia Armory, training their turrets on its still-smoldering ruins. Two tanks sat on the McGraw Street Bridge over Interstate 96 and covered the western flank of the armory.

With the tanks in position to cover all sides of the armory, the other two sections of the convoy disembarked more than 100 soldiers north and south of the armory, who took up defensive positions. Several cameramen and war correspondents were embedded with the assault teams to capture the troops as they secured the armory.

At least that was the plan.

Armor Crewman Specialist Christian Beck, a twenty-year old tank gunner from San Diego, felt a deep rumble through the periscope his face was pressed against. The world outside the tank trembled. Just as he pulled away from the periscope, however, the world turned upside down and he had the sudden sensation of falling. Then everything went black.

~ ~ ~

Twenty-year-old Private First Class Adrian Gonzales jumped out of a transport truck and got his first glimpse of Detroit. He let out an audible gasp. The truck was covered with a canvas, so Adrian and the other soldiers couldn't see anything during the one-hour trip from Selfridge. Adrian kept up with the news before being deployed, but nothing could have prepared him for what he saw.

It wasn't just the smoldering remains of the Olympia Armory and the acrid smoke it produced. It was the lack of people and buildings. The city was desolate. To his right, straight down Grand River Avenue, the tall buildings of downtown Detroit loomed four miles in the distance. The five towers of the Renaissance Center with its Marriott Hotel at the center, still the tallest building in Michigan, was instantly recognizable.

Apart from downtown in the near distance, Adrian could see only a handful of small buildings scattered here and there, all of which appeared to be long abandoned. Some were blackened by fire, but Adrian couldn't tell if the damage was recent or not. Overgrown lots crisscrossed filled the spaces between the derelict structures. Interstate 96 ran parallel to Grand River, and it was eerily devoid of traffic in one direction, but full of abandoned cars in the other. Most sat with their doors open and windows smashed. Some were burnt husks. It was a scene straight out of a post-apocalyptic movie.

Adrian grew up in suburban Phoenix, whose worst neighborhoods—at least from what he could tell—looked downright posh compared to this one. *This ... this isn't even America. How can this be the USA?*

Adrian and his squad had been dropped off next to an abandoned strip mall that sat across the street from the smoldering armory. They had gathered behind the mall as two tanks took positions on the bridge over the interstate, their turrets trained on the smoking ruins of the armory.

"Move out!" his squad gunny barked.

Adrian felt a deep rumble, followed by an earth-shaking *CRASH*. A massive cloud of roiling dust, mixed with black smoke, blanketed the highway.

Soldiers dropped to the ground and trained their rifles on the dust cloud where the tanks should have been.

"What the fuck was *that?*" someone loudly exclaimed.

The dust cloud slowly spread out and faded. Adrian saw that the tanks were not there anymore. Nor was the bridge they were parked on. *Did the bridge collapse?* "I think the bridge collapsed!" he shouted.

The McGraw Street Bridge was an unremarkable urban bridge that crossed Interstate 96, linking the east side of the Northwest Goldberg neighborhood with the west. It was also unremarkable in being one of 200,000 bridges across the United States deemed to be structurally deficient by the American Society of Civil Engineers. So, when the two M1A2 Abrams tanks, with a combined weight of 288,000 pounds, took up positions on the bridge, the structure disintegrated beneath them in the blink of an eye.

~ ~ ~

Aaron Jones awoke to the deep *thump-thump-thump* of helicopters flying low. It was not the more normal sound of low-flying police helicopters. These were military helicopters flying overhead, one after another.

The sun shone brightly through the bedroom window curtains.

Aaron rolled out of bed and sat for a moment. His mind was empty.

Another *thump-thump-thump* and the house really rattled this time. But Aaron remained frozen in a Zen-like position.

With a grunt, he got up to see what was happening.

"Something's going on outside, Ma," he said, walking into the living room. A small television set was on, but his mother wasn't there. He went to the kitchen, tore open a pop tart and munched on it. He looked outside and saw crowds of people standing around, peering at the sky. His mother was among them.

Aaron grabbed his coat and walked out the back door through the kitchen, texting Michelle, Xavier, and Devin.

Another *thump-thump-thump* passed over the house. Aaron

looked up at a low-flying, double-bladed Chinook helicopter.

Cool. It looked like the helicopter was landing just a few streets away, and he chased after it.

It was actually about a mile away when the Chinook finally landed, but before it did, another one lifted off. It, too, looked like it had taken off from a few streets away, but the distance didn't seem to lessen as Aaron chased after the first Chinook. Two Black Hawk helicopters, meanwhile, circled in the distance.

Unexpectedly, a third Black Hawk appeared as it lifted off the ground near the spot where the Chinook had landed.

"Yo, Aaron!" It was Devin, jogging to catch up. Aaron waited momentarily, and then the two tentatively approached the crumbling Kronk Gym.

It was their first time back to the corner since Nathan and Dwayne were shot. Aaron and Devin kept an eye out for River Gees, but they didn't see any. Xavier and Michelle waited for them the next block over, amid a crowd on Warren Avenue.

"Check it," said Xavier, nodding to the broad street. "Army's here."

Michelle snuggled up to Aaron when he and Devin stepped on the curb. Army trucks, one after another, drove past them. They stopped about four blocks to the west near a Coca-Cola Bottling center and an auto parts factory. Dozens of heavily armed soldiers disembarked.

Aaron maintained eye contact with Xavier, who nodded toward the other side of the street.

There, among the weeds alongside the little building, were two sets of bare feet sticking out from beneath cardboard boxes and other trash.

Tears welled in Aaron's eyes. Surely it was Nathan and Dwayne. It had been five full days since they were killed. Rumor had it that the River Gees let them lay where they fell for days on end.

More Army trucks barreled toward them. The air brakes on the trucks hissed, and they came to a stop in front of the growing crowd. Dozens more soldiers began disembarking, and Aaron saw more Army trucks coming down the road.

The soldiers massed in front of the lone business still in operation here, a Citgo gas station. The five other buildings clumped along the intersection were the burned-out hulks of abandoned stores and garages.

"Go home!" a soldier barked over a bullhorn. "Disperse or you will be arrested."

"We *are* home, muthafuckas," muttered a middle-aged man.

"Stay off the streets!" another soldier with a bullhorn ordered. "You will not be warned again!"

"Come on," Xavier said, pulling Aaron. He and his friends made their way to the more residential McGraw Street, as did some other onlookers.

But McGraw, too, was crowded with soldiers and their trucks.

Another crowd stood in the middle of McGraw Street as Aaron and his friends approached. They couldn't quite see what the Army was doing, but they were doing something big.

"What's going on?" asked Devin.

"Bridge collapsed," said an older man. "Took down a couple of tanks," he added. "It's a big-time rescue operation."

The older gentleman looked the kids over. "You boys best be careful. The Army isn't going to mess around after something like this. They'll be looking to round up young folks for just about nothing. Something to show they're *doing* something."

"Uh huh," mumbled Aaron. His mind was on the bodies a few blocks behind him.

Chapter 21

The sound of helicopters jolted Lamar Griffin out of bed. He didn't want to, but something was happening outside again, causing his heart to jump in his chest. A pang of fear shot through him. Not a fear for his own well-being. This was a daunting fear of what the day would bring, because the last two days were the worst two days of his life.

He kept replaying it in his head. He couldn't stop. First, his little cousin dead. He and his friends, just lying there with all of those people standing around. And the sound of his auntie and his own mother crying—no, *wailing*—it was like a knife in his back that he couldn't dislodge.

That Army Humvee in the middle of the road, burning.

No one knew what to do. Everyone just flailed about, screaming. Then Marlon Greer, with his own mother right there, pulled out his gun and started shooting at Army guys running down the street. People scattered. Others got their guns out, too. It was bedlam.

And then it was just Lamar and a few others left to stand over the bodies of Dominic, Shawn, and Chad. Women hovered over Auntie Sheila, Dominic's mother, as she lay in the middle of the street, sobbing. Lamar saw his own mother—it was like she was somebody else, unrelated—trying to console Auntie Sheila, her sister.

Shouldn't we help Dominic? Lamar wondered. But looking at

him—and Shawn and Chad, too—clearly, they were dead. It was just...definitive. A cold fact. You knew.

Lamar squatted beside the body of his cousin, facing away from it. He couldn't look at him anymore.

"We have to take him home," said a quiet voice. Lamar looked up. It was Felix, from the neighborhood. Worked at a warehouse or something. Lamar never spoke to him before.

"Can you help me get him home?" Felix asked. Lamar wiped his eyes and nodded.

When they gathered him up—Lamar taking Dominic's feet, Felix struggling to carry him by the armpits—the finality of the boy's death hit Lamar like a ton of bricks. He reeled in a daze as they carried his cousin's body, shuffling their feet as they went, for a full three blocks to his Auntie Sheila's house.

There was nothing dignified about how they struggled to carry him, and Lamar quietly seethed.

The neighborhood seemed to follow Lamar and Felix. They walked alongside, talking in hushed tones, sharing the news with others who were coming out to see what the commotion was. That led to more screams, more wailing. There was Christina, and her friends— schoolmates of Dominic and his friends—now screaming and crying.

When they arrived at Auntie Sheila's house, others met them there, laying out sheets and blankets for the body. They wrapped up Dominic's body and laid him on the couch in the living room.

Auntie Sheila, helped by a group of women and men, followed them in, wailing nonstop. "Oh, *gawd,* my *baby!*" she cried over and over.

Lamar found a quiet corner and stayed as a procession of family, friends, and neighbors crowded the small house throughout the day. Someone squeezed his shoulder, and Lamar stood up. It was his mother, and she hugged him tightly. He had to gently push her away after a moment because she didn't want to let go. Angelica, his girlfriend, was next, and now *he* didn't want to let go.

Men talked in hushed tones in the small dining room, away from Auntie Sheila. "He can't stay here," said an older man with a whitish goatee. "Not overnight," he said.

"No one is going to come for him," said another. "Not with all that's going on."

"Hendrick's Funeral Home ain't answering the phone," said yet another. "Ain't no one working in the middle of a damn riot."

The men and family organized a sort of funeral procession for later that evening. A friend of the family drove a pickup truck, and they loaded Dominic's body in its bed. Lamar, Felix, and five others acted as pallbearers and rode in the back of the truck with Dominic's body. A couple of the others were part of some remnant of the BMF, Dominic surmised, and they sported what looked like military-grade automatic rifles slung across their shoulders.

They trekked slowly for the one mile straight down Grand Boulevard to Henry Ford Hospital, the whole neighborhood walking alongside the pickup truck that crawled at pedestrian speed. Another car followed from a distance, and a third even further, bearing the bodies of Chad and Shawn.

The following day was full of rage. Lamar was consumed by

it. It was nonstop, all day long. Lamar, friends, and neighbors poured up Grand Boulevard into New Center. The big, official-looking buildings and businesses up and down the boulevard in New Center were always so close, but so far away. He sometimes wondered what was in those buildings, what it was like to work in them. One multi-story office building of bland 1960s architecture with "Work Force" in big bold letters followed by "Solutions" in a smaller font, the words spelled out in red, single-letter signage along the top of the building, stood authoritatively at the intersection of Grand Boulevard and Woodward Avenue. Work Force Solutions, a temporary employment agency, was just the latest company to occupy the building.

It was the first large, uninviting building the crowds had come across. They smashed their way into the lobby and found the building empty. All day long people went in and went out, looting what they could, some just taking out their anger on another cold and indifferent corporation. WFS wasn't GLEE, and it wasn't the Army that shot Dominic, but it was surely cut from the same cloth.

As the day gave way to night, several fires big and small burned in the various floors of the eight-story WFS Building. Three blocks over stood the historic thirty-story art deco Fisher Building skyscraper on Grand Boulevard and, across the street from that, the historic four towers with fifteen stories each, comprising Cadillac Place. Once the headquarters for Cadillac, Cadillac Place now housed state agencies. The Fisher Building housed a restaurant and bar on the ground floor, a law firm on the second floor, and Detroit Public Schools occupied all of the floors above the second.

These buildings were warmer than the WFS building. They were embraced by a patina that told of Detroit's history as a onetime center of manufacturing, commerce and culture, which somehow took the edge off the raging crowds, leaving both complexes largely untouched, at least in terms of looting floor by floor. In the central tower of Cadillac Place, however, someone had set fire to the trash cans in the lobby bathrooms, which had set off the building's fire alarm and sprinkler system, destroying and damaging hundreds of computers and furniture throughout the building.

The large buildings in the heart of New Center were not the only ones to bear the brunt of the neighborhood's ire. Even dentists' and doctors' offices were sacked and looted—anything that reeked of authority or economic gouging.

And now Lamar was spent. After a long day of running with his friends and even family members—other cousins, uncles, and aunts—all through New Center and along Grand Boulevard, throwing rocks, lighting up Molotov cocktails, and looting whatever was left of already looted pharmacies and stores, he made his way back to his own street and sat on a curb with Angelica and listened to gunfire near and far, and helicopters crisscrossing the night sky.

They laughed when he emptied his pockets of random, pointless loot from a nearby pharmacy: a Snickers bar, a small bottle of antacids, and a small bottle of some kind of laxative. Lamar tossed the bottles aside but tore open the candy bar and shared it with Angelica.

When he returned home, the events of the day before came rushing, crushing, back. *Dominic...*

Eventually, impossibly, sleep enveloped him.

And now something was happening. Something more. And it was not even 9:00 a.m.

Lamar threw on a T-shirt and jeans and looked out his bedroom window. He could hear some distant shouting and commotion but couldn't see anything. Only when he stepped out into the frigid morning air did he see others looking tentatively around and walking toward the boulevard.

As Lamar approached Grand Boulevard, his routine for the week now, he saw crowds had already gathered at intersections all along Grand Boulevard. Army trucks streamed along the boulevard, stopping and disembarking soldiers dozens at a time. And the trucks kept coming.

~ ~ ~

Gino Napolitano was the first to hop out of his troop transport truck. A sergeant and squad leader, Gino quickly barked orders and organized his young men and women. He passed each member of his squad a small card outlining the rules of engagement, and went through various scenarios.

Other squad leaders did the same as more trucks and squads arrived.

Squared away and ready for patrol, Gino only now smelled the acrid smell of smoke in the air. Then his eyes took in the buildings scarred black. Points of orange light danced in random windows high up on various floors of the surrounding buildings.

At only twenty-four, he was the veteran of the group. He had been deployed to Iraq, a country endlessly under siege by various armed groups, a situation that began with the United States' invasion in 2003, but he didn't know anything about that because it had happened long before he was born. Nothing could have prepared him for what he would see in Iraq. The bombed-out cities, the stoic faces of Iraqi citizens, including children. The constant awareness for potential attack. Maybe a sniper. Sometimes a mortar barrage. Every car, truck, even camel, was a potential bomb.

That same palpable sense of danger that enveloped him in Iraq came right back to the fore. This was a war zone. *But this is America,* his mind protested.

Despite the early hour, throngs of people gathered along Grand Boulevard and watched the soldiers as they went to work.

Their faces were stoic, brooding. And their eyes...their eyes had that blank stare of the Iraqis.

Trouble, his mind flashed. There was going to be trouble.

A glass beer bottle smashed to the ground off to his right.

Here we go.

~ ~ ~

Jayson Avery was back at Uncle Fave's house. Fave sat watching the television intently. News helicopters filmed from above as the Army sprawled out across the city—from downtown to Eight Mile in the north; from the initial unrest centered on Bernadette Price's house in Jackson/Mack in the east to Redmond Charter in the northwest to Dearborn in the southwest.

The Army was everywhere, and their Black Hawk and Chinook helicopters filled the sky.

But the biggest story was the rescue operation occurring at the McGraw Street Bridge. Fave could hear the commotion from his house, which was only blocks to the south.

What captured Fave's attention—indeed, he was intensely focused on the television—was what was happening two miles to the east of the rescue operation along Grand Boulevard. Protesters in New Center and the surrounding neighborhood were confronting the Army. News helicopters could only film from afar with zoomed-in cameras, but what they showed was a real melee. Rocks and bottles rained down on gathering soldiers wielding shields.

Fave leaned back and stroked his chin. New Center was Grand River Gees territory.

Chapter 22

It was a busy night for the Army. Despite the deployment, protesters still gathered at the major flash points during the overnight hours. But the Army methodically descended on the crowds with shields and rifles—and, in New Center, tear gas. They arrested anyone they could get their hands on. It was after dark and, if you were outside, you were breaking curfew.

The Army arrested more than 1,000 people overnight, but the soldiers' presence had kept the city mostly peaceful.

In the morning, Governor Krueger and Mayor Murray encouraged businesses to reopen and for people to begin the clean-up following the worst urban riots since Los Angeles. The dusk-to-dawn curfew would remain in effect, however, and so businesses had to close early enough for their workers and customers to return home before nightfall.

Army soldiers continued to patrol the streets of Detroit, particularly along the city's major roadways and boulevards. Kiowa Warrior observation helicopters kept tabs on the city and, wherever protestors tried to gather, they quickly found themselves outnumbered by armed soldiers. They would be very quickly set upon, subdued, zip-tied, and placed into the back of M35 troop transport trucks. The arrested would face charges of unlawful assembly.

~ ~ ~

The Ayalas—Arturo, Jacqueline, and Frederick—spent four whole nights at the Children's Hospital of Michigan. It sounded like World War III outside the hospital campus, and the massive explosion at the Olympia Armory on their very first night ensured that they were going nowhere until they found Martín.

The hospital staff, though very busy with walk-in injuries and gunshot victims, were very accommodating. They checked each day with other hospitals in the region, but there were no records of a Martín Ayala being admitted.

After their third night, with the Army being deployed across the city, the family walked back down Brush Street, but once again found the downtown closed off. The Army was everywhere—convoy after convoy passed them by, and soldiers patrolled the streets. They were stopped and questioned by young soldiers (Jackie was shocked at how young they were) nearly ten times on their trek down Brush Street and, when they reached the bridge over I-94 into downtown, it was manned by a police checkpoint.

The police remained on edge despite the presence of the Army, but at least they appeared more approachable this time. They wore helmets and sported riot shields, but they weren't wearing gas masks. So the Ayala family approached a group of police loitering on the bridge. "Go back," yelled an officer as they approached, while the others kept an eye on them.

"Our son is missing!" shouted Arturo.

"Please!" pleaded Jackie, "it's been four days!"

"Go back!" the same officer shouted, as an older officer, approached them. He listened as Arturo and Jackie told their story and was sympathetic. Since the boy had not turned up at any of the hospitals, he advised them to return to the city the next day and head for DPSH, the police headquarters. The city should be reopened then, at least partially so, and it was possible that their son was among the more than 5,000 people in police custody. If he was, he should be in the database.

And so they spent yet another night at the Children's Hospital, then returned to downtown at first light.

The sympathetic officer was right. A single police car remained parked to the side on the Brush Street Bridge into downtown, but the family wasn't stopped as they walked across, nor were they interrogated by patrolling soldiers on their way in.

They made it to DPSH and found a mad house. Police came and went, and they were ushered from one big office to another. And it was loud. People were talking everywhere, all at the same time.

They had given their story and Martín's name and age to several different police officers, anyone who would listen for a few minutes, but they were forced to wait.

It was almost four hours of waiting before a policewoman found them in the lobby of the main entrance. The boy was in their database and was being held at the Cobo Center. He was slated for release within the hour.

"Oh, my God," sobbed Jacqueline. "Thank you so much," she said to the policewoman.

"Good luck," said the officer as the family headed for the door.

The family left one mad house and found another at the Cobo Center. When they left DPSH, they counted themselves lucky to have arrived so early. A line of people outside DPSH snaked for more than two blocks. When they arrived at the Cobo Center, several thousand people stood around the main entrance.

As the Ayalas worked their way through the crowd, people were crying and hugging all around them as loved ones re-connected. "There he is!" exclaimed Frederick, pointing.

"*Martín!*" Jackie squealed, nearly tackling him where he stood. "My baby!"

Martín absorbed the hugs and kisses, his face alight with joy. Tears streamed down his face. Frederick lightly punched him in the arm before hugging him as well. Both pulled away after a moment, wiping their faces.

"These are my friends," Martín said, turning to the group of young people standing beside them. "This is Ian and Tina," he said, introducing a slight Asian kid and a white girl with curly brown hair.

"He did really good," said Tina, and ruffled Martín's hair.

~ ~ ~

For Matt and Maria, and for their hosts Maxwell and Linda Levine, the war across the border in Detroit was relentless. It was a long four days since Maria and Matt has been taken in. The constant din of small arms fire day and night, and of helicopters flying overhead, made it seem much longer.

Maria felt safe with Maxwell and Linda, and she couldn't be more grateful for their refuge. Her children were safe. That was what mattered most. In fact, it was the *only* thing that mattered.

Maria was able to contact her parents in the Mexicantown neighborhood of Detroit, and she checked in several times a day. Her parents were trapped in their home. There were no police or other services. It was a free for all until the Army arrived the day before. Thankfully, they hadn't experienced any trouble.

Most frustrating, strange even, was that her parents were just a mile away as the crow flies. Maria and her parents were on either side of the Detroit River, but they might as well have been a million miles apart.

While the U.S. Army was just getting a grip on Detroit, Canada's Essex and Kent Scottish had Windsor under wraps for three days going. Matt was able to phone his company and, luckily, they didn't think he was completely mental when he told them that their truck was still sitting on the Ambassador Bridge. He had learned through television news that, after they had arrived, the Essex and Kent Scottish had gone right to work to clear the Canadian side of the bridge of abandoned vehicles, and that the U.S. Army was in process of clearing the American side.

Matt wasn't sure which side of the border the truck was parked on, but he figured it was past the half-way point. After a few phone calls, he found his truck. The Canadians had it. It was impounded in the Police Services lot on the east side of town. The truck was in good shape, and he still had a delivery to make. It was time to move on.

After a teary goodbye between Matt and Maria, Maxwell drove Matt to the impound and, after paying the fees and filling out the paperwork, Matthew was on his way to deliver his goods to a warehouse in Hamilton, Ontario.

~ ~ ~

The unrest in Detroit came to an end with the deployment of the 10th Mountain Division. Much of the violence beyond Detroit also subsided. But unrest continued in Flint, and General McIntyre ordered a battalion of 500 soldiers into the city, augmented by an additional 1,000 National Guardsmen.

The four Marine F-35 joint strike fighters temporarily on duty at Selfridge did another flyover, this time over Flint, as did several Army Apache gunship helicopters. The small National Guard Armory in Flint was located alongside Interstate 75, away from the downtown and any commercial district, so it didn't suffer the same fate as the Olympia Armory in Detroit. The Flint Armory and Dayton Park, an open field that abutted the small armory, became the staging area for the National Guard troops. The 10th Mountain Division soldiers shuttled between Flint and Selfridge Air Base.

The appearance of the combined force of 1,500 soldiers quickly put an end to the unrest in Flint as well.

Chapter 23

Moe stood in the smoking ruins of the Olympia Armory near the front of the building, even as the Army continued its clean-up following the McGraw Street Bridge collapse. Chinook helicopters continued to land and lift off on the freeway astride the wreckage of the bridge.

An Army Explosive Ordnance Disposal (EOD) team combed through the crater where the rear of the building had stood, looking for and marking unexploded HIMARS rockets and other ammunition. The EOD technicians were dressed in full bomb suits.

Moe was forbidden to be on site until the EOD guys gave the green light, but the officer in charge acquiesced somewhat, allowing him to explore parts of the premises after he gave a withering glare that said "try and stop me."

He soon understood why a burned-out Caterpillar excavator sat in the midst of the ruins. *That's how they got in.* No doubt, he would soon learn that the Caterpillar had been stolen from a nearby construction site. His team was already tracking that lead.

Also sitting in the smoking rubble were the burned-out hulks of three HIMARS trucks, but the number of parking spaces suggested there should be more. Was it possible that local gangs had driven away with several artillery-launching vehicles? What would local goons want with a platform that launched artillery shells more than 150 miles?

Moe looked around at the surrounding neighborhoods and highways. This was professional, even if opportunistic. You don't just drive off with military-grade weapons systems if you're a local drug gang. No, this was organized crime. *Had to be.*

~ ~ ~

Ian and Tina were met by Trevor, Sarah, and Dakota after leaving the Cobo Center. They were surprised and relieved to find their three cross country friends waiting for them. They were tearfully hugging each other when Martín's family stepped up and embraced their son. Ian and Tina were doubly relieved that Martín had reunited with his family.

Ian and Tina spoke with the Ayalas for a few minutes to exchange contact information and see the family off.

"How's Roland?" asked Ian, turning to his friends as the family left.

Trevor, Sarah, and Dakota looked at each other. "We thought he was with you," said Trevor.

Tina broke down and sobbed. She and Ian told them what had happened.

"Oh, shit," whispered Trevor. "He must be in the hospital, then."

The Wayne State students walked back toward campus, stopping at the Detroit Receiving Hospital complex, part of which encompassed the Children's Hospital of Michigan. There was no record of a Roland Morris.

The following day, the students called other hospitals in the area, and again there was no record. Even the Detroit Police said they had no record. Ian called and asked again, to no avail. A tingle went down his spine. *What could it mean that the Detroit PD said they had no record of Roland when they had obviously taken him?*

Ian and his friends went back to the hospital and asked about bodies. They were desperate to find Roland, and eventually a concerned nurse accompanied them to the morgue, where more than twenty bodies remained unclaimed.

The nurse examined the tags on multiple bodies before coming to one with an age and description matching their friend. When she unzipped the body bag, a shaggy-haired boy stared back at her. He was listed as a John Doe, but fit the description they had given her.

She let only the boys in. "I can't be sure, but...," she said, her face grim. "You have to brace yourself," she said before leading them to the table.

Ian looked in and immediately looked away, his face breaking. He nodded that it was Roland and sniffled. Trevor just stared, his face pale. The nurse closed the bag.

"We have to notify the next of kin," said the nurse. "Do you have contact information for his family?" Ian nodded again and wiped his face.

~ ~ ~

Michigan's governor had ordered that the state of emergency and dusk-to-dawn curfew for Detroit and Flint stay in place for another week following the deployment of the Army. But things appeared to be slowly returning to normal. With widespread unrest now effectively over, the 10th Mountain Division focused on clearing the freeways and major roadways of abandoned and burned vehicles, tires, and other debris.

Businesses, schools, and government offices reopened.

National and global media largely moved on, except for some stories focused on the clean-up and costs of the unrest. Thankfully, the damage in Detroit was estimated at less than $1 billion. Although many businesses were looted, and some burned, most of the estimated 10,000-plus fires were in abandoned and deteriorating homes, factories, and long boarded-up businesses.

Seventy-eight reported fatalities occurred during the unrest, making the "GLEE Uprising" second only to the 1863 New York City Draft Riots in terms of fatalities. Seventy-two of the dead were civilians, two were National Guardsmen, and four were active duty soldiers killed in the McGraw Street bridge collapse. One hundred twenty people had been killed in the Draft Riots of New York. It was not known how many of the seventy-two deceased civilians were rioters. Three were known to have been killed by the National Guard in New Center, and several others by armed motorists and business owners. Some of the civilian fatalities were bystanders or motorists set upon by angry mobs. Other fatalities appeared to be gangland murders, with gang members apparently taking advantage of the breakdown of civil order to target rivals.

Local media focused on police efforts to investigate the seventy-two fatalities and other major crimes, like the raid on the Olympia Armory and other National Guard armories around the state. Various federal law enforcement agencies—the FBI, DEA, ATF, and the U.S. Army's CID—had deployed to Selfridge along with the 10th Mountain Division. Each agency conducted its own investigations and aided the Detroit Police Department as much as possible because, according to crime statistics, nearly ninety percent of murders had gone unsolved in Detroit each year for nearly a decade.

It wasn't long before federal law enforcement made its presence felt. Early in the pre-dawn morning after the initial deployment of the 10th Mountain Division, an all-black Lenco BEAR armored personnel carrier pulled out of Selfridge Air Base along with four black SUVs and three police vans. Selfridge was well beyond the city limits of Detroit, and thus outside the designated geography under a dust-to-dawn curfew. Traffic on the I-94 Edsel Ford Freeway was light at 3:30 a.m., but the appearance of the Lenco BEAR in the midst of police vans and black SUVs traveling at breakneck speed nevertheless garnered attention from motorists.

In the city, some people still ventured out in their neighborhoods despite the overnight curfew. Most stayed close to their homes in case Army trucks or Detroit Police patrols appeared on their street. Even with a few people breaking curfew, there was practically no one out and about at 4:00 a.m. when the speeding convoy entered Detroit. Nevertheless, the convoy did not go unseen by lookouts and night owls.

Within minutes of passing into the city, the Lenco BEAR and convoy housing an FBI SWAT Team had merged onto I-96 and exited on Livernois Avenue.

To those who caught a glimpse of the BEAR and convoy, there was no doubt that they were law enforcement. The all-black Lenco BEAR looked particularly ominous, earning the hashtag #batmobile by observers. Even before the SWAT convoy pulled up in front of a 100-year-old two-story SEARs catalog home on American Street, in what Neighborhood Scout deemed the most violent neighborhood in the country, hashtag #batmobile had become a thing.

The hashtags #batmobile, #SlavePatrol and #GIJoe came to life on Twitter, Whatsapp, SnapChat, Instagram, YikYak, and other social media, producing a moment-by-moment play-by-play update of the BEAR's direction and location.

A few selections of the #batmobile / #SlavePatrol / #GIJoe social media storm, with users and accounts redacted, are listed below:

I, Detroit @I_Detroit 4:05AM wakie wakie yall #SlavePatrol on da go #batmobile

I, Detroit @I_Detroit 4:10AM #SlavePatrol #batmobile gr2liver ('gr2liver' for on Grand River Avenue and turning onto passing Livernois Avenue)

I, Detroit @I_Detroit 4:11AM #SlavePatrol #batmobile stop@american (for the convoy stopping at a location on American Street)

By the time the social media hashtags became a thing, it was too late for nineteen-year-old Cedric Hart, the unlucky winner whose name was randomly pulled from the Detroit Police Department's database of unserved arrest warrants. Young Cedric was wanted for aggravated assault and other charges for a strong-armed robbery weeks before the unrest. He had so far been able, rather easily, to avoid apprehension. The Detroit PD simply didn't have the resources to track down wanted suspects for anything less than murder, and even there they weren't having much success.

And suspects like Cedric Hart didn't have a permanent address. The house on American Street was the address of a girlfriend, information provided by the Detroit PD's Gang Intelligence Unit (GIU). Cedric's name had come up in other investigations by the GIU, who suspected that Cedric might be an enforcer for some crew that had gone independent after the fall of the Black Mafia Family.

The FBI SWAT Team and police gang unit scored. Cedric was found scrambling shirtless out the back door just seconds after the front door was smashed in with a battering ram.

Four more suspects were caught before sunrise. And, with each movement of the BEAR and convoy, the hashtags #SlavePatrol and #batmobile became more established.

A system of observation and intelligence regarding law enforcement and Army convoy movements was organically born.

~ ~ ~

North of Baltimore, Maryland, nestled amid the rolling green hills of Baltimore County's Horse Country, was Coventry Estate. This was the grounds and mansion of the esteemed William Coventry, Esquire, president of the private Standard & King Investment House.

Standard & King dated back nearly 150 years. It kept a low profile and managed the portfolios of multiple billionaire executives, two former U.S. Presidents, several U.S. Congressmen and Congresswomen, and a few presidential appointees and members of the Senior Executive Service—and all by invitation only.

August Coventry, William Coventry's great-great grandfather, was one of the founding partners of Standard & King, which included Frederick Calvert IV, a direct descendant of one of the original barons of Baltimore. The stories that circulated down through the generations were so outrageous that they were not to be believed but, when they were accompanied by a wink—and they were always told with a knowing wink—they left one wondering if maybe, just maybe, there was some nugget of truth tucked away inside the hyperbole.

Among the esteemed class of alumni clients were Rowland Hussey Macy, founder of the now defunct Macy's department store empire; John D. Rockefeller, Jr., founder of the once-dominant Standard Oil Company; Rear Admiral Sidney Souers, the first Director of the Central Intelligence Agency; and none other than President Franklin Delano Roosevelt. Joseph "Don Peppino" Bonanno, an early boss of the Bonanno crime family, one of the Five Families of the New York Mafia, was rumored to have also been a client.

Throughout the decades, Standard & King consistently produced returns that outperformed larger and more recognized Wall Street-based investment firms like Goldman Sachs or Merrill Lynch. It took money to make money, and so S&K limited its client list to a particular threshold of wealth, somewhere in the range of $10 billion. But to stay ahead of the market, this was where particular government and ex-government clients with strong connections to certain levers of policy-making were important. They could help undergird investments by steering government spending into particular places, or by being knowledgeable of regulatory loopholes. Or by being privy to classified information.

On this very day, for example, Paul Rinnier, S&K partner and a former U.S. ambassador to the Netherlands, had lunch with a flag-ranked naval officer at the elegant Army and Navy Club on Farragut Square in Washington, DC. The two had been teammates on the Swimming and Diving team at the U.S. Naval Academy some thirty years prior, before serving as officers with the Navy SEALs, albeit in different Teams. Paul left the Teams when he completed his service time and entered the world of finance. Vice Admiral Baltzer Oberkirsch remained with the Teams and carved out a distinguished career in the Navy. Now he was at the Pentagon, working directly under the Chief of Naval Operations.

The two old friends met once a month at the club for a few rounds of racquetball and then lunch. They'd banter as they played, swapping sea stories and catching up on family happenings. And Paul always brought his tablet with the latest numbers in Oberkirsch's portfolio that he could share over lunch.

After an hour of racquetball, the two friends freshened up and then met in the club's Eagle Grill room for light fare and beer. Oberkirsch was quiet today, clearly distracted.

"Trouble at the office?" asked Paul, taking a swig from his bottle of beer—a Burley Oak IPA, a regional staple from Maryland's Eastern Shore.

"Busy," the admiral said after popping a steamed shrimp into his mouth and taking a swig from his own beer, a 3 Stars IPA. "Lots of chatter right now." "Chatter" referred to intercepted communications among known and suspected terrorists.

"Yeah?" said Paul.

"Something's afoot in the Middle East," Oberkirsch said, his voice lowered. "We're going to have to shift some assets around, maybe put a carrier in the Gulf. A ton of logistical stuff to work out."

"Sounds like business as usual to me," said Paul. "What's got you spooked?"

"They're buzzing about the unrest in Detroit. They think we're distracted. Whatever they've got planned, they want to move it up. Something is imminent."

"Well, I hope they're wrong. I have a meeting in Dubai next week with a prospective client. That could muck things up."

"The State Department will probably issue a travel alert."

"*Great,*" said Paul. In his head, he did a quick mental calculation. A travel alert would cause insurance rates to spike for oil tankers and other corporate assets in the Middle East. That, in turn, would translate into higher oil prices. Never mind an actual incident in the region, or news of a carrier's deployment to the Gulf.

Following lunch with Oberkirsch, Paul would head back to Baltimore and alert the partners. The admiral's tip would allow S&K to discreetly move a few billion dollars into the insurance and oil markets before the prices spiked, and to move money out of markets that might be affected by a rise in transportation costs.

Plying some discretionary funds into the defense industry would also be prudent in times like these.

~ ~ ~

As for the *other* clients of Standard and King—the Bonanno types—they, too, were important to the success of S&K. They were able to persuade—as a last resort—other businesses, and sometimes low-level government officials, to make decisions that weren't detrimental to the investments of S&K and its clients.

Giorgio Santacroce, of Naples, Italy, who divided his time between Italy and Philadelphia, was one such client. He was the patriarch of the Santacroces, who were rumored to be part of *la camorra,* the Naples-based crime syndicate linked, to Blue Planet waste management and recycling, which operated in Philadelphia, New York City, New Jersey, and Boston. Other businesses—some big, some small, some linked to the Santacroces, some not—included Donato's Pesce e Pasta (Donato's Fish & Pasta), a quaint Italian restaurant in Baltimore's Little Italy.

It was a very rare occasion when William Coventry patronized Donato's at lunchtime. The news coming out of Detroit, and the projections of investment losses there, necessitated his visit. But he didn't like dealing with the Italians. They were useful clients, to be sure, and he immensely enjoyed the air of mystery and the hint of menace they lent his business, but he didn't trust them for a minute. He considered them dirty and uncouth, and unworthy of the investment opportunities that he provided. But he could use their services now and again.

Donato Picucci recognized the silver-haired blue blood when he walked in. He could tell that the man looked upon him with disdain, but he did business with his Zio (uncle) Giorgio, and Zio considered him important. And so Donato would humor him by talking about the O's, and the old devil played along even though it was clear that he knew nothing about baseball.

He had ordered his favorite dish, glazed salmon with angel hair pasta and a touch of olive oil, and a glass of vino rosso. Donato never presented his bill, but Mr. Coventry always dropped a fifty-dollar bill on the table. As he did so, the blue blood said, "I would like to meet with Signore Santacroce. It's urgent."

That was a day ago. Now, he stood by the large double doors to the promenade in the back of the estate and watched as a navy blue-and-orange "Go the Distance" Air Charter Service Sikorsky S-76 helicopter landed on the pad adjacent to the tennis court. Go the Distance, of course, was one of the businesses owned by S&K.

Sixty years old, with jet black hair flecked with gray, Giorgio Santacroce stepped from the helicopter in a gray suit that was finely trimmed. At his side was a young man, fit and trim, and impeccably dressed in a skinny black suit that accentuated his own jet-black hair.

William stepped onto the promenade and greeted Giorgio and his companion, Fausto Santacroce, his youngest son and head of the Santacroces' American operations. William learned that he was a graduate of Harvard Business School.

Facades. Lipstick on a pig.

After a brief walk through the promenade to stretch their legs, the three men retired to the Coventry Library, beers in hand, where William laid out the problem in the simplest terms he could manage.

In normal economic times, S&K invested the bulk of its funds in global blue chip companies and promising start-ups which, in turn, provided solid returns. A scattering of investments in commodities, currency trades, real estate, and derivatives rounded out a diverse and solidly performing portfolio for each client.

But these were not normal economic times, and hadn't been for a decade. Global financial crises had left the blue chip companies of the world facing a crippling lack of demand and weak sales, and they in turn left investors with anemic returns and even losses. Investors were forced to seek better returns from riskier assets such as currencies, derivatives, real estate, and venture loans. Anything that produced a decent return resulted in a stampede of investors, inflating the costs of the asset and potentially producing a bubble that, when it burst, would be financially ruinous to anyone without a seat when the music stopped. These were dangerous times.

The voluminous wealth of its clients enabled S&K to scour the earth for investment opportunities, no matter how small. They found Pleasant Peninsula Bank, a small regional bank in the Detroit are, which performed quite well by serving a market few dared to enter. They offered very modest loans in a highly depressed housing and commercial real estate market. This enabled them to charge higher interest rates, but the way they saw it, the market in Detroit had been depressed for so long that it had nowhere to go but up.

And they were right. Pleasant Peninsula Bank saw its assets double, then triple, within a few months, then triple again. They snapped up thousands of foreclosed properties to rehab and flip, further growing their assets. Pleasant Peninsula was one of the reasons that S&K performed so well compared with other investment firms, especially in tough times like these.

S&K purchased many of the higher-rate mortgages from Pleasant Peninsula and Apex Superior and packaged them as securities in the form of Collateralized Debt Obligations. These securities offered a higher rate of return to investors, so long as homeowners and business owners paid their mortgages.

But then the riots hit, and all hope for Detroit's housing and commercial real estate market was abruptly dashed. Real estate values in Detroit were poised to crash again, leaving most homeowners and businesses underwater. If history was any guide, then there was little chance of a rebound anytime soon. Areas hit by unrest during the Los Angeles riots of 1992 still hadn't fully recovered. The collective value of the Pleasant Peninsula and Apex Superior CDOs held by S&K, worth five billion dollars just a week ago, was now almost zero.

"Pretty soon and we're talking real money," quipped the blue blood.

To avoid further losses, S&K had to deleverage and extricate itself from the Detroit market. The only way out was insurance. But out of the estimated ten thousand fires that raged in Detroit, barely a fraction included Pleasant Peninsula or Apex Superior mortgaged properties.

"The issue," said the esteemed Mr. Coventry, "is one of scale." He paused for a moment before he spoke again.

"We need the city to burn."

Chapter 24

Life in Detroit was slowly returning to normal, including its nightlife. For the Grape Vine Bar & Grille on Monroe Street, smack in the middle of downtown and a block up from the Greektown Casino, "normal" was greeted with subdued enthusiasm. That's because the club didn't really skip a beat, save for a couple of nights, during the unrest. When the downtown became a police fortress, the Grape Vine became a favorite among the cops—and then Army soldiers—to the amusement (and profit) of its true owner, William "Pops" Jefferson Avery.

It was rare for the Avery brothers to actually patronize the Grape Vine, but the venue seemed appropriate for the business at hand. The Italians wanted a meeting, and what place was safer than a cop bar?

"Bring the Marine," was the last thing Frank Auletta had said on the phone, and so Jayson was present.

Pops, Fave, and Jayson sat in a booth downing Motor City Ghettoblasters, while Elijah and the other crew members kept tabs on everyone in the joint. Marquis McKinnon, formerly Darrell's lieutenant, spotted Frank and Freddie Auletta along with a twenty-something as they came in the door, and he led them to the Averys' booth.

"This is Fausto, a cousin," Frank said, introducing the young man who, to Pops and Fave, looked like Damien, the devil child of the old Omen films. "He's from Philadelphia." Pops nodded. Maybe it wasn't Frank's intention, but Pops under-stood Philadelphia to mean that the kid represented the powers behind Auletta.

"Thank you kindly," the young man said, "for bringing some business our way."

"Hear, hear," said Frank, raising his beer. The six men clanged their beer bottles together and took a sip.

The devil child laid out the business before them. "We would like to further our partnership. It comes with a bit of urgen-cy, and isn't without risk."

"You don't say," cackled Pops.

~ ~ ~

Reggie kicked up his skateboard with one hand and tapped Aaron on the chest with the other as he gazed down the street. Aaron followed his eyes, and nearly slipped off his own board as adrenaline flooded his body. A black, raised Cadillac Escalade EXT with darkly tinted windows and spinning rims pulled up so fast, he didn't have time to react. He thought they were dead when all the doors opened and members of the Avery Gang stepped out, including Jayson Avery.

"The Scooby Doo Crew," said Jayson in his baritone voice, stepping out of the driver's seat. The other men clamoring out of the car included Willie James, Elijah Freeman, and Marquis McKinnon—well-known Avery Gang enforcers.

Xavier and Devin went swagger, squinting their eyes and raising their shoulders, even while holding their skate-boards. Reggie dropped his board, hopped on, and rolled a bit, seemingly oblivious to the presence of killers. But Aaron's heart pounded so loudly in his chest and ears that he was certain it drowned out the traffic.

"Want to make some cash?" Jayson asked Aaron. Given the way he said it, with his enforcers hovering behind, it wasn't a question.

Aaron nodded.

"Hop in," said Jayson.

After a short ride, the Escalade stopped and, when Aaron and the gangsters got out, Aaron saw they had stopped at Small's Bar-B-Que across the street from the once grand and now beautifully apocalyptic Michigan Grand Central Station, which had been abandoned thirty years ago.

"Damn, nigga. Move!" commanded Jayson, opening the wooden gate to the restaurant's outdoor patio. Aaron was ushered in.

"Mr. Jones," said an older man with braided hair and a beard. He stood, wiped his hands on a rag, and extended a hand. Aaron took it, hesitantly, and flinched at the man's solid grip.

Catty-cornered to the man who spoke was another older man. He sat with his head tilted slightly, his eyes squinted but locked squarely on Aaron.

With the wave of his hand, the first man indicated that Aaron should sit beside him, across from the squinting man. Jayson and his crew stood at different ends of the patio, legs spread and arms crossed behind them, like Secret Service agents.

On the table was a mountain of barbequed pulled pork.

"Do you know who I am, Mr. Jones?" asked the man.

"Yes, sir," said Aaron, barely audible. "You're Pops Avery."

The man leaned back in his chair and chuckled.

"*Sir,*" Pops said, and laughed even more deeply. "Jayson *said* you had manners." He nodded at Fave. "This is my brother, Forrest." Pops eyed Aaron, who was starting to feel like somebody's next meal. "And you also know Fave, I take it. Listen, Aaron, I need young men from across our community who can help us with a significant project. It's an unusual project, and we need juveniles to do it."

Pops wiped his face with a wet rag and pushed the dish of pulled pork away. "We need to burn some buildings down, my man. I mean that literally."

Pops slowly leaned forward and *his* eyes squinted, sending a chill through Aaron. "This," said Pops, his pointer finger tapping on the picnic table, "is a big responsibility."

Pops leaned back again and eyed Aaron. "I understand you have a crew of your own, little man," he said.

~ ~ ~

It had been nearly two weeks since Ian and Trevor identified Roland's body. Campus had reopened, and classes were once again underway.

It was surreal for Ian. Campus and his classes were abuzz about the unrest, but the professors still had a job to do, and so they carried on with their instruction. Ian tried to busy himself with studying, and lose himself running, but he couldn't get the sight of Roland in the morgue out of his mind. His head was misshapen, and his eyes and mouth were open. He looked small, like a scrawny little kid. His physical energy, his fearlessness, his mischievousness, were all gone. It wasn't him—it was some fragile, broken shell that kind of resembled Roland, but wasn't him.

Trevor, Tina, and Sarah were gone. Tina's parents had taken her home. She texted Ian that they were transferring her to another college after the summer, probably to the University of Akron in Ohio, where she had also been offered a cross country scholarship before she chose Wayne State.

Trevor went back home to Lansing. He said he would probably transfer to Western Michigan University.

Sarah told Ian that her parents pleaded with her to come home to Findlay, Ohio. When she told him that, Ian broke into a silent sob. When she hugged him, he bawled like a baby. He couldn't help it. "You'll be okay," she assured him.

Would he? Ian wasn't so sure. They were breaking up. Meanwhile, his own parents seemed oblivious to the unrest in Detroit. Either that, or they didn't realize that the university was in the thick of it. Their lives revolved entirely around the Viet Taste Restaurant that his grandfather had started some forty years before in Sterling Heights.

"I don't know anything about politics," was his mother's response when he told her about the unrest. He didn't tell them that his friend was killed by police. How could they understand such a thing?

It was a small, hot kitchen in a restaurant with only a few tables. It was suffocating and claustrophobic, but his parents had always assumed that Ian would take over some day.

Ian decided that he would complete the semester but, after that, he had no idea. Home wasn't an option. It probably never was.

~ ~ ~

Federal and local law enforcement reviewed hundreds of hours of video captured by news helicopters, ground-level reporters, and security cameras during the unrest, just as Fave Avery had warned.

Local television replayed over and over the scene of the vicious young man brutally smashing a brick over the head of a young driver commuting to work on the I-94, killing him. The scene was filmed from a distance, and the image wasn't entirely clear. The young man had looked straight up at the helicopter and held up his middle fingers, and the news would freeze the image each time. But it was blurry.

Fave was certain it was Dmitri Johnson, the bloodthirsty young River Gee who, along with Caleb Sessions, was trying to consolidate control of the Motown Mafia by waging war on any faction that dared to be independent. It was Dmitri and Caleb who ordered the attack on his house and killed his guys. Of that he had no doubt.

True to his out-of-control nature, Dmitri was Public Enemy Number 1, or soon would be. He would be quickly identified by police and the feds. He was probably already in hiding after seeing his face all over TV and the internet.

Fave had no doubt that the police would quickly locate the stupid piece of shit. But that would not be the end of the war. Dmitri was just one guy, and the River Gees were full of other reckless punks. He needed the whole lot of them neutralized. Then he could deal with Caleb.

For Fave and his family, there was no getting to either Dmitri or Caleb. They couldn't just drive into that territory without being seen. They'd never get close enough. And there was still the issue of the rest of the Gees.

He had to be bold. He had to go big. So, it was End Times.

One of Jayson's crews was able to park a rusty Ford Econoline van in front of an abandoned garage on East Grand Boulevard, in the same neighborhood where the National Guard had killed those poor kids.

The neighborhood still seethed, and that part of Grand Boulevard was thick with patrolling soldiers. It also happened to be the heart of Grand River Gees territory.

They drove from the east along I-75, parked the van, and drove off in a following car back to the interstate. The van carried a Lockheed Martin-built HIMARS MGM-140 missile.

The explosion was massive. Almost four miles away, Fave's entire house shook. Armed crew members rushed outside to see what had happened, and spotted the mushroom cloud of dust rising above the city in the near distance.

Fave sat at the kitchen table, waiting for an update, though he didn't really need one. A once-familiar knot of fear, which he'd buried in his youth, tightened in the pit of his stomach. There was no going back now. He *had* to see it through.

End Times...

~ ~ ~

After nearly a week of patrolling, Gino Napolitano's fears were not assuaged. Not at all. The hard stares continued. The hostility was palpable.

The first day saw a barrage of glass bottles on Grand Boulevard, and he and his soldiers were ordered to suck wind and take it.

Despite these orders, Gino and his soldiers went after the hard-looking young men snickering amid the crowds. But the crowds wouldn't part for them, and when they forced their way in to apprehend the young punks, it became an out-and-out street brawl between soldiers and civilians.

Some major ordered Gino and his men to pull back, and it went downhill from there. The crowds threw anything they could find at them. They also piled tires and assorted debris into the middle of the boulevard and set them on fire.

It was a mini riot, and it threatened to spread all over again. When word reached General McIntyre, he reassigned the major and ordered a whole brigade to flood into the "zone" and clear Grand Boulevard once and for all.

But the crowds kept gathering. They gathered each day, all day long. Gino didn't understand it. No one seemed to have a job or go to school. The Army refrained from entering the neighborhoods themselves. They stuck to the commercial districts. Young men and teenagers would taunt the soldiers, and then dash back into the neighborhood when the soldiers reacted.

The only forays into the neighborhoods would come in the dead of night when the FBI, DEA, or some other law enforcement agency served warrants, arriving in armored vehicles with Army squads in tow for security.

Grand Boulevard itself, though, was saturated with soldiers on foot patrol. Army vehicles traveled up and down the boulevard, dropping off supplies and running errands.

Businesses were reopening. Residents ventured out as well, to grocery and convenience stores, gas stations, doctors' appointments, and the like.

Gino and his squad neared the eastern end of Grand Boulevard, where they would turn around and patrol back to their starting point. On most days, Gino and his squad would cover the entire length of Grand Boulevard at least once. They often stopped and chatted with the dozens of other patrols they passed. They had come to know quite a few other soldiers. It was Gino's job to keep them moving; his squad had made all kinds of friends. A chatty bunch, he started calling them "ladies."

"Keep it moving, ladies," Gino ordered as another patrol passed them. One soldier wordlessly offered a high-five to each member of Gino's squad as they passed. Just as it was Gino's turn to high-five the passing soldier, the entire street in front him disappeared in an orange-and-black ball of flame that rose over the boulevard as a fiery mushroom cloud.

It was like a slow-motion silent film. There was no sound.

Gino's eyes and mouth widened as he tried to order his men to *get down,* but the order wasn't necessary. Everyone was slammed to the pavement by the explosion's shockwave, which arrived a millisecond before a concussive thunderclap split the air. Near the explosion's epicenter, people were tossed about like ragdolls.

After a moment, Gino stood, covered in dust from head to toe that gently trailed from his body in a soft breeze, giving him a ghostly, ethereal appearance. A young private, himself in shock, ran to him. When Gino turned and looked at the private, the man stopped, his mouth agape. Looking into Gino's eyes was like looking into a black, bottomless pit, and then the young sergeant crumpled to the ground in a rattle of bones.

~ ~ ~

Moe Adil was at a desk on the fifth floor of the Patrick V. McNamara Federal Building in downtown Detroit. The FBI had lent him and his team an office and a desk. The desk was Moe's since, well, since he was the boss. His team of five CID agents had their laptops and could use the floor. God Bless the FBI.

The building shook. The FBI offices stirred. "What was *that?*" more than one person asked. Moe watched as people moved with urgency.

Moe knew what it was. And, for just a moment, he thought he was back in Iraq. *This isn't Iraq,* he thought to himself. *I am not in Iraq, goddamn it.*

No, this was worse. This was home. Moe walked to the window and looked out on the downtown. Everything was fine. He craned his neck in order to see uptown. A gray-and-silver dust cloud hung over New Center, slowly drifting over the neighborhoods east of downtown and toward the river. A wisp of black oily smoke, meanwhile, curled into the air in swift patchy waves. It was a familiar sight from his days in Iraq and Afghanistan. *Car bomb.*

He was pretty sure he knew where the bomb had come from.

Chapter 25

Nine miles to the west, the Channel 13 newsroom was abuzz within minutes of the explosion. So it was for all local television newsrooms and print media. All of them soon dispatched a helicopter or a news van to get as close as possible to the site of the explosion.

There was a lot of confusion. Cell phones buzzed, land lines rang, and editors and reporters shouted commands.

Reporter Wally Mickiewicz was in the thick of it, and his own desk phone rang off the hook. He snatched the receiver. "Wally," he barked into the speaker end as he took notes from the director, who shouted orders from across the newsroom.

"Is this Wally Mickie-witz, the reporter?" asked a calm voice.

"*Yes, goddamnit,*" snapped Wally.

"We are the People's Armed Resistance. The Army is killing of our people, and occupation of our streets is an act of war."

The voice was electronically distorted, Wally realized. He held up his hand and waved for everyone to quiet down. They did.

"We demand a full withdrawal of the U.S. Army and police,"

the voice continued. "These streets are our streets. The people's streets." The phone line went dead.

"I got a claim of responsibility!" Wally yelled out. "The People's Armed Resistance."

~ ~ ~

Bobby 'Bones' Bailey disconnected the phone, removed the battery, and dropped both into the Detroit River. He'd made five calls and said the same thing each time. The phone was a burner, so there was no tracing it back to him or the Avery Organization.

Bones, dressed in a track suit, made his way back to the Grand Arnault Casino and Hotel where, two hours earlier, he'd booked a room. He made sure that his room overlooked Michigan Avenue, just as Jayson Avery had instructed.

Across the street was the DPSH complex, which had its back to the M-10 John C. Lodge Freeway. The short and narrow 5th Street ran between the DPSH complex and the M-10, and was off-limits to the public. Strategically-placed Jersey barriers prevented cars from entering 5th Street, as did a manned security gate on both ends. This was where police vehicles entered and exited the complex, including the Lenco BEAR armored personnel carriers.

This was where the FBI and police SWAT convoys departed.

Bones unpacked a telescopic camera from his suitcase and set it up on a tripod. The camera was equipped with night vision, an expensive piece of tech provided by the "Corleones," according to Mr. Avery. *What the heck was a Corleone?* Bones wondered. He didn't understand how old people talked sometimes.

He then broke open a cell phone box, one of five in his suitcase, and activated it. He did the same for the next four. Once all the burner phones were activated, Bones was ready.

He ripped open a bag of crispy onion rings, and sat with his feet propped up on the room's desk, peering out the window through the camera.

~ ~ ~

As the news media sought to understand the meaning of the car bomb in New Center, Bernice Hamandawana and Wayne State's newspaper, *The South End,* were suddenly thrust into the limelight. She'd published the first article of a planned three-part series about the killing of three teenagers by the National Guard. No other news outlet had covered the event. Much of the city was considered too dangerous for reporters to visit during the unrest, but rumors swirled in Midtown and New Center. Bernice explored the rumors, and she and fellow journalism student Daniel Rush walked from Wayne State to New Center to interview witnesses.

A shaggy-haired white kid, Daniel was scared to tag along, but Bernice was fearless. "If you're scared, major in accounting," she said.

She and Daniel were led to the spot where the three boys had been killed. The concrete driveway of a gas station was still stained with blood. Bernice interviewed orderlies and nurses at the Henry Ford Hospital. Lastly, she saw the bodies herself, still in drawers in the hospital morgue. Her news story had been picked up by the Associated Press, and since the unrest had ended, the *Detroit Free Press* was in the process of independently verifying her story when the car bomb exploded.

Surely the killing of the three teenagers was the impetus for the car bomb. It happened on the very block where the boys were killed. More than fifty people were killed in the explosion, including forty U.S. Army soldiers. At least 100 people had been injured. This *must* be about revenge.

General McIntyre surveyed the scene with an entourage of senior officers. Soldiers had swarmed in and cordoned off Grand Boulevard for the full three-mile length between I-75 and I-96. Army CID agents inspected a crater that swallowed the entire width of the westbound lanes of Grand Boulevard, plus its sidewalk and part of an adjacent parking lot. Tiny flags marked fragments within the crater.

"Welcome to the Occupation, General," said a large black man wearing a CID jacket. General McIntyre glared at the man, but the man held his gaze. "Moe Adil," the man said, "CID special agent in charge."

"The British Army was initially welcomed by the Catholics in Northern Ireland," Moe said. "It was supposed to be a brief operation, not unlike your deployment. That brief deployment lasted for thirty-eight years, from 1969 to 2007," Moe said.

"Tell me something I *don't* know, Mr. Adil," said the general, annoyed by the history lesson.

Moe looked into the crater and nodded to an axle in the center. "Looks like a Ford Econoline van. Car bomb. The explosive appears to be a rigged MGM-140 missile taken from the Olympia Armory."

"You can ascertain all of that already?" the general asked.

"Not definitively, not yet, but we're pretty sure," said Moe. "I've picked through enough MGM-140 fragments in after-battle postmortems in Iraq and Afghanistan to make a good guess."

The general nodded to the west, in the direction of the Olympia Armory. "From there?"

Moe nodded.

"You think this is the work of locals?"

"Right over there," Moe said, pointing a block to the east, "was where those three teenagers were killed after tossing Molotov cocktails at a National Guard Humvee."

The general continued to look around, arms folded across his chest. Moe remained silent.

~ ~ ~

William "Pops" Avery was an extroverted man. It was a personality better suited to a politician, but his loquacious-ness—the complete opposite of his brooding younger broth-er Fave—was disarming, and it opened doors.

He'd met Lynn Edwards two decades earlier, when they were both in their early thirties, and more than a decade before she landed a job as a records keeper for the Detroit Police Department. It was a pittance, what she made, and Pops plied her with jewelry and cash.

Her bosses preached a good game: God and country, law and order, us versus them. But "them" were people like her—people struggling to make a living and getting the power turned off. Having little or no health insurance. No way to afford college for the children. Driving While Black. The list went on. She feared for her boys when they were teenagers. She feared that the police department she worked for would ultimately kill them.

So whenever Pops wanted information that didn't require off-the-charts risk-taking, she was happy to oblige.

Pops wanted Lynn to text her on Whatsapp whenever the police were suiting up for a raid and whenever the Lenco BEARs were rolling out.

That was all. It wasn't like she was stealing anything.

~ ~ ~

Fave's phone buzzed on the kitchen table. The small television on the counter played the news. The video of the I-94 killing was shown again and again, but now there was also a mug shot of Dmitri Johnson with the word "WANTED" beneath it. A ticker at the bottom read: "I-94 suspect identified as Dmitri Johnson ... Suspect is at large and considered armed and dangerous..."

Fave answered the phone.

"I've got an address," said Freddie Auletta.

"9-1-1, what is your emergency?" said the dispatcher.

"Hello, I think I've seen that awful man on TV, the one wanted for that terrible murder on the freeway," said the woman. "I was walking my dog when I passed a house with a man on the porch smoking a cigarette. He looked right at me and I knew right away it was him. Then he went inside the house."

"I'm scared," she added. "He saw me. Please hurry."

Fave took the burner from Greta, removed the battery and sim card, and broke the phone and sim card into pieces. He wrapped his arms around Greta from behind and gently kissed the back of her neck.

Jackson Mills and Jayson Avery climbed the stairs to the top floor of the fifteen-story Lee Plaza Building before sundown. The building had been vacant since 1997 and was in a sad state of repair, despite being listed in the National Register of Historical Places.

Jackson had misgivings when Jayson found him on Grand Boulevard. But he was a fellow Marine, and what did he have to lose? They weren't aiming to shoot anyone. Just hold the Army at bay as part of some bigger plan.

Shooting target practice with Jayson brought back fond memories. He was a Marine again.

Jayson kept an eye on his smartphone as they settled in for the night. He thought it was a really nice phone for a burner.

The phone buzzed. It was a text message from Bones. "It's on," it read.

Jayson dialed a number and relayed the message. "Stay sharp," he added. "Could be any time now. Keep the line open."

He and Jackson peered through their rifle night scopes.

Twenty more minutes passed. And then, there they were. An armored personnel carrier sped toward them on Grand Boulevard, followed by several vans and a convoy of Army Humvees.

They were a quarter-mile away, but close enough to engage.

"Not yet," said Jayson. "Just wait."

A massive explosion followed by a deafening *KABOOM!* momentarily blinded them.

The whole building—already in poor condition—rattled and creaked in its frame. Dust fell from the ceiling. Jackson felt the air pressure change in his ear drums. He opened his mouth wide to equalize the pressure in his ears.

Jackson and Jayson peered through their rifle scopes again. After a moment, the dust started to clear. The armored carrier wasn't there anymore, nor were the vans. Jackson scanned the road with his rifle. The mangled remains of a vehicle lay burning in the parking lot of a vacant apartment complex. An entire row of retail stores, mostly boarded up, was also demolished.

The dust cleared further, and the Army Humvees came into view. They had stopped about a half mile down the road. Soldiers piled out of the vehicles as their commanders assessed the situation.

Several soldiers ran to what was left of the law enforcement vans.

"Now!" said Jayson.

Jackson fired four rounds into the lead Humvee's windshield.

It was bulletproof, as Jayson and Jackson knew, but the sudden appearance of bullet-sized pockmarks on the windshield was what they wanted.

Soldiers dropped to the ground and scrambled for cover.

Jackson fired a round once every minute to keep the soldiers on their toes.

Jayson kept an eye on the time. After several more minutes, he spoke into his phone.

"Now," he said.

Two stories below Jayson and Jackson was Team C. Composed of six shooters, they were facing the residential neighborhood to the north.

They opened fire, not with sniper rifles, but with M-4s, shooting haphazardly toward an area that covered five to ten streets. However, one particular house was their general target.

~ ~ ~

Dmitri's phone buzzed. His girlfriend, snuggled in his arms, moaned. He looked to see who was calling, but it said *Re-*

stricted. Agitated, Dmitri hit the answer button.

"Who the fuck is this?" he said, sitting up in bed.

"They're coming," a voice said.

"Who is it?" asked Jamaica, laying naked beside him.

Just then, the whole house seemed to collapse around him. The windows blew in, and he scrambled to the floor. It was an explosion.

"They're here," said the voice on the phone.

Logan burst through the bedroom door, slinging an AK-47. "Dmitri! You okay?"

Jamaica, backed up to the bedrest with her knees and bed sheets drawn up to her chest, screamed incessantly.

"Yeah, muthafucka!" Dmitri said, ignoring Jamaica as he pulled on a pair of jeans. He scrambled to the closet and retrieved his own AK-47.

"It's the *police!*" Dmitri said, catching his breath. "Let's *go!*"

Dmitri and his crew turned out the lights and looked outside. They didn't see anything.

Dmitri nodded to Logan. He cracked the door open. Cold air filtered in. Logan went out, crept low, and darted for the line of cars parked out front. He waved the next man out.

The whole crew came onto the street like an Army scout unit, rifles at the aim.

They heard gunfire and dropped.

Silence.

A fire burned a few streets over. Another shot rang out.

They saw movement, dropped to their knees, and were ready to fire when they were seen. It was Jamal Parkins and his crew. They were running from their homes a couple of blocks away.

"Don't shoot!" Jamal yelled, holding a rifle aloft.

There was more gunfire, a distant but nonstop *pop-pop-pop-pop*. Bullets seemed to rain down haphazardly on their street.

"Go, go, go!" ordered Dmitri. The combined crews worked as a large fire team. They took turns providing covering fire as they moved.

"*There!*" shouted one of Jamal's crew members. It was the Army, a line of Humvees sitting in the dark.

More gunfire sent the crews ducking for cover. Then they opened fire on the Humvees.

~ ~ ~

"I.E.D.," Major Jose Hernandez said into the radio. "We have many casualties."

Major Hernandez was calm, but chaos was all around him. "We're beginning rescue. We need medevac." His soldiers exited from the Humvees, and ran to aid the guys in the demolished FBI vans and personnel carrier.

"Sniper fire!" yelled a sergeant, and everyone dropped to

the ground. Looking back over his shoulder, Hernandez saw the tell-tale pockmarks of bullet strikes on his Humvee windshield.

"Take cover!" shouted Hernandez. He snatched the radio microphone from the radioman at his side. "We're under attack," he said. "Sniper fire."
Hernandez barked more orders to his men. A tall brick building, maybe twenty stories high and a quarter-mile straight ahead, was his best guess for the sniper's location. Several more shots sharpened this assumption.

Soldiers reached the smashed FBI vans and began treating the injured. The vans had been sent rolling fifty feet. Several men were dead.

The personnel carrier was a different story. It wasn't even recognizable. None of its occupants could have survived the blast.

~ ~ ~

At the New Fort Detroit command center, everyone felt the blast. The ground shook. Men came out of their tents and ran to their posts. Everyone looked north to see the gray mushroom cloud rise against the night sky.

Awakened by the blast, General McIntyre hurried into the command post. He arrived as Major Hernandez radioed in. Men could be heard screaming in the background as the executive officer assured Hernandez that backup was on the way.

"We're taking fire," Hernandez reported, and a distant *pop-pop-pop* of automatic rifle fire was heard at the command post.

McIntyre ordered a rapid reaction force into action, and their convoy sped out of New Fort Detroit and straight up Grand River Avenue to 14ᵗʰ Street, which took them straight to the gun fight while avoiding the likely source of sniper fire.

McIntyre called the Pentagon.

~ ~ ~

Other sniper teams were stationed on each of the three floors below Jayson and Jackson to cover all approaches to the building. The Army quickly ascertained that the Lee Plaza Building was the likely source of sniper fire, given the angles of attack, even as the gun battle raged below.

Through his scope, Jayson could see more soldiers arriving alongside the first convoy to join the gun battle against the River Gees, who were firing from the neighborhood north of the boulevard. Jayson and Jackson watched as cars and trucks full of men armed with pistols and AK-47s tore down Grand Boulevard from the opposite end. They stopped and scattered when army troops opened fire.

Other gang members arrived on foot, streaming in from Wildemere, Lawton, and Linwood Streets. These were the territories of the factions comprising the Motown Mafia—of which the Grand River Gees were but one. Many of the GLEE shutoffs and subsequent house fires had occurred in these very neighborhoods—LaSalle Gardens, Petosky-Ostego, Northwest Goldberg, New Center, and Boston Edison.

The gunfight was expanding. Other crews of the Motown Mafia had gotten word that Dmitri and his crew were putting up a fight after police tried to arrest them. They came to join the fight. The spontaneous anti-GLEE protests and riots were one thing. This was something else entirely. The

Army was attacking them.

This was all-out *war.*

~ ~ ~

Fifteen minutes into the attack, the appearance of a lone Humvee inching from the opposite end of Grand Boulevard suggested that more troops were arriving to flank the gangs.

Team B fired on the Humvee, halting its progress. It tore backward in reverse until it was blocked by a church at the intersection of Dexter Avenue. Team B reported that they could see Army trucks unloading soldiers beyond Dexter.

Seconds later, Team C opened fire on troops gathering at the smoldering remains of the Olympia Armory south of the Lee Plaza Building. The soldiers were surrounding them from a distance.

Jayson decided that they had done their part and it was time to vacate the building. First, however, he and his men set multiple fires to confuse any drones and helicopters armed with infrared cameras.

They also changed their clothes and used hand sanitizer to wash away any gunpowder residue. They used their discarded clothes as kindling, and placed their weapons in various piles to allow the fires to cook off the remaining ammunition. It was a long shot, but ammo being cooked off might make the Army and the River Gees think they were still being fired upon, even after Jayson and his crew had gone.

As they headed down the stairs, soldiers from beyond Dexter Avenue opened fire on the building from a distance of nearly half a mile. Jayson smiled as bullets tore through the upper floors while they bounded down the stairs. The Army fire would likely draw the attention of arriving crews of the Motown Mafia and Grand River Gees.

He was right. When they exited the building, they were met with a cacophony of gunfire that echoed down Grand Boulevard. It was a crossfire of bullets from beyond Dexter and into the LaSalle Gardens neighborhood, with return fire from the neighborhood.

Jayson and his crew scrambled away on foot. They had a van parked on Ferry Park Street, a residential street a block south of the Lee Plaza Building. With the Army now engaged with Motown Mafia crews, Jayson and his crew melted away. The plan had worked like a dream.

Chapter 26

General McIntyre stood in the double-wide command trailer, hands on his improvised desk, his steely eyes fixed on a large wall map as he listened to reports from the battle on Grand Boulevard and up-and-down Grand River Avenue.

Gunfire reverberated throughout the city. It was like Fallujah out there, and McIntyre was angry and aghast.

He had visited dozens of soldiers and civilians in the hospital who'd been wounded from the previous day's car bomb. He saw the bodies of the dead. And here they were, less than twenty-four hours after that attack.

The general wasted no time. He had to clamp down—*hard*—or risk another "Blackhawk Down." He shook his head in disbelief. *A major freaking firefight in the middle of an American freaking city. Un-freaking-believable.* And to worry about a "Blackhawk Down" scenario *in an American city was...unconscionable.*

McIntyre declared martial law. He ordered the remaining tanks at Selfridge into battle. They were on their way, along with more convoys of soldiers.

What gnawed at him was the Lee Plaza Building. Snipers kept his soldiers pinned down. They couldn't get medevac helicopters for the wounded FBI team until the snipers were neutralized.

Major Hernandez—a cool customer, the general thought—had requested close-in air support. McIntyre shook his head. *Air support! In an American city!* Yet another point of disbelief. They were coming fast. But he had a job to do, and he had to protect his soldiers. Days earlier, he had requested four Marine Corps F-35s as part of his deployment, mostly for show. He hadn't expected to actually *use* them.

He straightened, nodding to a captain with a radio in his hand. "Authorized," he said.

Fifteen minutes later, a U.S. Marine Corps F-35B Lightning II stealth fighter took off from Selfridge Air Base in the dawn's early light. Armed with two 500- pound bombs, the Lightning II banked left as its sensors honed in on the laser-designated target twenty-two miles to the south. The jet covered the distance in seven minutes, traveling at 440 miles per hour.

Major Luke Schmidt, the thirty-three-year old pilot from Tampa, Florida, let the aircraft do most of the work. He simply released the trigger on his joystick when the target-acquiring system emitted a high-pitch screeching tone.

"Bombs away," he announced into his helmet microphone. He felt the aircraft shudder and lurch upward as two 500-pound Guided Bomb Unit (GBU)-12 Paveway II aerial laser-guided bombs dropped free of the aircraft. He banked sharply to the right and accelerated to 600 miles per hour.

General McIntyre stood outside the command trailer facing the northwest, scanning the early morning sky. Plumes of black smoke rose from the nearby battles like monsters. The general heard the unique sound of a lone fighter jet ripping across the sky. He didn't actually see the jet, but there was no mistaking the orange flash of light followed by a thunderous *boom.* The ground shook beneath the general's feet.

A second *boom* announced that the unseen jet had broken the sound barrier as it peeled away.

A gray column of dust, smoke, and debris rose rapidly and angrily over the urban landscape. It rose high into the morning sky and drifted lazily to the east toward Windsor.

The general sighed. He himself gave the order, but still ... *An airstrike on an American city.*

A taboo had been broken.

~ ~ ~

Private First Class Adrian Gonzales of Phoenix, Arizona, lined up with his squad mates to await the morning brief before they boarded a troop transport truck. They would deploy to Martin Luther King Boulevard to relieve the overnight squad. MLK Boulevard split the Corktown neighborhood, which was one of the most violent in the nation, according to FBI crime statistics.

Grand Boulevard and Grand River Boulevard that were at the center of the current unrest, while MLK Boulevard was quiet. No protestors had gathered there, no cars were attacked, and no stores were looted.

And so, for Private Gonzales and his squad mates, deployment to MLK Boulevard was pretty boring. They walked all day long, back and forth, back and forth, "protecting" stores. Local residents plied them with water bottles, sandwiches, and baked goods. The night shift was jealous.

"Gather around, men" ordered the squad leader, Staff Sergeant Dan Culver. "We have new orders."

Culver explained that they were deploying to a different location.

They were going into battle.

Their convoy sped past downtown Detroit, taking a circuitous route to engage the "terrorists" from the rear.

As the convoy crossed northbound on Livernois over Grand River Boulevard—a gas station on the corner flew the U.S. flag upside down—, blood splattered into Adrian's face. The soldier sitting across from him fell forward, blood spurting between his hands as he clasped them to his neck.

He thrashed on the floor of the truck as Adrian and others tried to administer first aid.

Adrian helped pull the gurgling kid from the truck. He and two other soldiers half-carried and half-dragged him across Livernois Avenue to a gas station with the upside-down flag, but it was so far away. When they got halfway across the street, the kid went totally limp, so they dragged him by the arm pits.

When they reached the gas station's canopy, they laid the kid down and saw that he was dead.

The convoy commander, Major Thomas Warren, reported to base that the convoy was under fire, more than a mile and a half from the fighting on Grand Boulevard. Another sniper, it appeared.

The soldiers identified an eight-story building, which once housed a furniture company—as the likely source of sniper fire.

~ ~ ~

Major Schmidt circled the city aloft as he awaited new orders. He could see that the fifteen-story brick building was now a ten-story pile of rubble.

A red light on the heads-up display in his helmet visor caught Major Schmidt's eye. It was an engine fire light, and he pressed the lighted red button on the cockpit panel. It flickered and went out, but came right back on.

"Selfridge, I have an engine fire light, requesting emergency landing," Jason said into his headgear microphone. He steered his plane northeast toward Selfridge.

Multiple alerts came on all at once—fuel, engine power, hydraulics, and others—along with a beeping alarm.

Jason could see Selfridge in the distance, but his plane shuddered and lost power. It started to descend. "Mayday," he announced, calmly, "no power." Acrid smoke filled the cockpit. Jason reached for the ejection seat cord and pulled, but he was a hair too late.

The F-35B stealth joint strike fighter exploded in a fireball fifteen miles west of Selfridge. Debris rained down for two square miles over suburban Troy.

McIntyre hurried out of the trailer and looked to the north. He saw a single black cloud in the distant sky with multiple contrails tracing to the ground. *What the hell just happened?*

"Get me Selfridge," he ordered. "Jesus Christ! What else can go wrong?"

"Sir," said a radio operator, "Charlie squad is taking sniper fire on Livernois and Grand River. They've got casualties."

General McIntyre slammed his hand on the main table in the command trailer. He took a deep breath.

"Okay," he said to no one in particular. "Okay," he said again, nodding to himself.

"We're going to seal these neighborhoods off. We go door to door, house to house. The President has already declared the city to be in insurrection, so it's time for the gloves to come off."

He stood straight, chin jutted out. "I warned them," he sighed. "God knows I warned them."

~ ~ ~

The city may have been officially on lockdown, but it took a while for word to spread, despite being announced on TV and radio. It was the neighborhoods of West-Central Detroit that the Army focused on. The rest of the city was fine.

Aaron Jones and his friends didn't watch the news or listen to the radio. They were too busy. They had a lucrative job to do, and it took every night of the past week to perform.

They had a list of twenty-five addresses programmed into their phones. They didn't know it, but there were twenty other crews just like them—all with lists of addresses programmed into their phones.

Half of the houses they hit were abandoned. Others appeared to be lived in, especially in the suburbs, like here in Sterling Heights and Utica. These houses were all occupied.

They had it down pat now. They needn't torch the entire place. Just enough to do damage. They quickly learned to aim for the roof. Fires on the roof that burned long enough would mean that the whole house would be condemned. That was the key. And, if there was anyone inside, it gave them enough time to get out. At least that was the thought.

In their van, they had several gas cans, loads of oily rags, and hundreds of empty glass beer and soda bottles. There were so many glass bottles that the unlucky kids in the back had barely any place to sit. Or breathe, for that matter. The fumes were overpowering. When they got to an address, they filed out, filled up, lit up two Molotov cocktails each, and firebombed the roof. If they had time and the house appeared vacant, they bombed all sides of the house.

Then they climbed back in the van and drove to their next address. The whole process took thirty to sixty seconds. If they were seen, which was rare, no one could identify them or even get a license plate due to the speed with which they operated. Most people questioned what they saw, because it happened so fast. But the fires soon confirmed that what they'd seen wasn't a dream.

They started work on the first night that the curfew was lifted. They hit three houses that night, and Xavier nearly set himself on fire at one point. They were paid $1,000 per house, and so each night they tried to hit more. They got up to ten per night, and they were making money hand over fist.

Each of the twenty crews averaged seven houses a night. In ten nights, they torched 1,400 homes. The Averys contributed only a few of the crews. The rest came from other groups throughout the city that, together, comprised the Motown Mafia: the Brightmoor Boyz, the Corktown Crew, the Barton McFarland Gang, and others—even factions of the Grand River Gees. Fred and Frankie Auletta put ten of their own crews on the job, and enlisted groups they'd done business with in the past.

Twenty crews grew to fifty. The Santacroces even flew in crews from Philadelphia and Brooklyn. Ten fires the first night grew to an average of 140 fires by end of the first week. It was 250 a night by end of the second week, and 500 a night by the end of the third week.

The Army, police, and federal law enforcement agencies were entirely focused on restoring order to West-Central Detroit. By the time the fires caused them to take notice, the gangs had already set fire to 40,000 buildings.

~ ~ ~

Alex Cooley sat in his office, looking over the first of twelve new vanilla folders on his desk. Twelve new folders meant twelve new fires. All in the same week. It was crazy.

That meant twelve more—*twelve more!*—tedious multi-page insurance forms that he had to fill out. It had been a busy week, and the work continued to pile up. *So many fires.*

Outside his window, Alex could see the Ambassador Bridge in the distance. Helicopters buzzed around the bridge and the two cities it connected. Thousands more people had converged on the bridge to cross the river into Canada. It was strange that so many people were still fleeing the city.

It was weird to see the Army everywhere but, except for that, everything was pretty much back to normal. The unrest had ended, and that somehow opened the floodgates. The riots in Detroit might have been the catalyst, but Americans were now fleeing to Canada in droves.

It was all over the news. The government of Canada was teetering. Conservatives railed in Parliament against "illegal" American immigration, a crisis on the border. And it wasn't just the Ambassador Bridge anymore. The Blue Water Bridge in Port Huron was also swamped with American refugees. Regular commercial and non-commercial traffic had completely ceased as refugees from Detroit—"false refugees," according to prominent conservatives in Canada—overwhelmed the Canadian border stations.

American conservative media were equally vitriolic about the refugees—and Canada. "What a laughable irony," taunted the bombastic George Bruttale on Alex's computer. "Even liberal Canada doesn't want American liberals!" he snorted. And, in the next breath he applauded the refugees. "A brilliant idea," he thundered. "Yes, go to Canada! Take your Hollywood with you! Take your Starbucks, your lattes, your electric cars! Take it all with you! And don't let the door hit your liberal asses on your way out!"

Alex heard a commotion in the hallway. He got up from his desk to see what was going on.

A group of twenty men in suits, the leaders gray-haired and austere, stormed into the executive suite, some marching straight into Donnie Tillman's office.

After a few minutes, a grave-looking Donnie Tillman emerged from his office with the men.

"Everyone, these gentlemen are with the FDIC, the Federal Deposit Insurance Corporation," said Donnie. "I've been informed that…"

Alex's mind drifted. Just a week ago, PIG, or Pontchartrain Insurance Group, collapsed and was seized by the federal government. The week before that it was the Motor City Insurance Group. Forty thousand fires was too much. Motor City and Pontchartrain insured many of those buildings.

The collapse of the insurance companies left tens of thousands of home and business owners with no insurance to cover their losses. And, with their houses and businesses burned to the ground or damaged to the point of condemnation, they were no longer paying their mortgages. That meant trouble for local banks like Apex Superior and Pleasant Peninsula. Even worse, the local housing market was collapsing. Housing prices across Metropolitan Detroit were now in freefall.

The FDIC was here to seize the bank. Alex and his fellow executives, with the exception of the bank president, vice president, and the executive administrative assistant, were escorted to the exit by the men in suits. They could only gather their coats. Everything else was left "as is," even Alex's computer with George Bruttale streaming vitriol from its speakers.

Alex and his friends stood on the sidewalk outside the Pleasant Peninsula Bank building. They were stunned and, as of now, unemployed.

Chapter 27

Aaron Jones and his friends drove to the next house on their list.

Xavier was driving.

The homes on this block were single-story ranchers, a thousand square feet on average. They rode in a rusty Ford Econoline van on loan from Freddie's Garage and Auto Parts, its vehicle identification number tags ground out. The license plates were no longer valid. They could not be traced back to Freddie's.

It was early morning, and most of the suburban neighborhood was just starting to stir. Adults were getting ready for work, and kids were readying for school. Xavier stopped in front of the house, and then backed into the short driveway.

The friends piled out of the van, took up stations around the house, lit their Molotov cocktails, and heaved them onto the roof. Four separate fires flared with a *whoosh,* and black smoke rose into the air. The four young men returned to the van where each one grabbed another rag-stuffed bottle. They lit up the bottles and threw them into the windows before scrambling back into the van.

Xavier was careful to pull out slowly, as they had been told to do by Mr. Avery. So far, they'd had no trouble with this project. They alone accounted for more than 200 fires over the course of three weeks.

They'd heard that some other crews had been busted, so Aaron and his friends were extra careful—at first. During the first week, they worked only at night, but they became more daring with time, starting before sunset and ending after sunrise, like now.

Warren Police Sergeant Adam Davis, driving east on 13 Mile, noticed a wisp of black smoke rising above the rooftops of the suburban tract housing to his right. At first, he dismissed it, thinking the smoke was birds, but it soon became clear that there was a fire nearby.

There had been a number of fires in the Warren area, so Adam turned into the neighborhood and tried to determine where it was coming from. He turned onto a street and sped up, passing an old van driving in the opposite direction.

He made eye contact with the driver. It was a young black kid, probably not even twenty. He looked nervous, and so did the kid in the passenger seat.

A few seconds later, Adam saw the fire.

~ ~ ~

Xavier giggled, nervously. "Oh, my God," he said in a high-pitched voice. "That was so close!" He repeatedly peered into the rearview and side view mirrors, making sure the police car hadn't turned around. "The dude looked right at me."

"Maybe we should wait until tonight," offered Aaron in the back, "you know, to be safe."

"What's next?" asked Xavier as Devin scrolled to the next

address. It was in Harper Woods, to the southeast, which they could hit on the way home.

"Okay," said Xavier. "We'll go back and wait for tonight, but we can get one more on the way."

That seemed reasonable.

Xavier turned southbound onto Schoenherr Road. A few minutes later, they were eastbound on 7 Mile, following the directions of the GPS on Xavier's phone to Harper Woods. A Detroit Police car sped up from behind and turned on its emergency lights and siren. It pulled directly behind the van.

"Oh, *shit,*" exclaimed Xavier, "where did *he* come from?" Everyone scrambled to get a peek of the police car behind them.

"What do I do?" asked Xavier, his heart jumping in his chest.

"Go, man, *go!"* said Devin.

"No way, man, pull over!" shouted Aaron.

Xavier gunned it.

The van leapt forward and sped east on 7 Mile, which turned southeast and became Moross Road as they crossed into Harper Woods. No matter. Detroit police were officially in hot pursuit. They followed the van into the suburban township.

More than one siren screamed in the near distance now. They were had.

Xavier turned right onto a residential street. He took the

turn too fast, and the van side-swiped a parked car, sending the van careening to the right and flipping it onto its side. It slid across the road and slammed into another parked car.

Aaron, soaked in gasoline and gagging on the fumes, scrambled out of the back of the van on his hands and knees amid the broken bottles. Reggie, bloodied, was right behind him, limping and coughing.

Several police cars, sirens screaming and lights flashing, came around the corner and screeched to a halt.

Aaron reached back to help Reggie out of the van when, in a sudden *whoosh,* flames engulfed the van, knocking Aaron backward on his haunches.

Reggie, like Aaron, was covered in gasoline, and flames enveloped him. He emitted a blood-curdling scream, waving his arms and staggering toward Aaron.

Aaron, horrified, sat and stared up at Reggie, his eyes wide and mouth agape.

Reggie lurched toward him, and Aaron scrambled away, knowing that he, too, would erupt in fire if Reggie touched got too close.

Aaron turned his back on his screaming friend and ran. He sprinted across the front lawn of a house and into the backyard as Reggie wailed behind him.

Aaron tried to put distance between himself and the police as quickly as possible.

After the van flipped, Xavier wound up on top of Devin.

"You okay, man?" asked Xavier as he frantically untangled

himself from Devin and kicked out what remained of the windshield.

Devin didn't respond. When Xavier looked at him, the fact that he was dead didn't register, despite the contortion of his body, the unnatural tilt of his head, the staring eyes, and the alarming amount of blood streaming from his nose and mouth.

With all the adrenaline flowing through Xavier's veins, he didn't notice that Devin's body was caught in the van's remains. So he reached under Devin's armpits and pulled, nearly ripping the kid's clothes off as he dragged the body from the wreckage.

He also didn't notice the half dozen cops shouting commands and aiming their pistols at him.

As Devin's body came free of the wreckage, the van erupted in flames. Xavier dragged Devin from the van and heard Reggie's screams. He looked to the back of the van and saw someone stagger into the street, engulfed in flames, before collapsing in the middle of the road. He knew it had to be either Reggie or Aaron.

Movement from his right caught his attention for the first time. It was the police, lined up in a semi-circle, all of them aiming guns at him. Their faces were contorted as they shouted commands, but Xavier just stood there, stupefied. He couldn't hear a single word, just his own heart beating loudly in his ears.

Xavier was also unaware that he was holding a handgun in his right hand the whole time, even as he dragged Devin from the wreckage. He'd seen it on the floor and picked it up without thinking.

Xavier laid Devin's lifeless body on the pavement and stood up, still gripping the gun. He was met with a hail of bullets. The autopsy would later reveal that he had been shot twenty-six times.

~ ~ ~

Aaron ran and ran, fueled by adrenaline. He ran from front yards to backyards, again and again. He stumbled across a high school—a mile away—in just seven minutes. School was about to start, and kids were everywhere. Aaron stopped running and tried to blend in, but he smelled strongly of gasoline.

He tried to act nonchalant, just a kid walking to school. He remembered his cell phone and pulled it out. It was intact.

He called Michelle. When she answered, he burst into tears. "Reggie's dead," he told her.

"Whaaat?" asked Michelle, thinking he was somehow joking. But he was crying. She had never seen or heard Aaron cry.

He told her everything. About how Jayson Avery and his organization hired him and his friends. About the house fires.

About Reggie catching on fire and how there was nothing he could do to save him. About Reggie's screams.

"What about Xavier and Devin?" asked Michelle.

"I don't know," sobbed Aaron. "I ... I think I heard gunshots."

A helicopter made a wide circle above, but he didn't think they were circling *him*. It looked to be circling the site of the crash. Probably looking for him, though. "I'm *scared*," Aaron said. "What am I going to do?"

"Call Mr. Avery!" Michelle offered. "I mean, it sounds like he had a plan in case something like this happened, in case you got busted."

"I don't know." .

"How are you going to get home with the police looking for you! Do you even know where you are?"

"Uh, no," said Aaron, sniffling, looking around. A street sign said "Kelly," and headed toward a cluster of long-abandoned storefronts.

"Call him! And be safe, please! Call me right back."

"Okay," Aaron sighed, and hung up. He dropped back among the abandoned stores, momentarily seized by panic. A police car was coming down the street.

When it passed, Aaron exhaled a deep, trembling sigh of relief. It was a taxi. Then he dialed the number that Jayson Avery had given each of them.

"Yo," someone answered.

"This is Aaron Jones. Reggie is dead and I don't know what happened to Devin and Xavier." He burst into tears all over again.

"Stop," said the voice. "Stay where you are. Mr. Avery will call you." The man hung up.

Within a few minutes, his phone buzzed. The number was restricted. "Hello?" asked Aaron.

"Yo, Mr. Jones," said a familiar baritone voice. It was Jayson Avery.

"Mr. Avery, I don't know what to do." He told Jayson everything that had happened.

"Listen, Aaron," said Jayson. "Take a deep breath. Tell me where you are."

"I'm on Kelly Street," said Aaron, "and … there's a church. I don't see a sign. I think it's abandoned."

"Okay, I'll find it," said Jayson. "Stay put, stay calm, and stay out of sight," he ordered before hanging up.

Aaron wiped his nose and held his phone, staring at it. He felt better. Mr. Avery was going to make things right. He called Michelle back.

"He's coming," he said.

"Oh, thank God," said Michelle. "You sound better."

"I can't believe Reggie is gone." He started crying again.

"I'll stop by your house later. Hang in there, and stay out of sight until Mr. Avery gets there."

"Okay," said Aaron. "I love you."

Michelle chuckled.

"What?" he asked earnestly.

"Just, you've never said that before." Aaron could practically *hear* her smile through the phone, and it made him feel good. "I love you, too," Michelle said before hanging up.

Aaron stayed hidden behind brown shrubbery. In the summer, the shrubbery would be green, lush, and wild. He peeked out whenever he heard a car coming, but he was careful to not reveal himself, fearing the police.

Thirty minutes passed before he spotted a black SUV coming down the street. He stood up, but then ducked behind the shrubbery. It might be a police SUV.

The vehicle sped up, and then stopped in front of the shrubbery.

"Yo, Mr. Jones!" yelled the familiar, baritone voice. It was Mr. Avery, after all. Aaron stepped out from the shrubbery. Jayson Avery was in the back seat, waving Aaron over. Aaron recognized the driver as Elijah Freeman.

Aaron jogged to the Cadillac Escalade and returned Jayson's smile with his own—a shy smile of gratitude.

A single gunshot to the sternum sent the slender teenager reeling backward, tackled to the pavement by an invisible force. A violent spasm jolted his body.

Jayson got out of his car and briefly stood over the boy. The kid's eyes were open wide with surprise and then dulled into a smoldering, empty stare. He was dead, his arms splayed out over his head. Blood pooled on the street beneath him. Jayson knelt beside him and fished out the boy's cell phone from his pocket. He shot him again to be sure he was dead, and then climbed back into the car. Elijah drove off, morosely eyeing the body in the rearview mirror.

~ ~ ~

Adrian vomited after feeling for a pulse on the young private's neck. The kid was unnaturally pale, and his skin had shriveled. The amount of blood that had poured out of him was unimaginable. There was no escaping the fact that he was dead, and his death was nothing like on TV or in the movies. It was ugly and unclean.

Adrian and two other soldiers stood vigil over the corpse as their unit continued taking fire from a sniper or snipers in the abandoned Dynasty Furniture Building a few blocks west. Every time someone moved, a gunshot echoed loudly amid the flashy but sad-looking fast food joints and dilapidated industrial buildings.

The private's body lay on the gasoline station's grease- and oil-stained tarmac, which was strewn with trash. Adrian watched as a pool of blood from the dead private seeped across the parking lot and enveloped a cigarette butt with lipstick on it.

They waited a long time. The silence and stillness among the soldiers, all hidden behind cover, left an eerie pall over the already dystopian landscape.

The screech of a jet followed by a *KA-BOOM,* as if in exclamation, broke the eerie silence and marked the destruction of the Dynasty Furniture building. Hidden soldiers hooted and applauded. One of the soldiers with Adrian peeked around the gas station's convenience store and saw nothing but smoke and dust where the building once stood.

"I think it's gone," said the soldier.

"Target neutralized," said a voice over the radio, confirming the soldier's observation.

A Humvee with a bright red cross on its doors pulled into the gas station. Medics went to work on the private, largely out of protocol, given that he was obviously dead. Soldiers, meanwhile, came out from behind cover. They seemed to be everywhere all at once.

"Contact, contact!" someone shouted. The soldiers once again scrambled for cover.

Adrian and his squad took shelter between an outdoor Kentucky Fried Chicken Drive-thru menu and the restaurant's building, laying prone on the ground. Adrian could see that crowds of people had gathered on the boulevard in front of them, probably drawn by the airstrike.

It was Livernois Avenue that stretched before Adrian and his squad, and the crowds gathering along its sidewalks and center island had that hard look on their faces. Young people darted onto the roadway as far as he could see, dragging tires and debris and setting the pyres on fire.

Detroit was stirring again.

A Humvee sped ahead of the troops, and stopped a half-mile up the road. Adrian could hear a bullhorn barking orders to the crowds, but he couldn't hear what it was saying.

The crowds appeared unmoved. No one seemed to be leaving.

Adrian looked back at a group of officers hunkered around a Humvee, with a radio and a street map laid out on the hood. They seemed hesitant about what to do with the crowds. Two miles to their right, they could hear that the gun battle was still raging.

Adrian and his squad mates remained prone on the ground. Waiting. The officers presumably were communicating with the head honcho, General McIntyre. After a while, the officers began issuing orders.

They were going into battle, it seemed, but they would have to wait a little while longer.

Nearly an hour later, a large low-flying cargo plane, a gray Army C-130, passed overhead, startling Adrian. He watched as it banked hard to the right. A steady stream of *something* poured out the back of the airplane. Papers, Adrian realized. They floated down en masse, fluttering all over the neighborhoods.

~ ~ ~

Bernice Hamandawana was awakened by the pre-dawn car bomb, and had immediately known what it was. It sounded just like the first one the day before and, like that one, her apartment shook so hard that she thought the building might come down. Within minutes, there was a pounding on her door. It was her friend and fellow journalism student Daniel Rush. He brought his camera.

Bernice threw her clothes on, grabbed her cellphone and book bag, and met Daniel outside. Her nostrils were assaulted by a bitter smell, and the sky glowed orange to the west of her.

"What's going, Daniel?"

"Don't know. I think it was another car bomb."

"Let's go," Bernice said, and the two began a brisk walk. As they walked, the unmistakable sound of automatic gunfire in the distance punctuated a growing cacophony of sirens near and far. They both instinctively stopped and dropped down.

"Whoa," whispered Daniel, "*that's* new."

They picked themselves up and renewed the brisk pace. As they approached Grand Boulevard in the heart of New Center, several police cars whisked by at high speed, sirens blaring and emergency lights flashing. Two fire trucks, moving not much slower, followed. Daniel, his camera held up to eye level, captured the police and fire vehicles as they sped past.

Bernice and Daniel had to dart across the boulevard. More vehicles— Army Humvees and trucks—were approaching fast. A sea of flashing lights and Army vehicles filled the boulevard about a mile away. A few blocks to behind them was the scene of the first bomb. Incredibly, the second bomb also appeared to be on Grand Boulevard.

Sirens from more police cars hurt their ears as they, too, sped by. Daniel grabbed Bernice's arm and was saying something, but she couldn't hear him.

"What?" she shouted.

"That guy is calling you!" he yelled over the sirens, nodding to somewhere across the street. Bernice followed his gaze to where several people stood watching the commotion, some dressed in night gowns and robes despite the cold air. With them was a man wearing jeans and a tweed sports coat, waving his arms.

It was Walter Clay.

"Walter!" Bernice yelled.

Bernice and Daniel ran across the street to Walter, who briefly hugged each of them.

"Daniel, good to see you again, my man," he said with a hug after greeting Bernice. "Should've known you'd be out here covering this mess."

"What's going on?" asked Bernice as Daniel turned his attention to filming the passing emergency vehicles. "Another car bomb?"

"Looks like it, and now it sounds like a war is going on down there," Walter said.

The police and fire departments were closing off the boulevard, so they decided to take a longer, alternate route to the scene.

It was a leisurely walk. The sky was a vibrant red and orange as the sun peeked over the southeastern horizon. The gunfire had largely subsided, but there was a distinctive single shot that occurred every minute or so, echoing off the buildings as they walked. When they approached the Seward Street bridge over the M-10, they found it blocked by police, so they continued north to the next crossing at Euclid Street. It was also blocked, and so they trudged on. A pedestrian-only bridge at Pingree Street was clear, so they crossed there. As they walked over the M-10, Daniel filmed the highway from the pedestrian bridge. An Army convoy was passing beneath. Daniel could see two bridges to their north, each of which was occupied by an Army M-1 Abrams tank, their turrets pointing west into the Virginia Parks neighborhood.

Their cell phones buzzed with an official alert. The Army had declared a State of Emergency for Central Detroit, and the city was officially on lockdown. A U.S. Army operation was underway, the alert read, and warned residents to stay indoors.

As if on cue, a single F-35B Lightning II stealth fighter roared high in the sky. Daniel panned his camera to follow the plane. Daniel lost it behind rooftops and a billboard, but he could hear its roar like a scratch in his ear.

"Oh shit!" Daniel exclaimed. A roiling gray mushroom cloud filled his lenses and lifted angrily some distance behind the rooftops. A massive *BANG* followed, shaking the bridge they stood on.

"Holy shit!" Daniel exclaimed again, "that was an airstrike!"

"Tell me you got that," said Bernice.

"Hell, yeah!"

After Daniel uploaded his brief video to the free and independent newspaper *Motown Mirror,* Wayne State's *The South End* student newspaper, and various social networks, the three of them jogged across the bridge for a better view, but none was to be had. The airstrike was too far away. So they did their best to follow the dissipating gray cloud. Another, muffled *bang* reverberated through the air, but this one was much farther away. Was it another airstrike? If it was, it was too far away for them to immediately investigate, so they turned their attention back to the first one.

After an hour of walking they were closer, but the gray dust cloud had drifted away, and a low-hanging shroud of dust had spread over a wide area. They still couldn't pinpoint the location of the airstrike. Another loud aircraft made them turn their heads up to the sky, and Daniel captured the low-flying C-130 as it unloaded its cargo of flyers.

It wasn't until they were six blocks north of Grand Boulevard that Walter noticed the unusually jagged top of the Lee Plaza Building. In fact, the top few floors of the red brick building were practically gone, reducing the building's height by a third.

Daniel zoomed in with his camera while Bernice recorded an impromptu on-location report.

After uploading her report, the three students turned their attention to the throngs of people walking south, many dragging suitcases on wheels. It was clear that they were evacuating as ordered.

~ ~ ~

The massive overnight car bomb was less than half a mile from the long abandoned St. Agnes Catholic Church on the corner of South La Salle Gardens and Rosa Parks Boulevard. St. Agnes had once hosted Mother Theresa during a visit to Detroit in 1979. In recent years, a revolving door of up to fifteen young artists and musicians had taken up residence in the church as squatters, using the wide open spaces as art studios and theaters.

LeRon "The People's Mayor" Gordon was among the current residents. He had met his current girlfriend, Rachel Lamont, there. She sketched and painted. LeRon wrote poetry and rapped out lyrics.

After the explosion rattled the old church, nine young artists, including LeRon and Rachel, kept wary eyes on the ceiling and walls. They were unsure if the grand high ceiling of the nave could absorb the abuse.

Then the jackhammer gunfire began, amplified by the church's open space. The young artists joined in on an impromptu rap, led by LeRon, in an effort to drown out the gunfire.

The war outside
A shiver down my spine
This old rickety church
A black birch
My sanctuary, my Hail Mary

Enough for LeRon to scribble down what he could to keep up as they took turns sketching out verses on the fly. And so it went on through the night until sunlight filtered into the nave from the high cathedral windows that still remained.

The constant barrage of gunfire had largely died down, but it didn't go away completely. Fits of machine gun fire would flare up into sessions of various lengths even after the sun had risen.

The gunfire was close, that much was certain but, as dawn drew into the latter hours of morning, the young artists ventured out into the neighborhood.

For LeRon, it was like stepping out into a war zone after a bomb had gone off. A bomb *had* gone off, and it *was* a war-zone, he had to remind himself. Papers fluttered around all over the streets and in the air. LeRon had seen that before, on the internet. In videos of the 9/11 terrorist attacks in New York City years before he was born, papers fluttered in the air and clogged the streets. It was one of the images that stuck with him.

Looking down at the papers gathering in the street gutters, he could see that there were at least two different flyers. One of the artists picked up one of each and the others gathered around to read over his shoulder. One flyer said that they had to evacuate the neighborhood. The other flyer had wanted photos of nine people on both sides. The largest photo was of Dmitri Johnson, the freeway killer.

No one spoke. The young artist that picked up the flyers let them go, and the wind took them away. The kid walked away without a word and seemingly without a care in the world.

"Are we in the evacuation zone?" asked Rachel, grabbing LeRon's arm with both hands and pulling herself into him.

"Guess so," said LeRon, "we black, ain't we?"

"What do we do?" asked Rachel.

LeRon's eyes went distant. He sat on the curb and pulled a ragged notebook from his shabby book bag. Rachel sat beside him, resting her chin on his shoulder as he wrote.

> *Exacerbate*
> *Infuriate*
> *Discriminate*
> *Annihilate*
> *Invalidate*
> *Premeditate*
> *EVACUATE*

"Seriously, LeRon?" said Rachel, smiling.

LeRon heard sirens as the backdrop to the lyrics.

"An artist *documents,* baby," he said.

"Where are we going to go?" she asked. LeRon didn't answer.

A pickup with several men, armed with machine guns, tore past LeRon and Rachel. One of the men in the truck bed flashed a "V" sign and a big smile.

LeRon and Rachel were too close to the gathering troops and police to head south. So they walked north, in the direction of the pickup truck, unsure of where they were going.

As they walked north along Rosa Parks Boulevard, they ran into friends and acquaintances. LeRon was a minor celebrity of sorts. Bernice Hamandawana's filmed interaction with him ("they're lining up against us") during the initial GLEE protest had gone viral. Various DJs added beats to his rhyme. The unkempt hair, toothy grin, and charisma of "The People's Mayor" generated more than ten millions views.

The boulevard, meanwhile, was crowded with people and car traffic heading in the opposite direction. The car traffic thickened into bumper-to-bumper, barely moving vehicle traffic. Some people on foot pulled suitcases on wheels, and some dragged little red children's wagons stuffed with belongings, with children in tow. The boulevard was strewn with the flyers dropped by the C-130, and many residents were taking heed.

Some of their friends were among those that were evacuating. Others were staying. In fact, most people seemed to be either standing around or wandering about as though it were a big block party. One of their friends—more like an acquaintance, really—was a brooding kid, seemingly older than his nineteen years. The neighborhood did that.

The kid was Lamar Griffin. He stood among an armed and tragically dangerous-looking group of kids. An assault rifle was slung over his shoulder. "The People's Mayor," he said, nodding to LeRon and Rachel. "How's it going, Mister Mayor?"

"Not bad, little nomad," LeRon answered. "What's up with the guns, shogun?" LeRon asked.

"Do you want to die?" added Rachel in her child-like earnest way.

Lamar lit a cigarette and studied her and LeRon while he inhaled. Both of their faces were open and sincere, like always, and devoid of sarcasm or edge. After a moment, Lamar, his face impassive, exhaled a cloud of smoke and answered. "This ain't living."

After more walking, someone waved their arms and yelled "LeRon!"

 It was Walter Clay and the two journalism students. LeRon flashed a grin and, when they approached, hugged each of them.

And, of course, he rapped.

A brotherhood, a sisterhood
in my neighborhood.

Chapter 28

Antonio Gonzales and his squad mates waited no longer. It was almost noon, and the crowds gathered along Livernois had not dissipated. Instead, they grew larger. Pyres of tires and trash were burning everywhere.

It was time.

An M-1 Abrams tank roared to life, drove to the intersection of Burlingame Street, and stopped. Anthony and his squad were directed to the next street, residential Woodside Street, which stretched for only three blocks. Squads ahead of them stormed homes on either side of the street. Anthony and his squad stormed the third house on their left. It was boarded-up, so they smashed through with a battering ram, sweeping through the dark, spooky house as fast as they could.

They had to be fast, but also careful. The floorboards creaked under their feet, and they weren't certain they wouldn't fall through, especially when they went upstairs. Finding no one in the house, they painted a bright orange "X" on the board that stood in place of a front window, indicating that the house had been swept and cleared.

Antonio and his squad mates walked briskly to their next assigned house.

General McIntyre had ordered a full-on assault on the neighborhood adjoining the two firefights, the one on Grand River Avenue marking its western border, and the one on Grand Boulevard marking its south.

Soldiers cordoned off West-Central Detroit from I-96 in the west to I-75 in the east to the M-10 in the north and I-94 in the south. Pretty much all of Central Detroit, save for downtown.

The President had given McIntyre full authorization to neutralize the so-called Motown Mafia by any means necessary. She wanted Detroit out of the headlines *yesterday*.

That made things easier for McIntyre and his army. It was now a matter of cold and methodical execution.

Soldiers surged south of Grand Boulevard into the six blocks in New Center between Grand Boulevard to I-94, and into the troubled Northwest Goldberg neighborhood between West Grand Boulevard and I-94.

They faced mild resistance in New Center as they went door to door. Soldiers encountered several gang members who didn't seem to understand the gravity of the situation. They refused orders as soldiers stormed their homes. On two occasions, a young gangster flashed a pistol—only to be cut down by soldiers in CBQ assaults. A third had an AR-15 semi-assault rifle slung over his shoulder, which he aimed at the soldiers as they rushed through the front door. He couldn't even get his trigger hand on the grip before a precision shot to his forehead and sternum flipped him backward like an acrobat. He was dead before he hit the floor. Soldiers stormed past the body with barely a glance.

As Northwest Goldberg was being cleared, protecting his southern flank, Major Hernandez led his men north into La-Salle Gardens. Here, Hernandez and the men faced immediate resistance.

In addition to the Army's two Kiowa reconnaissance helicopters flying above the area of operation, an Air Force MQ-9 Reaper flew high above the city to monitor the ground operations. The air surveillance teams found two primary areas of concern. The first was the LaSalle Garden neighborhood bordering all of Grand Boulevard, where Major Hernandez was deployed. Hundreds of young men, armed with rifles, wandered into and out of homes. There appeared to be a degree of coordination.

The second area of concern was along Livernois Avenue, but whether the hundreds of people gathered along the street were armed or not could not be determined. The units assigned to the north would find out soon enough.

Major Hernandez's forces advanced into the first block north of Grand Boulevard. An M-1 Abrams tank drove into LaSalle Gardens on Linwood Street, taking up station at the intersection of Linwood and LaSalle Gardens Avenue. They immediately began taking small arms fire. At first, it was hard to determine where the shooting was coming from; it seemed to come from almost every house.

A second Abrams tank lurched along Linwood, and stopped. Its machine gun opened fire on a house where muzzle flashes had been seen. At another house—this one abandoned—young men streamed out, taking positions behind other homes and parked cars. The Abrams' turret lowered, took aim, and fired a round with an earth-shaking *bang.*

The entire ramshackle Sears catalog house disappeared in a cloud of dust and splinters.

The tanks and soldiers behind laid down relentless fire as other soldiers advanced. Then, they would lay down fire as the soldiers behind them advanced. And so on.

Hernandez's company advanced in methodical fashion. Yet the gangsters continued to lay down fire of their own, and they appeared to be coordinated. They, too, moved as fire teams.

In the command trailer, General McIntyre watched live video from the Reaper as a convoy of tanks penetrated the Dexter-Linwood neighborhood, and took up positions at major intersections. The tanks fired their machine guns sporadically as the Army opened what was essentially a third front in the center of the evacuation zone. Convoys of troop carriers joined the tanks and discharged soldiers into the fight. Two separate companies were advancing into the neighborhoods, closing in like a vise.

It won't be long now.

~ ~ ~

Caleb Sessions lived six blocks north of the second car bomb attack in a colonial manor on a leafy portion of LaSalle Boulevard. Caleb bought the large home with cash two years prior. Today, it was crowded with multiple crews that had descended on Caleb's home after the car bomb shook the neighborhood.

In the morning, when one of his soldiers handed him a leaflet dropped by the C-130 with Dmitri and his picture on it, Caleb was stoic. Word came that Dmitri was holed up with one of his girlfriends a few blocks east.

Caleb and his crew walked over.

They found Dmitri's crews hunkered down. Several were bloodied from engaging with Army troops during the pre-dawn hours. Soldiers for Dmitri alerted him that Caleb and his crew had joined them.

Dmitri finished a rock of meth, passed the small bag to a soldier, and went outside to greet Caleb. When he saw him, Caleb's face was impassive and his demeanor deceptively humble. Dmitri could see it. He instinctively knew.

Caleb held his out hand and projected his shoulder for a bro-hug.

Dmitri shot him in the face.

~ ~ ~

Caleb's crew was caught entirely by surprise. Neverthe-less, they raised their rifles before Caleb's body even hit the ground. In turn, Dmitri's crew raised theirs. It was a Mex-ican standoff. If just one person pulled the trigger, a mael-strom of bullets would ensue, spelling everyone's demise.

"*I'm* the boss!" shouted Dmitri, shoving Logan aside and walking to a member of Caleb's crew. "*I'm* the boss," he shouted again, standing in front of the gangster's gun bar-rel. "*I'm* the man," he shouted, pounding his chest.

Logan, seventeen years old but going on forty, was numb. He could still hear the sound of that brick in Dmitri's hand as it hit the young white man's head, and now Dmitri pranced about again as he did then, pounding his chest, daring any-one to challenge him. He pulled out a pistol and held it to the head of the youngest member of Caleb's crew.

"*Hey, hey,*" a member of Caleb's crew pleaded. Everyone

adjusted their grip on their rifles as fear and adrenaline spiked among them.

"I'm the boss," Dmitri yelled again. *"Me!"* he shouted again and pounded his chest. He looked around at Caleb's crew, his face snarling. "Now get your guns out of my *face,* mutha-fuckers!"

Slowly, one by one, Caleb's crew lowered their rifles. When the last one lowered his gun, Dmitri lowered his pistol. Then, he immediately raised it again and shot the boy in the head. His eyes flared wide with madness and a deranged smile spread across his face after he pulled the trigger.

Before anyone could react, Logan raised his rifle behind Dmitri and shot him between the shoulder blades.

Everyone froze. Dmitri went ramrod straight and slowly turned around, blood drooling out of his mouth and down his chin. He faced Logan. *"You!"* he spit, his face contorted in anger and disbelief. He walked chest-first into the barrel of Logan's rifle, forcing Logan to take a step back. *"You!"* he sneered again. He tried to raise his pistol to Logan's face.

But Logan fired once, twice, three times, straight into Dmitri's chest, and Dmitri cartwheeled backward to the ground, his body rolling over limply to land face up. His back arched and a volcano of blood burst out of his mouth, painting his entire face red. The body deflated, then sank to the ground. It quivered and went still, the eyes bulging.

Several gang members of both crews stood mesmerized, gawking at Dmitri's body as if not believing that was really dead. But the spell was broken as more gunfire erupted.

The U.S. Army had begun its operation. Soldiers advanced west into the LaSalle Gardens neighborhood and fired on the armed River Gees gathered around the body of Dmitri Johnson. Several gang members fell dead or wounded in the initial barrage. Logan ran for cover between two houses, firing haphazardly over his shoulder at the advancing soldiers. It was kill or be killed.

He didn't make it. Before reaching cover between houses, a bullet tore through the middle of his back. He stumbled into another retreating gangster, and both went sprawling to the ground. The kid looked over at Logan, He was stretched out, dead, his eyes locked on the young gang member with a look surprise etched on his face. The kid tore his eyes away from Logan's body and scrambled to his feet. He was immediately cut down by another volley of gunfire.

Soldiers ran past the bodies of Logan and the young gang member and advanced deeper into LaSalle Gardens.

~ ~ ~

Bernice and Daniel interviewed dozens of evacuees as Walter, LeRon, and Rachel took turns holding the camera. The sound of gunfire in the distance had marked the start of the Army operation. Walter pointed to the end of the street where an Army tank had turned onto the road. Is turret faced the group as it lurched forward. From behind the tank, an Army Apache gunship helicopter soared past at tree-top level.

Daniel took the camera from LeRon, and he and Bernice jogged a few yards in the direction of the oncoming tank to get a better view, careful to stick to the side of a crumbling apartment building. Daniel had his camera automatically synced with DIYtv for live streaming.

A young man casually walked into the middle of the street with an AR-15 assault rifle, He took aim, and opened fire on the soldiers advancing behind the tank.

The presence of the Army over the last few weeks, and the omnipresence of armed gang members, had normalized the sight of weapons and sounds of gunfire. For this reason, perhaps, Bernice and Daniel didn't even notice that a gang of armed men had come down the street, not until the jack-hammer sound of gunfire nearly burst their ear drums.

Everyone, including the procession of evacuees and other pedestrians, dropped to the ground as the young men took turns firing on the soldiers. When there was a pause, LeRon scrambled to his feet and ran to Rachel, who stood with her hands over her ears.

"Take me home, LeRon!" Rachel pleaded as he put his arm around her.

"Let's go, baby," he said.

Another burst of gunfire drowned out his words, and they both stumbled and fell, LeRon falling on top Rachel.

Daniel had trained his camera on one of the armed kids, who suddenly fell, along with several others, after a fresh round of gunfire.

"Oh my God!" Rachel screamed. She tried to stand, but Le-Ron, though skinny, lay heavy on her. "Oh, my God!" she screamed again, getting her feet under her and pushing at him, but she was pinned underneath the body.

"Get out of the road!" screamed Bernice.

"They killed the People's Mayor," Daniel said in a hushed voice. He could see through his lenses that LeRon was dead.

Bernice ran to LeRon and Rachel. "Bernice, no!" yelled Daniel, scrambling after her.

Bernice stumbled into the road and then tripped as exploding gravel stung her back. She slowly sat up, a long moaning sob blending with the roar in her ears. Daniel lay on the ground beside her, his face turned up, his slender body stretched out.

Daniel was looking up at her, but his eyes were fixed. There was blood on his cheek. His jacket was open and his T-shirt rested above his bony ribcage. His mouth opened and closed like a fish out of water as his pale white diaphragm flexed and released every other second.

Soldiers swarmed them, and now Bernice was face-down on the gravel, a knee in her back and her wrists tied behind her. The world turned bumpy as a truck pulled alongside and she was lifted up.

"Daniel!" she finally managed as they carried her. "Daniel!" she screamed as they dumped her into the truck. "Daniel!"

Rachel, Walter and others were bundled into the truck with Bernice. Walter sat between them, silently. Bernice and Rachel sobbed. Walter stared ahead as tears silently streamed down his bloodied face.

~ ~ ~

Soldiers surged into all areas south of Grand Boulevard. They went door to door through every single home and building. They confiscated all weapons, registered or not, and illicit drug paraphernalia, and made multiple arrests.

North of Grand Boulevard was a different story. Here, soldiers progressed street by street, house by house, pinching from the east and west. They forcibly entered each and every house and building, working their way north: Horton Street, then Custer Street, then Bethune Avenue, then Smith Street.

The Army faced heavy resistance here. Armed men seemed to occupy every standing structure.

Tanks were brought to bear on the homes and buildings—abandoned or not—from which anyone fired.

A second airstrike flattened the Dynasty Furniture Building on Grand River Avenue, where the other sniper had kept soldiers pinned down. And, since the taboo had already been broken with the first strike, several more followed. With the tanks occupied, the remaining F-35s took turns circling above the city, diving in attack when called upon.

General McIntyre was now on the clock. Rather than allow his soldiers to get bogged down by single fighters or snipers, McIntyre ordered the tanks, Apache helicopter gunships, and F-35 Lightning IIs into action. Building after building was obliterated, and the soldiers advanced unmolested.

General McIntyre leaned on the railing of the short stairway grate outside his command trailer. He heard the intermittent scratching of the F-35s ricocheting across the sky, and a constant *tat-tat-tat* of distant automatic rifle fire.

It was the sounds of war. A massive *boom* drove home the point. The command trailer and the stairway grate shook and rattled.

McIntyre stepped inside for an update.

Battalions deployed to the north were working east and south from Livernois and the M-10. They had skipped right past the Russell Woods neighborhood where there was no resistance and were moving into Petosky-Otsego.

Major Hernandez and his company worked their way from the south, engaged in house-to-house fighting from the get-go. They had largely secured LaSalle Gardens and were moving into Virginia Park.

The major had sent cell phone photos of some of the dead, confirming they had killed more than ten of the most wanted members of the Motown Mafia, including Dmitri Johnson, the freeway killer, and Caleb Sessions, who was said to be the group's co-leader, along with Dmitri.

It would all be over soon.

Streams of people, meanwhile, continued to flee the neighborhoods even as the Army moved in and battle raged on. They were forced to walk, leaving their vehicles behind. People walked solemnly, carting suitcases carrying whatever belongings they could manage. They pushed shopping carts full of belongings, and dragged toy wagons loaded with clothes and other valuables.

These were families—elderly people, children, toddlers, mothers and fathers. They suffered the indignity of letting the Army search every box, every bit of clothing, every personal belonging, and even their bodies.

It was a sad procession. It couldn't be anything but. People walked all the way to East Adams Avenue in downtown with their belongings in tow, past the tents and trailers of the Army's New Fort Detroit. They headed to the domed Ford Field, home of the NFL's Detroit Lions, where they would be temporarily housed.

Red Cross volunteers set up stations along the way, handing

out water bottles, blankets, soup, and other aid.

Much of the procession detoured southward at 14th Street, however, following a few hand-drawn signs that read "Canada this way."

~ ~ ~

President Belle watched cable news in the White House residence. The airstrikes on the Lee Plaza and Dynasty Furniture buildings in Detroit were played over and over again. It was like watching old World War II footage, except this was now, and this was in America.

"An *air strike?*" Cynthia fumed. "In Goddam *Detroit?*"

Vice President George Wartmann was folded into a leather backed chair, one leg draped over the other. He was tall and lanky, so much so that he was often referred to as "Daddy Longlegs." The moniker was either endearing and derisive, depending on which side the side of the aisle one belonged to. A long-time Senator from Ohio, Wartmann was Cynthia's conduit to Congress and also her in-house foreign policy guru.

Wartmann somehow looked comfortable in the chair despite barely fitting into it. He nursed a glass of Kentucky bourbon.

"You did authorize MacIntyre to use 'whatever means necessary,'" Daddy offered.

"I sure as hell didn't mean bombing the city! I meant deploying active-duty Army—arresting criminals, preventing looting, stopping the unrest. *Not* fucking air strikes on American soil." Cynthia shook her head in utter disbelief.

"Well, it certainly sends a message," Daddy said.

Cynthia looked to Wartmann, her eyebrows raised.

"Those soldiers were pinned down by sniper fire after a car bomb took out a slew of FBI and ATF agents. You don't fuck with federal law enforcement or the United States Army."

Cynthia paced back and forth. "News and social media are going *bonkers!* They're calling me a *Nazi.*"

"Fire him," Daddy offered. "Not right away, but as soon as this is over. And make it public."

Cynthia grunted.

"Wait. One minute you're defending him, the next you want me to *fire* him? Which is it?"

Daddy took a swig of his bourbon and smiled. It was his signature mischievous smile. "Both," he said.

"It had to be done," he continued. "MacIntyre had to lay down the gauntlet. How do you think all of this is playing in Beijing, or Moscow? To them, we undoubtedly look divided and weak. As shocking as it is—and it is quite shocking, the imagery of American air strikes on American soil—it sends the message that we aren't fucking around.

"*Firing* MacIntyre when this is over, if not sooner, reinforces a basic tenet of American democracy—that the ultimate authority of the armed forces rests with elected civilians, not military officers."

A pundit on the television ranted about how the President was unleashing the military on harmless, helpless American civilians.

Cynthia sighed.

Damned if you do, damned if you don't.

281

Chapter 29

For Ian and the students of Wright State University, surrealism had returned. Campus was on lockdown again, and, once again, classes were canceled. It was start-and-stop, and it was old already. So long ago it had all seemed kind of exciting—the first protests, the march on downtown, even the tear gas. Scary, yes, but exciting nonetheless.

For Ian, the luster had worn off long ago. Even before Roland. *Roland. That sound.* Ian fought a sudden wave of emotion as the scene played in his head one more time. The baton coming down across Roland's temple. *He never saw it coming.*

Dakota looked at Ian and smiled. Ian, Dakota, and some twenty other students stood on the roof of the Belcrest Apartments, the historic twelve-story building nestled in the northern part of the urban campus. Invited up by a more senior cross-country teammate who lived in the building, they had a clear view of the battle raging just a mile to their north across I-94 in North End, New Center, and LaSalle Gardens.

They had watched as Major Schmidt's F-35 bombed the Lee Plaza Building to their west.

Small arms fire echoed nonstop like jackhammers. Multiple Apache helicopter gunships circled the neighborhoods to the north like angry bees. Plumes of smoke dispersed across the northern horizon, rising high into the sky, each of them vigorous at their base. The air was pungently acerbic and stung the eyes.

It was all so weird; the war, of course, but even that had become old hat. The presence of so many soldiers and Army vehicles and helicopters constantly flying overhead had surprisingly become normalized so quickly. It was amazing what one could get used to.

What was truly weird was watching it all from the comfort of an apartment building roof as the war unfolded just blocks away. Like what was happening was not actually real, but some kind of intense virtual-reality video game.

But Ian and Dakota knew it was all too real, and they were leery that the Army could easily fire on *them*. They would be written off as some horrible accident—a stray rocket, a misidentification. *Oops.*

Ian was glad that Sarah, Tina, and Trevor were not here anymore. They were safe.

Ian looked out on the city, sweeping all around in a circle away from the battle in front of him to the neighborhoods stretching out to the suburbs at his left and right, and the downtown behind him, and back to the battle raging across the way. It all seemed so inevitable to him now. The Downtown and Renaissance Center, the University and Hospital District, and New Center—all little islands of glitz surrounded by a vast sea of decay.

Desolation and destitution were always around, manifest in the crumbling infrastructure, abandoned and burned homes, countless empty and unkempt lots, and the hundreds of long-abandoned and crumbling factories and retail centers, all remnants of a bygone era. Ian had grown up in the midst of economic and social artifacts. But he never actually *saw* it. It was all around him but kind of invisible, hidden in plain sight.

Perhaps it was Romanesque, the abandoned factories and stores and homes not unlike the ruins that dot the landscape throughout Rome and Italy. Maybe. But it was jarringly contemporary. The blight was more than the relics of a bygone era. People lived amid the crumble. It was slow-motion economic and social collapse. Modern ruins of a faded, and fading, American empire.

Ian looked east where, on the horizon, he could see a line of filled-in spaces of dense housing and trees that marked the end of Detroit and the beginning of the affluent burg of Grosse Pointe Park, and the other Grosse Pointes beyond. That line was Alter Road.

Alter Road is perhaps the most startling boundary between neighboring communities anywhere in America. It's not only a political boundary, but also an economic and social boundary between the mostly poor and black City of Detroit, and the mostly white and largely affluent townships of the Grosse Pointe. The stark contrast between Detroit and the Grosse Pointes that Alter Road etched in the ground was startling. The America beyond Alter Road was the America of television and movies, the America of news and social media, the America of dreams. But there was another America this side of Alter Road. An Alter America of abandonment and have-nots.

A flash and debris tossed high into the air caused Ian to flinch and duck, followed by a massive *bang* that shook the building.

It was another airstrike.

~ ~ ~

William Coventry, Esquire, sat at the large oak desk in his oak furniture-filled office at the Standard & King Investment House in Baltimore's historic Mt. Vernon district. S&K was housed in a modest brick building on the corner of Charles and Madison Streets, with a direct view of the Washington Monument.

"Come in," said William after a soft rap on his oak door. It was his nephew, Charles "Carlo," who quietly stepped into the room, closing the door behind him. He was young, trim, blonde-haired and tanned, the Hollywood ideal of a sun-kissed All-American Californian.

And he was a Coventry.

William liked his young nephew. He was a recent graduate of Harvard's Department of Economics. Although he didn't excel there, he did the work that was necessary and gradu-ated. A Coventry understands that a little bit of living, some youthful indiscretion, was more important than pure aca-demic excellence. It seemed that Carlo had taken a liking to Martha's Vineyard, Ogunquit, and the Hamptons in Long Island. He especially liked the nightlife in Manhattan, with its assortment of recreational substances.

"May I?" asked the young scion, gesturing to the oak cabine-try that housed a large flat-screen television behind sliding doors. He carried a leather portfolio under his arm. "Some breaking news," Carlo said. Carlo was soft-spoken and re-spectful around his uncle, another thing that William liked about him. He knew whence his charmed life emanated.

William nodded, and Carlo fished out the remote control, opened the cabinet doors, and turned on the TV.

~ ~ ~

It was 5:00 p.m. and Khalid Husseini wasted no time calling it a day. He didn't have too far to go—about two and a half miles as the crow flies—but getting from Point A to Point B quickly in a crowded and bustling city like Manama could be a daunting task. He had to walk nearly a half mile to the parking lot of the U.S. Navy facility to pick up his car, then drive out on Avenue 22 heading east to the Moharraq Third Causeway, then up Al Fatih Highway into the heart of the northern quadrant of the main island of Bahrain. Once on Al Fatih, he'd make his way to Exhibition and then Qudaibiya Avenues before turning onto Road Number 2108. All in all, the trip took about forty minutes in the heavy traffic.

It was Friday, and Khalid had put all thoughts of work behind him just as soon as he stepped off base. The weekend had officially begun. He looked forward to going to BJ's with his friends Ali and Ghazi.

BJ's was an upscale nightclub in the Al Asasiin Hotel (the Americans called it the "Assassin" Hotel, but in Arabic, "Asasiin" was more akin to "Standard") in Adliya, which was hard to get into. But a couple of the American Navy guys whom Khalid had become friends with would meet them there. Americans didn't have any trouble getting into BJ's.

Khalid had just slipped the key to the front door of his flat into the lock when something caught his attention. He looked up and down the street. It was a muffled *boom.*

He didn't so much hear it as feel it. He felt it in his hand that pushed the key into the lock. He felt it through his feet as he stood in the doorway, the ground vibrating. He felt it in his ears because of the subtle change in air pressure mixed with the rattling of doors and windows. As he scanned the scene to the ends of his street, movement above the buildings caught his eye, and he looked up. Some sort of flare streaked across the dimming sky, leaving behind a dark contrail. It arched downward and disappeared from view as it descended behind the apartments far away. Khalid heard a delayed high-pitch whistling sound from the flare. Then, as he gawked, he heard a faint second and third whistle.

Khalid stepped back from his apartment, still looking up. He saw two more contrails that arched in the sky. One stretched far away to the northwest; the other looked sank a mile to the east behind his building. Then, like Godzilla rising, a orange-and-black cloud of fire, smoke, and dust billowed into the sky from behind his building. And it looked really *close.*

Khalid stood wide-eyed and open-mouthed as he watched the ugly, angry cloud rise and expand. Something, however, tapped him on the top of his head, breaking the spell. He looked around, a little confused. He tilted his head and listened: a pitter-patter filled his ears. He quickly realized that it was falling dust and debris, and when nearby car alarms began sounding all at once, he scurried into the doorway. Nothing hit his street, but he heard a few bangs and clangs echoing through the eerily quiet neighborhood.

Khalid walked briskly down the street, his eyes glued to the rising cloud. People stuck their heads outside their doors and looked around. Others pointed to the sky and covered their faces in horror. It was a surreal sight and, as Khalid rounded the street corner and joined a growing crowd gathered at the intersection of Qudaibiya and Exhibition Avenues, it grew even more surreal.

Looming on the southern horizon was a massive American aircraft carrier, the Ford-class USS *George W. Bush*, anchored just offshore from the Arab Shipbuilding and Repair Yard (ASRY). The cloud of smoke and dust looked as though it was standing on the back deck. Balls of flame glowed red-orange in the bowels of the ship, cutting through the shroud of black smoke that poured from invisible openings in the ship's structure. Flares intermittently streamed out from the flames like bottle rockets, whistling into and across the darkening sky before falling to the ground or into the sea.

Muffled popping sounds reverberated from the ship. A large blinding flash lit up the sky for a couple of seconds. Khalid threw up his hands to protect his face as he felt the heat of the blast. A massive *bang* reverberated so deeply that it seemed as if the air itself was vibrating.

I'm too close. He stumbled backward before turning and running. Others around him did the same. As he ran, he felt a searing blast of air against his back—a sudden gust that nearly pushed him down. He was able to stay on his feet even as others stumbled and fell. The windows of apartment buildings and the windshields of cars twisted in their frames and shattered.

Khalid dared not stop and look back anymore as he ran for his life.

~ ~ ~

The President sat quietly, eyes fixed on one of the large monitors in the Situation Room. She cursed herself for the sense of relief she felt, relief that *finally* Detroit would no longer be in the headlines.

But this—an apparent attack on a U.S. aircraft carrier in the Persian Gulf—this was pure dread.

She turned to the secretary of defense.

"Bernie," she said softly, and the room became quiet. "The

Detroit situation. It's time to end it."

~ ~ ~

Some 280 miles southwest of Washington, DC, twenty U.S. Air Force four-engine C-17 Globemaster cargo planes ferrying one hundred 82nd Airborne paratroopers each, lifted off, one after the other, into the morning sky at Fort Bragg, North Carolina.

It took the aircraft an hour and a half to reach their destinations. As they flew over Michigan—ten in the southern part of the state, and twelve over the northern part, including the Upper Peninsula—they each descended to under two thousand feet. Soldiers and their gear and parachutes streamed out of the aircraft in long lines. The lines lost their linearity with the blossoming of the soldiers' olive-green parachutes.

The sight of 1,000 soldiers landing in the bucolic fields and farmland was both graceful and ominous.

In Mackinaw City, twenty-year old Clyde Dodson, a part-time waiter and Superior Volunteers "soldier," was nervously manning the Jamet Street checkpoint to the Mackinac Bridge. At first, the job had been boring, but motorists were becoming increasingly hostile. The burned-out hulks of an SUV and a pickup truck in the median were testament to two separate attempts at breaking the checkpoint by angry motorists.

Four people were killed in the incidents, all of them gunned down by the Volunteers. The pickup truck driver was a Navy veteran who had gotten out of his truck armed with an AR-15 and threatened to kill the Volunteers if they didn't let him pass. They didn't, and an argument—and brief gun battle—ensued.

The second incident entailed the SUV speeding north along the shoulder against the turned-around southbound traffic. Volunteers had opened fire with hundreds of rounds when the SUV burst past the turnaround and sped toward the bridge.

The SUV swerved out of control and rolled several times before coming to a rest, wheels down, with bodies dangling out of the windows.

In both cases, Clyde had seen the immediate aftermath. He and his fellow Volunteers were startled awake by the commotion. A huge argument broke out among the Volunteers, both "officer" and "enlisted" volunteer alike. Clyde was afraid they would start shooting each other.

That tension remained.

Several Volunteers had left. Clyde was thinking about splitting, too, but he didn't know how he could escape without being seen. He didn't really know the guys who had left, and now he wished he had been more outgoing. And he didn't come in his own car. He'd come in Ricky Barksdale's truck. What could he do? Walk home?

Another commotion heightened Clyde's awareness. He looked around and saw Volunteers shading their eyes and looking skyward. Clyde followed their gaze.

Several military cargo planes flew low and slow on the horizon as paratroopers streamed out behind them. They floated to the ground like poplar fluff carried by a spring breeze.

The U.S. Army had arrived.

The Volunteers fell into a state of panic. The Army paratroopers were a ways off, but no one doubted that they'd reach the bridge in short order. And there was no doubt why they had come.

Someone argued that the Volunteers should greet the soldiers peaceably. After all, they were all on the same side. A grizzled Volunteer was certain that the Army paratroopers weren't going to cheerily greet and thank them for their work. He argued that they should leave *right now.*

Twenty-four-year-old Rickey Barksdale, tattooed and sporting a buzz cut, spoke up unexpectedly, arguing for guerilla warfare. He suggested that the revolution would start right here, right now. Multiple Volunteers snorted and began removing their camouflage uniforms and anything else that read "Superior Volunteers."

The company of militiamen disassembled and scrambled for their vehicles. It was a traffic clusterfuck. Horns blared and Volunteers shouted curses at each other. Several minor fender-benders were followed by scorching invectives from inside the vehicles, but no one stopped to argue.

Amid the chaos, some vehicles failed to start, and were abandoned in the middle of the road. Most of the pickups, cars, and vans beat a hasty retreat, speeding north across the Mackinac Bridge as fast as they could.

~ ~ ~

"Colonel" Jenkins was sitting at Chief Wendowski's desk when the "corporal" on the other end of his cell phone grew frantic.

"The Army's here!" exclaimed the young corporal. "They're parachuting in! Everyone's taking off!"

Jenkins stood up. "Now hold on there, boy, what exactly is

...” but the call was disconnected.

Jenkins rushed out of the police office, where his two boys stood guard. “Let's go,” he said. He scanned the sky as he walked briskly to his pickup truck with his two boys in tow. His two sons exchanged a look, but didn't say anything.

Jenkin's truck was parked in a diagonal across the street from the Mackinaw City Municipal Building. Tucker was too busy scanning the sky to see Village President Bob Mollen, flanked by Chief Ralph Wendowski and Officer Frank Carroll, waiting by his truck. His eyes fell on the three, and he stopped.

“Going somewhere, *Colonel?*” asked Bob. The two police officers held rifles at the ready.

“We'll take those,” said another voice, as more officers stepped from behind and stripped the “colonel” and his two boys of their weapons.

The “colonel” looked up while officers handcuffed him. Two F-35 stealth fighters screamed across the sky toward the Upper Peninsula.

~ ~ ~

When her name was called, Araminta stepped up to the podium. Brandon stood beside her, his head hung low and his shoulders slouched, but he looked around, stealing glances left and right and shifting his feet. Araminta nudged him with her elbow and whispered, “Stand up straight,” which the microphone picked up, eliciting quiet chuckles from around the packed courtroom.

The judge, Elizabeth Ault, peeked over the glasses at the tip of her nose. “What is the basis for your claim of asylum?”

asked the judge as she returned to the paperwork before her.

"Ma'am," Araminta spoke, "uh, Judge, Brandon—Brandon is my son here—Brandon's best friend, um, three of his best friends, were killed by the Army a—a few days ago."

"The United States Army?" asked the judge.

"Yes, ma'am," replied Araminta.

"It's 'Your Honor' when you address a judge in Canada, Ms. Cole, just like you do in the United States," said Judge Ault, sternly.

"I'm sorry, ma'am—um, your Honor," said Araminta, repeating "your Honor" in a trailing voice.

"I'm sorry about your sons' friends, Ms. Cole, but I fail to see the merit of your claim for permanent status. The current unrest in Detroit notwithstanding, the United States is currently at peace and is not generally a refugee-producing country. You have resources at your disposal in your country, Ms. Cole. I suggest you use them."

A court bailiff stepped up and held his arm out to usher Araminta and Brandon out of the defendant's box and allow the next defendants in. The docket was full, and the judge clearly wanted to move on to the next case.

Araminta hesitated, then pleaded with the judge.

"Please, your Honor," she said. "If you reject our case, then please..."—she grabbed Brandon by the arm and yanked him close to her— "please, I beg the court to put a *bullet* right here," she said, jabbing her left pointer finger into Brandon's temple. A collective gasp emanated from the public seating area. Brandon looked up at his mother, alarmed.

"Because," Araminta continued, pausing to regain her composure as tears streamed down her face, "because that's what you would be doing if you send us back, your Honor."

Murmurs passed through the courtroom as Judge Ault looked out on Araminta and Brandon over the glasses perched on the end of her nose.

"I feel your desperation, Ms. Cole," the judge said. "As a mother, I truly understand your desire to protect your son."

The judge looked down at Araminta's file and paused. She jotted something down in the folder. "I am denying your claim but, at the same time, I am recommending a full review by the federal court. Case adjourned," she said, and struck her gravel.

The court bailiff ushered Araminta and Brandon out of the defendant's box and toward the courtroom exit as the courtroom broke into applause.

"What does that mean, Momma?" asked Brandon.

"I don't know," whispered Araminta, "but I think it's good."

~ ~ ~

"The militias have scattered, boss," Moe said into his phone, "as expected."

On the other end of the line was Major General Teddy Rose, the commanding general of CID.

"The FBI and ATF picked up a couple of sheriff's deputies down in Lenawee County and a city councilman in Coldwater, all members of the South Michigan Militia that raided the Adrian armory," Moe reported. "Mackinac City Police gave us custody of the so-called colonel who took over the town and blocked the Mackinac Bridge. He fingered the lot of them—the entire leadership of the Superior Volunteers. They were also kind enough to maintain a website and social media accounts with their names listed."

"Very good," said General Rose. "Wrap it up, Moe, and get back here as quick as you can. You're needed in Bahrain. It's all hands on deck out there."

Moe disconnected the call. He looked out over the cold blue waters of the Straits of Mackinac as they crossed the Mackinac Bridge.

In the back seat, agent Maxim Yanayev hung up his own cell. "Guess whose nephew is in the National Guard?" said Maxim. "And guess which armory he drills at?"

Moe laughed. "Well, let's go get him too."

~ ~ ~

Floyd sat in his usual seat at the Bull Moose Restaurant on Route 2 in Brevort, sipping coffee and flipping through *Field and Stream.*

"Thank you, darling" said Floyd without looking up. He assumed that the shadow crossing his table was the waitress with his breakfast. He glanced up from his magazine, and recoiled at the sight of a distinguished-looking black man peering down at him with soulful eyes.

Floyd had never seen the man before in his life, but the man's eyes knew *him.*

"Floyd Barksdale," the man said, softly but firmly. It wasn't a question.

Floyd licked his lips and looked out the window. An unmarked police car sat in the parking lot with its engine running, a cloud of water vapor exiting the tail pipe. Farther up the road, two county police cars were blocking both sides of the four-lane highway, their emergency lights flashing.

At the restaurant's front door, two state police troopers hovered just inside. Amanda stood wide-eyed behind the counter, eyes darting back and forth from the two policemen to Floyd and the black man.

Floyd looked back to the black man. He opened his mouth as if to say something when his lower lip began trembling.

He burst into tears.

"I meant no harm," Floyd pleaded. "I meant no harm, I swear. Oh, sweet Jesus, help me!" he sobbed.

~ ~ ~

As they rounded a bend, Ricky and Clyde saw two state police cars blocking the highway ahead, emergency lights flashing. Several more police cars sat behind them.

"What the...?"

Ricky's voice trailed off as he took his foot off the gas pedal.

"Is it an accident or something?" asked Clyde.

"Don't think so," said Ricky. He peered into his rearview mirror. His heart pounded in his chest as he tried to make sense of it. "Roadblock," he finally said.

He brought his truck to a stop. Behind each of the police cars, state troopers were aiming rifles and pistols in their direction.

"Is it for us?" asked Clyde. "It can't be for us, right? What the hell, man? What did you do, Ricky?"

"Nothing," said Ricky as he reached behind his seat for his hunting rifle. A black SUV with flashing emergency lights, along with several state police cars, roared into view from behind and screeched to a halt.

A tall, intense-looking black man stepped from the passenger side of the SUV. He calmly approached the driver's side window and smashed it in with a single blow. He placed a large pistol at Ricky's head. "Let it go, Ricky," he said in an authoritative but empathetic voice.

"Get the fu—" protested Ricky, but he didn't finish his thought. He was yanked out of his truck in one graceful motion right through his driver's window. Before he knew what was happening, he was on his stomach on the pavement, being handcuffed as he gasped for air, the wind knocked out of him.

"Corporal Ricky Barksdale," the intense man said, now yanking Ricky to his feet. "You're under arrest."

Only then, as he was frog-marched to the SUV, did he become aware of the commotion around him. Police swarmed over his truck, removing their rifles, backpacks, and hunting gear. A tow truck pulled alongside his pickup and a helicopter buzzed overhead. From the backseat, Ricky watched as Clyde was handcuffed and put into the back of a state police cruiser.

~ ~ ~

William came from behind his desk and sat on the leather couch while Carlo sat upright in an oak-framed Victorian chair with red upholstery. William watched the television intently. He couldn't help but smile as the *George W. Bush* burned and listed in the water. The loss of life would be horrendous, he knew, but the price of oil had, in a matter of an hour or so, increased more than tenfold, shattering the historic highs set during the Great Recession of the late aughts.

And, in this instance, with an American supercarrier aflame in the Persian Gulf, prices wouldn't be coming down anytime soon. This was at least as momentous as the terrorist attacks of September 11, 2001, and all that flowed from them.

"There's going to be war," William said.

"You knew," said Carlo with admiration. He opened his portfolio and slid it across the table to William.

The business in Detroit, which had kept him up late in recent weeks, was wiped completely from the books. It was no longer even a blip in comparison to the windfalls that the oil and insurance markets were suddenly generating.

"Not really," said William, "but that's why we have the clients we have."

~ ~ ~

Petty Officer Second Class Jason Palmer looked up from the paperwork on his desk.

"Is that our boy?" asked Senior Chief Petty Officer Antonio Salerno, not even looking up from a file he was writing in.

It was the telltale spitfire sound of a blue low-rider Volkswagen Golf R with its muffler modified to be, well, less modifying, that caught their attention. They could hear the tinny rumble of the low-rider amid the pouring rain and the intermittent vibration of thunder. Jason spotted the car, pulling into a parking space facing the Navy Recruiting Station.

"Yep, that's our boy."

It was the seventh or eighth time, and four working days in a row, that the distinctive VW Golf pulled into the parking lot where it would normally sit for up to twenty minutes before it would leave. "Our boy" referred to the driver, an Asian kid, maybe eighteen.

"Why don't you go fetch him," suggested Antonio, again without looking up from his work, "and see if we can't help him make up his mind."

Jason stood. A suggestion by the senior chief was no suggestion at all; it was a command. Jason pulled on his ankle-length Navy-issue black raincoat. A flash of lightning followed by a crack of thunder made Jason pause before stepping out into the storm.

~ ~ ~

Ian sat in his car looking over at the Navy Recruiting Station as it rained loudly on his car roof and heavy metal blared from his car speakers. But he never saw Jaime step out of the Navy Recruiting office. Instead, he was lost in thought. Where would he end up with the Navy? Would he be in Europe? The Middle East?

Ian tried to imagine life overseas, and life in the Navy.

Would there be a war? And, if so, wouldn't the Navy be the safest branch? Maybe the Air Force? But it was the Navy that traveled the world, wasn't it?

How about the Marines? If he was going to go military, maybe he should go all in—and the Marines were definitely all in.

Ian dismissed the idea out of hand, as he had before. No, if he were to do it, join the military, it would have to be the Navy. It was the conclusion he kept coming to. *Travel.*

Ian jumped as someone knocked on his driver-side window. A young uniformed Navy man stood there in the pouring rain, holding an umbrella aloft. "Come inside," the Navy man shouted over the rain and the music.

"Let's talk!"

Note from the Author

Alter Road was my debut novel, first published in 2020 by Defiance Press and Publishing. I wanted to tackle—and dramatize through fiction—themes of deindustrialization and creative destruction: how new technologies reshape the geography of production, leaving older industrial cities like Detroit behind while newer centers of innovation, like Silicon Valley, thrive. *Alter Road* was the result.

What you've just read is the Second Edition. Despite the first edition's slow beginning and the rawness of a beginning author, the book earned some generous reviews. *New York Times* bestselling author Blaine Pardoe gave it "a solid five out of five stars," praising its ensemble cast and "terrifyingly realistic" depiction of protests and unrest. Ghostwriter Peter Gerardo described it as "so smart and plausible, I kept forgetting it was a novel." These reviews inspired me to keep going.

My second novel, *Friendship Games*, went on to earn the prestigious Kirkus Star and a Bronze Medal from the Military Writers Society of America. I mention that only to show how far my writing has evolved since *Alter Road*. *Friendship Games* is a kind of sequel—it moves from Detroit to the Middle East, picking up after the explosion aboard the *USS George W. Bush*. It's more of a geopolitical and military thriller, launching what became *The Wartmann Series* and introducing Vice President George "Daddy Longlegs" Wartmann. He actually appears briefly in *Alter Road*, though his role here is small—a quiet prelude to the force he becomes later.

When I returned to revise *Alter Road*, I tried to strengthen the narrative with more dialogue, especially that first quarter—without sanding away its rough edges. Beyond that, I kept revisions to a minimum. I didn't want to lose the rawness of a beginning author that's still evident here.

If *Alter Road* spoke to you in any way, I'd be grateful if you left a short review on Amazon or wherever you found your copy. Reader feedback means more than you know.

You can find me online at markjamesauthor.com and northarrowpress.com, or on social media (X/Twitter, Substack, Facebook, LinkedIn, Instagram, and BlueSky). I always enjoy hearing from readers.

Thank you for reading—and for walking down *Alter Road* with me.

With gratitude,
Mark James